Gracie.
Enjoy Genoa –

THE

SCHOLAR

THE GENOA CHRONICLES

JJ Anden

BOOKS BY JJ ANDERS

The Scholar
The Warrior
The Queen

FOLLOW JJ ANDERS

www.jjanders.com
fb.com/jjandersauthor
twitter.com/jjandersauthor

THE
SCHOLAR

THE GENOA CHRONICLES

JJ ANDERS

GRAYTON
PRESS

This is a work of fiction. Names, characters, places, and incidents are either the product of the author's imagination or are used fictitiously, and any resemblance to actual persons, living or dead, business establishments, events, or locales is entirely coincidental.

THE SCHOLAR

DIGITAL ISBN: 978-1-942896-89-0
PHYSICAL ISBN: 978-1974255740
Copyright © 2017 Grayton Press

Published by Grayton Press

SUMMARY

Time is running out for the world of Genoa and its magical peoples. A wizard's past mistake must now be set right if Genoa is to survive the battle that is to come.

Anna is clearly different from others. With obvious physical differences and powerful abilities, she's never quite fit in... anywhere. Having no knowledge of her parents, she sets out to discover her true origin. On the run for most of her life, she's become a master at eluding capture, even a little cocky you might say. When a sticky situation forces her hand, she hitches a ride with a wizard, who whisks her away to another world, where, according to him, she'd been exiled from as a child. This new magical place seems oddly familiar as Anna discovers powerful enemies and treasured allies on her quest for answers. The dangerous journey thrusts her headlong into the arms of Kriston, who finds himself caught between sworn-duty and insatiable curiosity.

JJ Anders

DEDICATION

To Spencer and Mason,
the best adventures in my life...

Imagination will often carry us to worlds that
never were. But without it we go nowhere.
- Carl Sagan

JJ Anders

Full size map available at www.jjanders.com

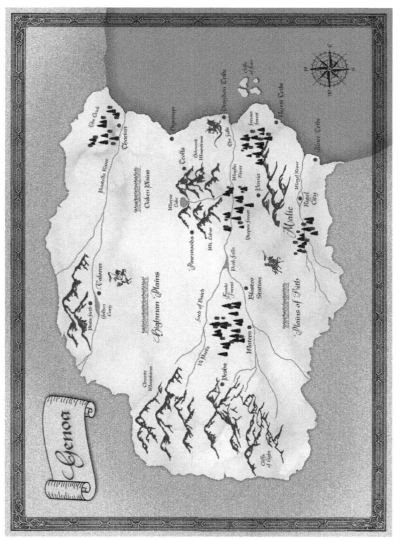

CHAPTER ONE

The Great Escape

She didn't know how much longer her little legs could run. In her young mind, she had been running for years, when in reality, she and the man had only been running for minutes. But she'd been often told that the young had less experience when it came to the passing of time during danger. Especially when it came to life or death. Hers.

When she fell and landed on the gravel, the man stopped running and turned around as red light flew from his hands, lighting up the dark night that surrounded them.

He shot the red lightning bolts into the darkness behind her so quickly, she didn't have time to blink. She heard a distant scream in response as bright colored lights flashed.

She sat up quickly as her protector reached

down and hauled her over his shoulder.

She closed her eyes as the lights continued to flash around her. She tried to cover her ears as the siren's screaming continued around them.

"Hold onto me!" Orden, her protector, shouted as he snatched her up, then pushed off the ground and flew over a large gully.

As they sailed across the darkened ditch, she glanced back and saw what followed them. Military machines of various sizes raced over the dark ground towards them. Each machines headlight sought to capture them in their glow. Lights from helicopters blinked overhead trying to find their quarry on the ground.

Fear almost over took her as she watched the military draw closer and felt a quick stab of guilt. She started to cry, shame and fear finally washed over her. This was all her fault.

When they finally landed on the other side of the ditch, she heard Orden give a cry of dismay as his old legs gave out from under him. She flew out of his arms and landed hard in the dirt next to him.

By the time she sat up and shook her head clear, Orden was once again next to her. His old face showed concern and fear hidden behind his blue eyes.

"I broke my leg." He said and brushed her pale hair from her face as he looked deep into her eyes. "My princess, it's time to get you to safety." He said with a sad smile on his old face.

"No!" She screamed as the lights and noise

grew closer. "You will not leave me!" She said with a pout. Her face was covered with dirt and tears. But she didn't care.

"My child, I will never truly leave you, but this is my doing and I must first protect you." Orden said as he dragged himself to his knees next to her. "Remember all I have taught you."

Anna's tears doubled as he started to wave his big hands around her small body. She knew this was the end, if he sent her away now he would not survive what was coming towards them.

When a loud screech sounded several feet behind her, she watched as Orden stopped his incantation and looked up with fear. Anna watched as hate filling his eyes.

"Don't move!" Anna heard from behind her, the order came from a very familiar voice. "I have you now. You and that freak are mine." The man she knew as Uncle Wil shouted at them from a few yards away.

"She has never been a freak." Orden said as he looked once more down at Anna. This time she saw a small smile play across his face. "She is greatness, and I am proud to die for her."

Anna felt the bullet whizz past her before she heard the sound of the shot from the gun.

As if in slow motion, she watched in horror as it ripped into Orden's body and the tiny bullet embedded itself into the old man's chest, causing him to fall backwards.

"No!" She screamed, rushing over to Orden's

side.

He lay there as his life's blood poured out of the hole in his chest into the dirt.

"My princess, be safe." He coughed, and then raising his right hand towards her. A bright green light engulfed her quickly. She felt the magic's warmth take over as she continued to shout and cry for the older man.

When she finally used her dirty hands to wipe the tears out of her eyes, she noticed that she was no longer kneeling on the hard-packed ground in Texas. Instead, tall trees and green ferns filled her vision as rain fell upon her uncovered head.

She continued to cry, tucked tight in a ball, as her small fist beat the ground in frustration.

After several moments of crying, she stood. Tears and dirt covered her pale face as she lifted her chin to yet another new and odd world. Finally, after looking around, she accepted her fate with a heavy heart. She was uncertain of what she should do next, since the old man had trained her well for such a circumstance.

The only thing she knew for sure was that she was truly alone on this strange planet now.

Anna crouched low on the cold, wet cement near the mouth of a dark alley along one of Boston's many busy streets. Ignoring the smell of the full trash container that sat directly behind her, she focused on the building across from where she hid.

Not even the chill and dampness of the evening hindered her concentration. The heavy rain continued to fall in slow steady drops as she watched the large building across the street from her hiding place, she was deep in thought.

It had been raining for days without stopping, causing the rivers around Boston to flood well beyond their banks, filling the lakes and ponds, and wreaking havoc on all who ventured outside. The street drains couldn't handle the amount of water that had poured from the skies in such a short amount of time. As the streets continued to fill with water, rush-hour traffic slowed to a standstill.

A part of her wished she could be back inside, nestled in the small hotel room she had paid cash for last night. The room had been dry and warm, but most importantly, safe.

An occasional person rushed past Anna's hiding spot, no doubt seeking shelter as they continued along their daily route, hunched under rain jackets or large umbrellas, trying to keep the moisture and the chilled wind at bay. But she knew she was safe from view, especially since everyone appeared to be more concerned about watching for puddles than spying a slender woman hidden near yesterday's trash.

This time of day, most everyone on the streets was either on their way to or from school. One of Boston's largest college campuses sat just a few blocks away. You couldn't walk a street without seeing a statue of one of the college's founding father figures or pass a coffee shop that wasn't full of students trying to get more study time in.

A sudden change in the wind had a cold shiver running down her spine, causing her to pull the hood of her jacket tighter around her face. She was nervous so she kept her body low as she worried about her plan again.

She hated being nervous and scared, yet it seemed to her that most of her life had been spent either running or escaping danger. She had tried to change that about herself, but here she was again, hunkered down in a smelly alleyway, dripping wet, and on another dangerous mission.

Autumn was quickly approaching and the evening air was starting to get crisp, its cool bite a reminder that the seasons were constantly changing, and snow was just around the corner. She glanced up at the cloudy sky quickly, thankful it hadn't started snowing yet. It became harder to hide when your footprints showed your route in the snow.

Her eyes darted around once more and then focused on a tall tower building, beyond that sat a picture-perfect church with a tall spiral steeple. Beautiful stained-glass windows adorned most of its surface. Instead of enjoying the beauty of the building, she mentally marked its position in her head so she would know which direction to run if she needed a quick exit. Then she refocused on the building across from her once again.

She wouldn't have much time. By her

calculations, about two hours', worth of searching. Max. In the past, she had shorter timeframes and had succeeded in those missions.

Another quick scan showed her the way was clear and she felt confident she could proceed as planned.

Her heart kick into overdrive, pumping blood to every vessel in her body. Quickly, she unfolded her thin frame and wiped the moisture off the knees of her faded jeans.

She knew the risks of every step she had to make; she'd weighed them every time she took this chance, back when she'd started her very long and lonely journey. It had been so many years, she didn't really remember when it had all started. Let alone her life or time before the fear. She just hoped that this time it would be worth it.

Highly aware of her short white hair, her most identifying feature, she made sure the oversized hood completely covered every strand. She had pulled the short locks up into a clip to ensure her thick hair was kept fully hidden.

Closing her eyes for a moment, she took a couple cleansing breaths to calm her nerves before leaving her hiding place. When her hands stopped shaking, she hunched her shoulders, hoping the slouched stance would make her look like all the other college students in this area. Sometimes, deep down, she wished she could just be normal. She also wished she knew exactly what she was and where she'd come from.

One of her favorite Bruce Lee quotes flashed into her thoughts. *"The possession of anything begins in the mind."* This phrase held more truth in her mind than most and caused her to push herself even more.

"It's now or never," she said to herself. "Just don't get caught." She kept repeating the statement over and over like a prayer. For some reason, this simple action seemed to calm her.

Taking a deep breath, she glanced once more at the stalled traffic and cautiously started walking across the street. She forced her breathing to level as she tucked her cold hands deep into the pockets of her hoodie.

She was relieved when she finished crossing the street, and sent up a blessing as no one seemed to pay attention to her as she then moved toward the brick building.

Slowly she approached the large doors, taking mental notes of all the visible exits as her palms grew damp, deep inside her pockets.

Taking big risks, like she was taking now, meant you couldn't work yourself into a corner. Not like last time.

At one of the library's main entrances, she pushed opened the heavy wooden doors and felt the warm air rush over her thin body. The smells hit her next: paper mixed with old leather and the sweet aroma of coffee from the Map Room Cafe. The scent caused her mouth to water, making her realize it had been a while since she'd had a warm meal, or a good cup of coffee for that matter.

She didn't dare chance the distraction now, so she kept her eyes straight ahead and forced her body back into control.

As she moved over the threshold, she felt the essence of knowledge seep into her core; this feeling seemed to radiate slowly from the building itself. She shivered as it filled all her senses and pushed all other thoughts to the back of her mind.

Here, there was older knowledge than she'd ever experienced before, this fact caused her racing heart to almost double its speed. Her eyes watered in sheer excitement. Gone was her desire for food or sleep. Her mind and body were totally focused on only one purpose now, and she found it hard not to let a small smile pass over her lips.

Walking further into the library, she passed the return book desk. She kept her pace steady and glanced towards it casually while keeping her distance then made her way to the massive staircase. Not bothering to glance at the large domed ceiling overhead, as many first-time visitors would have done, she instead spared a quick look to the right. Two employees were working behind a tall countertop desk. An older woman stood engrossed in her work, her eyes glued to the computer screen. The other employee, a gentleman, was too busy stacking books on a roll cart behind the desk to notice her.

The bright overhead lights buzzed above her as she made her way silently across the crisp white tiles. She tried to keep her wet boots from making a sound on the dry floor and was glad she'd taken great care to wipe them thoroughly on the doormat before stepping into the building. She couldn't chance having heads turn in her direction because of squeaky shoes.

Continuing to roll her shoulders forward, she moved towards the stairs, hoping that she'd go unnoticed. She'd dressed, purposely, like most of the college students from the area and sent up a silent thank you to the movie industry. With the string of vampire movies showing at the local theater, the fashion around town had returned to darker styles, which would help her blend in while she was in the library and could also be of benefit outside if she had to flee.

Out of the corner of her eye, she noticed the woman glancing up from her computer screen. Not wanting to give the librarian too much time to contemplate her, she pulled her backpack higher onto her shoulders. Trying not to rush as she made her way towards the stairs, she held her breath as she walked slowly.

She'd been to enough places like this to know that a person who hesitated usually called attention to themselves. If anyone had looked closely at Anna, they would have seen that she didn't look like other students at all, despite her wardrobe. Actually, she didn't look like anyone else she had ever seen.

At a quick glance, she was tall and skinny,

which was one of the reasons she made a point to wear baggy clothing and walk slumped over. If she was mistaken for a young boy, all the better.

Usually, she was quite proud of her pretty heart-shaped face, with its straight nose and a small cleft in the middle of her chin. It was one of her favorite features about herself. However, the one thing that made her stand out the most was her pale skin, skin so translucent that she always covered as much of it as possible, to prevent second glances.

Not many people had ghostly white hair, at least not without using a lot of product. Even the vampire followers tended to migrate towards darker locks.

A few years back, she'd tried to dye her hair a darker shade, but it had washed out by the next morning, leaving an awful mess. Even permanent colors didn't stick to her thick white locks. She'd tried cutting her hair short instead, but that only emphasized her very pale blue eyes. She'd settled on keeping her hair in a short bob, using her longer bangs to help hide her eyes. She had added a bright pink hair extension clip to the left side of her face, hoping the punk rock look would lead people to think she had done the colors on purpose.

She could remember many years ago, the first time she'd realized she was different than everyone else. She'd been walking along in the mall and had stopped to look at a mannequin that had been stripped of all its clothing. A woman was trying to pull clothes on it, and the two figures were so strange in comparison to each other. The pale statue had seemed so out of place next to a living thing that she'd glanced at her own reflection and realized she, too, was different.

No one had ever made fun of her directly. Instead, they had stared and talked about her in hushed voices. She had always been able to see it in their eyes as they looked at her, which had hurt twice as bad.

She quickly jerked her mind back to her current situation and started up the wooden staircase. She fought the urge to trail her fingers on the shiny wood banister. Just a simple touch with something so old could set her back. She decided to play it safe and tucked her hands into her jacket pockets once more.

When she had researched the building, she'd found that the oldest books were housed on the third floor, hidden behind a locked door. Now, hoping she would find what she needed, she made her way up the stairs.

However, the richness of the wood and the beauty of the interior design didn't go unnoticed by her. Everything looked so shiny and new, even though the building was well over a century old.

Thinking of the age of the building caused her to think about herself. Just like the building, on the surface, she looked young, about nineteen, but she knew better than anyone that looks could be deceiving. Especially since she'd been alive for over forty years now.

Yes, she and the library of Boston had a lot in common.

As she reached the second floor, she quickly glanced out the windows which looked down into a huge courtyard. The rain continued to fall at a steady pace as a row of cars slowly crawled down the streets in the background.

She thought about the next step in her plan. Of how she had to access the private elevator on the second floor, which would lead her to the entryway of the secluded and very private rare book section. Taking this route, she'd be less likely to run into trouble. At least she hoped.

She headed towards the outer hallway of the courtyard. The elevator was on the south end of the building, and after making sure no one was paying attention to her, she continued into the next section, frustrated she was not finding a librarian here.

What she found instead was the history section, which caused her great joy. History was one of her favorite things to learn about and she secretly hoped that her answers might be hidden somewhere in the past. She confirmed that no one was around, and a great calm settled inside her. She allowed a part of her to surface, the deepest, most secure part of her.

Her magic.

Deciding on one of the oldest books, titled *History of the World*, she carefully picked up the book from the worn wooden shelf. Turning it around in her hands, she felt the weight of the leather, of its many pages. She could smell the paper and ink hidden beneath the covers. A book. Filled with knowledge, this item held its own power of sorts. Men had journeyed to unknown places, labored, toiled, and endured to fill its pages with their knowledge and beliefs. Now it sat here, in her hands, waiting to share its secrets.

It took her only a few seconds, seven to be exact, as the complete knowledge of the book pulsed from its core and moved quickly through the old bindings. It moved up her arms to sear into her mind. She held perfectly still as everything the creators had put into this wonderful item flooded her mind and she gained its knowledge.

During this time, she was as vulnerable as a sleeping baby. Gaining such knowledge physically drained her as if she'd lived through each moment written on the pages.

After the last of the images flashed behind her mind, she blinked a few times and realized she was spending too much energy. For her current mission, time was of the utmost importance.

Setting the book back down, she felt a little discouraged that the knowledge she sought wasn't hidden within this book's pages. But she was used to disappointment. Quickly, she moved on to the next book, this time only scanning the title and keeping her hands to her side.

Anna was very patient when it came to finding what she needed. She'd learned that lesson early on. It had been one of her first life lessons. She remembered the first time she'd picked up a book and scanned its pages with her mind. She'd been so excited that she'd instantly rushed around and grabbed hold of every book she could get her hands on. That experience had ended with her on the floor, gasping for breath, her body too tired to move. She'd spent almost a full day lying on the floor before she'd built up enough energy to get up.

Now, she continued down the aisles, searching the titles of books, looking for ones she hadn't already scanned before, stopping only when one caught her eye. Each time, she made sure the aisles were empty before absorbing their knowledge.

If these books didn't hold the information she was looking for, she knew what her next step would be. She kept telling herself that maybe the next book would be the one to answer all her questions which would allow her to skip heading into the secure room and deeper into danger.

After fifteen minutes in that section, she could feel her strength beginning to weaken.

Flipping open her backpack, she discreetly grabbed a granola bar. After taking a big bite and swallowing the sugary goodness, she felt a boost of energy and continued. She finished eating one bar and opened a second as she continued to scan the knowledge of more books into her mind.

When she finally reached the end of the section, she looked down the long corridor and saw the elevator that would lead her to the third floor and the section she'd come here for.

Deciding it was now or never, she quietly

moved towards the main staircase. She considered herself very lucky when a librarian, arms laden with books, approached the landing. The woman appeared to be in her early forties and was dressed like many of the others Anna had seen in other libraries from her past. The woman's drab dark brown hair was rolled into a tight bun at the nape of her neck. She wore dull gray slacks with a button-up white blouse, neither of which appeared to have any wrinkles, even though she now carried a pile of books.

Her smile was friendly when she spotted Anna.

Smiling, while trying to hide her crystal-clear eyes by lowering her eyelashes, Anna stopped in front of the woman and looked down at her.

"Hi," Anna began so the woman would keep walking towards her. "I'm looking for the restrooms. I guess I had too much coffee…" When the woman stopped on a step just below her, Anna reached out as if to offer to help with the heavy books she was carrying and quickly laid her pale hand along the woman's forearm.

It took just a light touch.

Anna watched as the librarian's eye color faded away, the brown retreating quickly as if the color was being drained like water in a sink. Her eyes turned the same pale blue as Anna's and stared blankly back. Now she was a clean slate for Anna to use and control.

It still shocked her after all these years that she could do these things. To take over another living thing so easily. To control. To manipulate. She hated using this power and only did so when it was necessary, such as now.

Quickly, Anna glanced around and noticed that there was a young couple in the entryway who might be close enough to hear their conversation. Using her mind only, she convinced the woman to speak out loud. "I can help you find what you're looking for," the woman said softly as they made their way back up the stairs.

The librarian was still weighted down with her armful of books. Making sure to keep in physical contact with the woman's arm, Anna helped her set the large pile down on a table near the top of the stairs. Then they continued walking past the rooms lined with bookcases and headed straight towards the private elevator.

Scanning the woman's mind, much as she had the book contents, Anna discovered the librarian's name was Sara.

Anna explained to Sara, in her mind, what she was looking for and convinced Sara to help her. She was pleased when she discovered that Sara could open the locked elevator and could also help her find the type of books she had been looking for, all without Anna having to push too hard for the assistance she required.

Anna didn't dive too deep into the woman's mind, knowing she was limited on energy. Plus, she felt any further intrusion would be rude and, more important, a waste of her time. What she was here to discover would not be found in the librarian's life story.

Together they finished making their way towards the secure elevator. Anna made sure never to break contact with Sara's arm as they moved. When the doors slid open, they stepped into the wood-paneled elevator together, keeping close to one another.

Anna knew this part of the journey was a bigger risk. There might be someone else already upstairs in the small secluded section and she could only control one mind at a time.

Praying the space was empty, she watched as Sara plucked a silver key from a chain attached to her belt loop and slid it into the spot above the elevator buttons. When the car started to move, Anna felt her nerves vibrating as excitement made her head spin.

She was getting closer to her goal.

Before they reached the third floor, she communicated her wishes to Sara and finished just as the elevator doors slid silently open. Then Sara said in a clear voice. "I'm sure we can find that special book your father is looking for up here, Ms. Chester."

Anna scanned the small space and discovered the hallway was completely empty. Releasing a sigh of relief, she and Sara walked towards the door labeled "Authorized personnel only."

After the librarian opened the heavy door, Anna glanced inside and saw a small lobby that held a table, a few scattered chairs, and a desk, which sat in front of another thick wooden door. She was relieved to see that this room was also empty.

Walking across the floor, they stopped in front of the second doorway. Hoping her luck would hold, she had Sara open the door and they walked in together.

The first thing Anna noticed was that this room had a different feel and smell to it. Here, the books were kept far away from the small square windows, which were covered with heavy curtains of deep brown. They were kept away from any light that might damage their fragile pages and the knowledge held inside. Knowledge that was locked away from the masses and allowed to only a select few.

Glancing around, she noticed another small wooden desk, which sat in the middle of the room. It was well worn and its dark wood scarred from years of use.

She asked Sara where she thought they should start looking and was guided across the hardwood floors to the shelves on their left.

Here Anna found books on astronomy and world history, some older than America itself, books that Anna had never seen or heard of before.

She could feel her excitement building and tried to maintain a firm hand on Sara's arm as she reached out with her free hand towards her destiny.

She grasped the first book and began collecting some of the oldest knowledge she'd ever encountered.

Five minutes later, Anna walked with Sara over to one of the narrow windows and lifted a corner of the curtain to check the street below. She hated feeling nervous but knew that it too was a lesson she'd learned in the past. There was a reason she was on guard, and that reason was strong enough to cause her to scan the streets below one more time.

She was content when she found everything still looked normal. The rain was continuing to fall and people on the streets were moving about their everyday lives.

Nothing looked out of place. She released a deep breath she'd been holding and relaxed slightly.

Moving away from the windows, she poured a quick drink of water from a pitcher, then set the empty glass on the desk. She headed back to another bookshelf to continue her search, as she dragged the spellbound Sara along with her every step of the way.

This time she focused on world geography instead of history.

After two more small breaks and three more granola bars, she checked the street below once more.

She began to feel the ticking of the clock and feared her time was running out. She was getting a little discouraged that she hadn't encountered a book with the information she'd been seeking.

Choosing to try the other end of the room where there were rare books from Europe, she pulled Sara along with her and scanned the titles only to discover that most of them were very old educational books with a few old fairy tales mixed in.

When her head started spinning five minutes later, she snatched another bar from her bag, thankful she'd stocked up before coming on her mission. For some reason, this time she'd grabbed enough of the energy bars to last her several weeks. It made her backpack heavier, but she'd known the extra weight would be worth it in the long run.

In fact, everything she owned was currently resting on her back. It had become a standard in her life to travel light and carry everything she'd need with her always.

She'd hopped from city to city, skulking in some of the lowest places she could scrounge enough money to stay at. This had been her life for so long, she could scarcely remember a time when life had been more than just living in fear and on the run.

Feeling the ticking of time once more, she headed back to the window and was terrified to discover that all the foot traffic on the street below had disappeared. The street was now completely empty and dark.

Something deep down in her gut told her that he had found her again. Her heart skipped a few beats and she felt her skin prickle with fear. Cursing herself for not keeping a closer eye on the time, she glanced over at Sara and thought about her next move. She'd planned for this, even though she'd hoped it wouldn't come to it.

Quickly, she relayed her plan to the librarian and they walked out the doors and back towards the elevator, leaving nothing behind.

Taking the car all the way down to the main level, she asked Sara to wait in the elevator for five minutes before leaving. Then she took the key chain off the woman's belt and finally broke contact with her just as the elevator doors were closing. There was a second before the double doors slid shut when she saw Sara's eyes returned to normal and a stunned and confused look crossed her face.

"Welcome back," Anna thought as she turned and quickly moved away. She moved down the hall to her right, which would lead her to the back of the building.

Using Sara's keys, she opened a door marked "Employees only" and made her way towards the service entrance near the back of the building.

As she passed a large employee bulletin board, she jolted to a stop when she noticed her own face looking back at her. Ripping the wanted poster off the bulletin board, she noticed that the grainy photo was from another library excursion she'd had in Baltimore. She was relieved to see that it was several years old and extremely fuzzy.

Her pale eyes had been hidden behind dark glasses, and her hair had been covered with a red ball cap which she'd lost several months back. Unfortunately, her physical description was listed below the photo, along with a reward amount of fifty thousand dollars.

After scanning the page, she shoved it into her pocket and continued past an open doorway. Apparently, the reward for her capture or information on her whereabouts had increased since the last poster she'd found. She was also frustrated to learn that she was now wanted in all fifty states.

Quickly glancing in an opened door that she was passing, she found herself once again looking at her own face. This time it was on several small television screens.

The room appeared to be a small security room. After her first glance, she continued at a quicker pace as understanding came to her.

There had been another flyer laying on the table under the monitors. It appeared the security guard had spotted her and called her location into the hotline.

Sheer panic rocked her entire body, causing her hands to shake once more. Her breath quickened, and she felt a bead of sweat roll down her back.

Trying not to rush too quickly, she reached the back door of the building and forced herself to stop so she could listen near the entryway. Caution. She had to remember to think and not rush into anything. That's how she'd been caught before.

Taking a deep breath to steady her racing heart, she listened and looked around.

"Move swift as the wind and closely-formed as the wood. Attack like the fire and be still as the mountain." The quote from *The Art of War* played over in her mind. Its wisdom soothed her into action.

After hearing nothing, she cautiously crept on her hands and knees towards a low window to peek out into the small alley behind the library.

She kept below the edge of the windowsill as she scanned the area. Trying not to panic, she stopped mentally berating herself for spending too much time in her search. She wasn't sure if it had been long enough to allow them to surround the entire place.

"Don't panic, keep calm. Think!" she told herself as she leaned against the wall and closed her eyes. Tapping the back of her head against the plaster, she quickly ran over every escape route in her mind.

"Think!" she hissed at herself. For some reason, only this back way came into her mind. She'd learned over the years to go with her first judgment. It had kept her alive thus far.

Forcing herself to move, she got onto her hands and knees and crawled past the windows, heading directly towards the door. If her luck held, there wouldn't be anyone along that part of the building, yet.

Sliding the heavy metal door open just a crack, she peered out and sighed with relief as she noticed the empty alleyway. The street was completely abandoned, and the rain continued to fall in a steady sheet.

Glancing up, she tried to see if there were any snipers on the roof of the surrounding buildings. Everything appeared clear. This was always a good sign.

Knowing it could be only a matter of seconds until men were in position, she took a deep breath, bolted to her feet, and ran from the open doorway. The familiar sound and feeling of her backpack hitting against her body as she ran helped her keep pace as she moved as fast as she could, counting the seconds and heartbeats in her head.

Sprinting down the side streets, she headed away from the building in her planned route of escape.

"So far so good," she thought as she hit the outskirts of the city park that lay directly across from the library.

She ran past large trees that dripped with moisture. A light fog started to gather around their huge trunks and crept slowly along the walking path. She knew the fog would help her escape and prayed it grew thicker.

Her breath was panting out of her lungs in little puffs of smoke as she ran through the icy rain. She felt her heart kick with each step and knew that she had only enough energy to run a few miles before she would be overcome with exhaustion.

She was halfway through the park when she bumped squarely into a large figure completely dressed in camouflage. His large gun rested in his arms, cradled like a little child. He glanced down at her with a shocked look on his face.

At least the heavy rain had helped shield her from the man's view until she had been right in front of him. He must have been just out of basic training because when he saw her, his first instinct was to take a step backward. Then he moved quickly.

She flipped around, using a move she'd learned in a book about Tai Chi. Her movements were smooth and well-practiced as she sidestepped the man when he raised his weapon.

He was quick, but so was she. He didn't have any time to respond before her fingers grazed his face. It took only a moment of contact and she had him quickly convinced he'd just seen her running north, towards the river.

She persuaded him to call in the sighting on his radio, passing the information to his team leader. Then she urged him to follow the phantom Anna. She had learned in the past that if she placed a belief into someone's mind, they would follow that belief for a brief time, so she wasn't surprised when he took off sprinting in the opposite direction, chasing the phantom Anna.

If she could make it to the highway and the turnpike, she could hail a cab and be on the toll road before they knew that she had slipped past their trap. However, before she made it to the next street, she ran into three more Special Forces soldiers.

She touched each of them, using the same methods she'd used for years to avoid capture, her body moving so much quicker than their larger ones. After touching them, she had them all running away from the freeway and her escape route, chasing an Anna they could only see in their minds.

She passed Stuart Street and hoped she was in the clear. Her sides hurt from running and she was in desperate need of an energy bar. She was just thinking she could stop and shove a bar into her mouth when she ran straight into a roadblock setup one street before the highway. The barriers blocked the entire road as lights flashed their harsh yellow and red into the air. Their glow almost blinded her in the thick rain and brought unpleasant memories to her mind.

More than two dozen armed men were blocking her last exit, all, it appeared, were waiting for her to join the party. She felt completely hopeless as she watched guns quickly raised in her direction. Her dark sweatshirt lit up with small red lights from their scopes. She could hear men shouting and moving into position as all eyes focused on her.

She stood, almost paralyzed, as she realized too late that she had run right into General Wilberg's ambush.

Glancing around without moving her head, she noticed the large military trucks parked along the side roads. There were even more trucks filling the parking lot directly beside her as men in camouflage appeared behind her, successfully blocking the exit back towards the park.

Glancing up, she spotted the snipers that were stationed on the tops of the buildings surrounding the lot. There were even a few across the street in a parking facility. She felt the red glowing dots of their guns move over her chest, pointing and aiming directly at her heart.

Over fifty of America's finest were now pointing their weapons directly at her. At that moment, she knew her freedom was truly gone. There was no quick thinking to get her out of this mess, no escape route. Nothing. He had finally caught her.

No knowledge she'd ever obtained could have prepared her for this situation. Slowly, she raised her hands in surrender and silently hoped there wasn't a trigger-happy soldier in the group.

Surrounded in the trap, her arms raised as the soft rain continued to fall around. Her shoulders slumped in defeat. How could it end here?

All the years she had spent on the run, hiding, evading his grasp, only to be caught now. Frustration and anger filled her as she turned a slow circle towards him in the parking lot.

Imagine it, getting caught and killed for just trying to find herself, her origins, her family.

Parts of her wished she had just settled somewhere years ago, had a career and raised a family. Heck by now she could have had a brood of children running around. Of course, it would have been hard to explain why she didn't age, but still, she could have had a somewhat normal life and maybe even a family of her own.

Just thinking of having someone else to rely on, someone who would be there to share her life with had kept her hopes raised. Each time she had snuck into a place and risked getting caught just to find any information regarding her origins, she had that one single hope of finding someone like that kept her going. Maybe this time she'd find something that would lead her to back to the open arms of her unknown family.

She had created so many different stories of why they had abandoned her to this lonely place. Stories where she had been stolen, whisked away from their loving arms, or even hidden for her protection from an unknown enemy. As a child on the run, she had years to imagine every possibility.

But with each story she made up, the reality sunk in deeper that she was left all alone in America. Alone and running from the US military and her enemy, General Wilberg.

Even now, surrounded by snipers with their guns pointed to her where her heart beat fast in fear, she held onto the hopes of one day finding her family.

She watched as General Wilberg himself got out of a dark sedan and walked towards her. Floodlights lit up the rain-drenched parking lot and burned her eyes, almost blinding her. When he got closer, he had the nerve to smile at her as if he'd won the game. She slowly lowered her arms as he approached.

One of the great lessons she'd learned from scanning *The Art of War* played in her head.

"Appear weak when you are strong, and strong when you are weak."

When dealing with General Wilberg, it was that book's lessons she'd used the most.

Even now, when she was surrounded, she was unwilling to concede the battle. Looking directly into his eyes, she raised her chin as she cocked her left hip out. She added insult to her stance by giving her head an offensive tilt.

He noticed her move and stopped three feet away from her, no doubt remembering their last encounter. The van they'd been traveling in had hit a bump in the dirt road, which had allowed her to fall slightly closer to the general and scrape a hand across his knee.

She almost laughed at the memory of Wilberg and several of his men standing along the dessert road as she drove away in the dark van, leaving them staring after her. He was too smart of a man to let her touch him again.

"Anna." He nodded to her as water dripped off the brim of his hat. His ugly face seemed to grow even more so when he smiled at her. "It's been a while."

Shaking her head and releasing a deep sigh, she

slowly lowered her hoodie and let the rain fall on her face. Her pale eyes focused on the general's muddy brown eyes, which were filled with hatred. However, she noticed a slight hint of fear behind the anger, which caused her smile to grow.

"Not long enough, General." She purred out his title as she jutted her chin out slightly. He may have won this battle, but there were still plenty of opportunities for her to escape and win the war. After all, someone had to step closer to her, eventually.

She tried to keep the memories of this man chasing her when she was younger from surfacing. She knew he'd spent most of his life looking for the girl who didn't age. She'd been so young when she'd first seen him. Then again, so had he.

Shaking her head clear, she turned from the memories and started mentally preparing to do some fast talking. A loud noise to her left had her and General Wilberg spinning in defense.

Fear of bullets ripping through her flesh made her crouch down on the wet pavement. She knelt there, prepared to either run or fight and was stunned to see a small red sports car barreling down the street directly towards them.

The car slammed into one of the trucks in the barricade, causing it to explode like it had been hit with a tank. Then the red car crashed between two army jeeps, squeezing through the tight space as if there was plenty of room. When it finally broke into the middle of the parking lot, it headed straight towards Anna.

She watched as fully armed military men dropped their guns and ran for safety, almost as if the devil himself had been set upon them instead of a small red sports car.

"What?" General Wilberg yelled, taking a step away from her, his eyes burning into her own as if she held the answers to this problem.

She could tell he was torn between getting out of the way or taking his chances and grabbing her again.

"Stop that car!" he finally screamed as he turned and ran back towards safety. He continued to yell orders as he moved to a position behind his men.

"Always the brave general," she thought sarcastically as she glanced over at him and remembered all the other times he'd run from her. Of course, he'd never had so many men with him before.

"During chaos, there is also opportunity" Another lesson from *The Art of War* flashed into her mind.

Glancing around for an opening to escape, she had just enough time to take two steps backwards before the car came to a screeching halt directly in front of her.

When the door flew open, she bent down to look into the interior, hoping the small body of the car would shield any bullets. It was dark inside, lit only by the dome light on the car's ceiling. The driver was a man around twenty years old with sandy blond hair that was sticking up in every direction. He had a large grin on his handsome face as he waved his hand at her.

"Get in, Anna. Quick!" he yelled.

Grabbing the door handle, she hesitated for only a moment. "Who are you?" she asked.

"Does it matter?" he replied, looking up at her with a lopsided smile. Except for the tone of his voice, his demeanor was totally relaxed. Almost as if he were enjoying the entire ordeal.

Shaking her head clear, she decided it didn't really matter who he was or how he knew her name. Just as long as he could save her from the General's clutches. Besides, she knew the small space of the car would make it easy for her to reach over and take control the situation if the need should arise.

Jumping into the small car as fast as she could, she watched as the military men finally pointed their guns in her direction once more. She ducked her head down quickly, expecting bullets to fly into the glass at any moment. Just then, the tiny car lunged forward, sending men running for safety as it gunned out of the parking lot. Its tires spun on the wet cement as the rain continued to fall around them.

She watched in amazement as the barricades exploded out of their way well before the car even reached them. She was shocked to see the wood splinter and the metal fly as if being pushed by some unknown force feet away from the front of the car.

There was no visible damage to the car. She could hear bullets hitting the car, but so far none had hit the glass.

When she glanced towards the driver, he still had a smile on his face. His shaggy blond hair lay longer over his forehead, and several times she'd seen him swipe at it to clear his vision.

The car took a sharp turn down one of the side streets as the sound of gunfire slowly faded behind them.

Anna sat up a little and blinked a few times when she realized that her rescuer wasn't even holding the steering wheel. One hand rested in his lap while the other lay on the headrest behind her head. Looking forward, she watched as the car turned another sharp corner, the wheel moving of its own accord.

Quickly, she yanked on her seatbelt and stared over at the man once more. Panic and shock set in as she saw he wasn't even using his feet to make the car drive. Instead, he sat back like he was sitting in the back of a limo.

She leaned forward and for the first time since getting into the car, realized that the engine wasn't even running.

"What the hell is going on?" she demanded, as the car made another sharp turn. Now they were heading straight for the freeway, which only a few minutes ago, she'd been so desperately trying to reach.

"This is an amazing device," he said, glancing over at her. "I cannot wait until we get back so I can tell Shiarra all about the towns and creatures I have seen here." He looked over at her as the car merged smoothly into existing traffic.

The vehicle was traveling well over the posted speed limit and was weaving in and out of traffic effortlessly by itself. Its windshield wipers were going full speed as if they were the heartbeat, pumping the machine full of life.

"I thought I would not get to you in time, but my calculations were correct and here we are." He pointed to her, then tapped the side of his head, taking another moment to swipe the hair away from his eyes. "I will have us back to the Orick in no time and before sundown we will be back in Tharian." He crossed his long thin arms over his chest and grinned at her as if they were old friends.

"Great. A crazy man has just kidnapped me." She mumbled as she leaned back in her seat. She calculated that they were traveling too fast for her to jump out. For just a moment, she thought about reaching over and touching him, taking control of him with her gift, but since she didn't know how he was controlling the car, she didn't think she should chance it.

Glancing back behind the car, she scanned the traffic for any signs that the army was following them. Sure enough, there were over twenty vehicles racing onto the freeway ramp at high velocity, their flashing lights blaring through the gloomy evening rain. She knew the General wouldn't have let her go that easily.

"Look, I don't know who you are or how you're driving this car, but could you step on it? We need to get out of here." She pointed behind them.

"I am not sure what 'step on it,' means, however, that is exactly my plan. To get you out of here, Your Highness." Then he leaned over in an attempt to complete a full bow from his waist up in the small car. "Wizard Leian at your service, my lady," he finally said with a smile as he pushed his hair once more away from his eyes.

"Wizard?"

There was a word she hadn't heard in over twenty years. She glanced over at the odd man sitting next to her. Could this man really be a wizard? And if so, where had he come from? Why was he just now showing up? And what did he want from her?

Anna took a hard look at the man sitting behind the wheel of the self-driving vehicle. His shaggy hair was almost out of control. Where it wasn't in his eyes, it was sticking straight up. His blue eyes were almost laughing at the predicament they were in as he watched out the windshield. His arms were now crossed over his chest.

She scanned him with her pale eyes, searching from his blond head to his boot-clad toes. He was wearing worn, deep brown leather pants, which were tucked into tall brown leather boots that looked like they'd been worn for years. He had a finely knitted vest which covered most of him along with a shirt that appeared to be made of a rough tan linen. What really caught her attention, though, were the clasps and buttons on each garment. She thought the buttons were made from bone, and she didn't see any zippers or modern clasps or snaps.

Around the man's chest, hanging sideways, was a leather bag. Next to him on the seat was a hat, or what was left of one. He looked around six feet tall, but since he was sitting, she couldn't really tell. He was skinnier than her and his unruly blond hair needed cutting, badly.

Finally, she glanced into his eyes and realized he was smiling at her with his lopsided grin. The look eased some of her fears. Maybe it was the little dimple on his right cheek that made him look younger and somewhat harmless. Whatever it was, she could tell that the man didn't appear to mean her any harm.

Once she was finished with her assessment, he bowed his head slightly. "Yes, Your Highness, I am from Genoa, your home planet. I am from a small village called Tharian to be exact. It is on the eastern border next to the River Pontella. I have come, as I said, to take you out of here."

Anna still couldn't believe it. While he spoke, he didn't even look at the road once or pretend to drive the car. His speech was funny, like he was from England, but with a twisted accent, yet for some reason, it was familiar to her. He also talked as if she should know where, or what, these places were, all while keeping the simple smile on his face.

"Look… Wizard," she said with disbelief pouring from her tone, "I'm not sure you're playing with a full deck of cards, so maybe we should just focus our efforts on trying to get away from the scads of armed forces following us right now. Then we can talk about your delusion issues later."

The wizard turned around and looked out the back window. Laughing, he turned back to the front and gave Anna another crooked smile. "Do not worry about them. I created a bubble. They will not bother us. Besides, we should reach the Orick soon. It lays just beyond that hill." He pointed off to the left in front of them.

"Bubble?" She shook her head in disbelief.

Boy! This guy was further gone than she'd realized. Peeking at the speedometer, she realized she couldn't even judge the speed the car was going since the motor was off. None of the gauges were even working! However, taking a guess, she estimated they were doing a little over 80 miles an hour and the car didn't show any signs of slowing down as they approached the hill he'd been talking about.

Glancing back again, she noticed that the army trucks that were chasing them were quickly gaining ground. Twisting a little more, she saw something else out of the corner of her eye. Occasionally a ripple would happen in the air outside the car, causing distortion in her vision. Removing her seat belt, she turned even further around, then propped her left knee on the seat and watched as it happened several more times. She began to understand what was happening.

The wizard's "bubble" was stopping the bullets that were flying towards them. The bullets, which were no doubt trying to hit their tires to disable the car, would cause a big ripple in the bubble, then fall quickly to the ground.

Anna prayed the protection would hold when the army tried the tire spikes, which she knew would be the next step.

"Where is your wizard?" The question had Anna turning back to Leian in shock. "Why are you traveling without Wizard Orden?"

Upon hearing the name, the memories she'd blocked out long ago rushed forward in her mind and consumed her.

General Wilberg was so young, she almost didn't recognize him. He was laughing as he tossed her little body up in the air. She was giggling and squealing with delight as she flew high above the man, then landed safely back in his waiting arms, begging to be tossed once more.

There was another man laughing beside the pair. She smiled over at the man she'd thought of as her father.

Orden, Wilberg had called him.

Another memory rushed forward into her mind,

49

this one from several years later. She'd been feeling ill, and Orden was hovering over her when Wilberg rushed in. He was in his late twenties now and was dressed in a starched military uniform. Seeing her in a desperate state, the man voiced his concern and reached out to grab her to rush her to the hospital.

She'd unwillingly scanned the man's memories, the first display of her powers. In his memories, she witnessed the young Wilberg being abused by another man. The acts done to him caused Anna's small body to convulse and she desperately tried to push the man away from her and break contact.

Finally, Orden had broken the contact using a warm soft green glow from his own power, something he never showed any other "human."

Wilberg and Orden had then argued a few feet away from her. Wilberg pointed towards her and yelled, "What is she?" Then he turned to Orden and his eyes narrowed as anger, fear, and hatred consumed him. "What are you?"

The shocked look on Anna's face must have been apparent since Leian grabbed her hand and gripped it tightly as her ears buzzed and her eyes swam with un-fallen tears "Has something happened to Wizard Orden?"

CHAPTER TWO

Finding Paradise

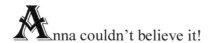nna couldn't believe it!

Orden was a name she hadn't heard since she was small.

Had anything happened to Orden? Yes, everything had happened to Orden, and it had been his own fault.

She remembered so much about him, the two strongest memories that stood out the most were his magic tricks and his death.

She also remembered he had been kind, an old man with dark gray eyes that would shine when they were doing "secret magic," as he called it.

He used to call her his little princess and would make her laugh by swinging her high up in the air, spinning her above his head for minutes at a time by waving his arms, something the other man she'd known as Uncle Wil could never do.

Orden had called it flying when he could keep her up in the air for as long as she begged. Then, when he brought her down, he would make a new toy for her or give her sweets to eat.

Orden had made sure she was fed and clothed, and had even given her an education himself.

She also remembered traveling a lot, always on the move from one place to the next, never settling down in one location for very long. But in all the places they had been, she had never seen anyone else do what Orden could.

Years later she'd assumed she had made up the strange memories. After all, she'd learned that most childhood memories are embellished. At least that's what she kept telling herself.

Hearing his name now, she remembered the day he died, seeing all the flashing lights and hearing the loud screeching. She didn't want to relive it now. Especially since she'd just been so close to being captured by the very man who'd killed the only father or family she had ever known.

"Yes, something happened to Orden," Anna whispered as she stared out to the rain-soaked windshield. "He's dead. Betrayed by a friend."

Leian removed his hand from her arm and whispered, "I'm sorry." He too turned and looked out the front of the car.

"How is it that you know who I am? How do

you know about Orden?" Anna asked as the car sped off the freeway and headed onto a side street next to a large swollen lake. Emotions swirled around inside her as she watched the tall trees with multicolored leaves surrounding the water's edge pass by her window quickly. There was a sign for a state park ahead, which reminded her of the last time she had camped in the Rocky Mountains, well over a year ago.

"I told you, I am from your home. I came here to bring you back so we can start to set things right," Leian said.

"Where is my home?" she whispered as she felt the car slow. She'd spent her entire life trying to find "home," and now here was this man talking about it as if it was just around the corner. All of a sudden, she felt weary. Running no longer seemed paramount, she had searched since Orden's death for answers. She was beginning to question if she wanted to really know the truth after all. How was it that the unknown was suddenly scary? Here was This stranger willing to give her all the answers and the only thing running through her mind was fear.

She saw a gap in the trees ahead and was shocked to feel the car take a right turn. It slid slightly, spitting mud and rocks into the air. The feel of the car spinning sideways caused her to snap on her seat belt again and grab for the bar above the window as her heart raced once more, bringing her out of the funk she had been in. She would try to listen this man's answers and decide for herself if the truth was worth it. All her years on the lamb, hiding in dirty alleys, sneaking into libraries while searching for one word that could help her figure out the magic she held and the place where she belonged. All while thumbing rides across the country that seemed determined to lock her up and dissect her because she was 'different'.

Once the car righted itself, the speed continued to slow almost to a crawl as they headed into a clearing that Anna realized was a large baseball field.

"Where are we going, why are we slowing?" she screamed as panic once again filled her, she knew that the General and his men were always behind her.

Looking back through the rain, she saw the large army trucks take the same turn. Some were not so lucky and ended in the ditch, others missed the gap entirely, skidding on the wet road and hitting the trees on either side. She couldn't stop the small smile; seeing the General have difficulty, always caused her joy.

"We are here and I do not want to hit the Orick going too fast. A forest lies on the other side and we may hit something." As he spoke, the wizard took a handful of what looked like small round cookie sprinkles, in assorted colors, out of his pouch and spread them over the car's dash. The car was heading to the far side of the field where a forest of large trees sat. Between the trees, she saw the edge of another lake.

"You have got to be kidding!" she screamed as the sound of bullets hitting the bubble echoed around the car. "You're going to get us both killed!"

"Take another look," Leian said while he moved his hands over the now jewel-encrusted dash.

Anna bent forward just as the dash started to shimmer. Looking up she realized they were still heading right for the lake, now at an alarming speed.

Thinking she would try to jump out of the car, she grabbed the door handle just as the front of the car disappeared before her eyes.

Blinking twice, she leaned forward in time to see the windshield and dash vanish. She tried yanking on the door harder but it didn't budge.

She screamed as her high-tops vanished before her eyes, and by the time her legs went missing, she felt like she was going to pass out. Her breathing was faster than it had ever been. Her fingers gripped the door handle so hard, they turned an even lighter shade of white.

Her voice didn't work, but her mind continued to scream in horror as she watched her entire body disappear before her very eyes.

The car did hit something, just as Wizard Leian had said it might.

It careened off a small spruce and headed

straight for the biggest tree Anna had ever seen. She screamed again, just before they struck it with a bone-jarring crunch.

The car finally jerked to a halt after getting its bumper tangled in the bark of the huge tree, slamming both Anna and Leian forward. Since Anna had her seat belt on, she stopped short of the dash, but Leian smashed into the windshield headfirst and slumped back into the seat, apparently unconscious.

Not sure if the bubble was still surrounding the car, she released her seat belt and jumped out prepared to do battle with the army that was surely surrounding them.

As her feet hit the ground, she felt the ground give and gripped the door of the car to prevent herself from falling. The dirt gave a small shake and a puff of white smoke moved outward from her high-tops in a large ring. It traveled away from her at a very fast speed until it disappeared.

"Weird." Shaking her head in doubt, she glanced around and was instantly confused by her surroundings.

As far as she could see, there was no sign of the military trucks. In fact, there was no park, no rain, no lake, and nothing she recognized for as far as she could see. Her surroundings were so unexpected that her uncertainty almost overtook her causing her to worry that she had hit her head in the crash. It was as if her eyes couldn't focus and her brain was unable to comprehend what it was she was actually seeing.

Worry began to set in. Then, her years of training took over and she instantly knew that action was needed. She pushed her apprehensions to the back of her mind and walked around the car, she opened the driver's door and checked on Leian. When she shook him lightly, he moaned and started moving.

"Don't move too much, you may have hurt your neck. Take it slow," Anna said as she grabbed her backpack and searched for her first aid kit. "Here, let's stop the bleeding. You have a nasty gash on your forehead." She pushed a gauze pad against his left temple, trying to get the blood to stop.

Leian's eyes rolled around to Anna as he pushed her hands away.

"That will not be necessary, let me get my salve and I will be just fine." He reached into his bag and produced a small square tin. Opening it, he rubbed two fingers into the purple mixture and then wiped it straight over the gash. She was amazed to see the split skin start to close itself. His skin drew tight and pulled together as the blood flow stopped altogether.

He grabbed the gauze from Anna and used it to wipe the blood and remaining salve off his face, leaving a clean and unscarred forehead.

"What the hell was in that, and where can I get some?" Anna said taking a step back with a shake of her head as she felt her life and everything she'd ever known slip down the rabbit hole a little bit more.

"That, Your Majesty, was Winnept sap, and as to where I got it, you may not want to know. Quite a nasty journey that I hope not to repeat for quite a while," he said as he extracted his tall frame from the car.

"You're what?" Anna asked, panic laced her voice. She watched him reach back into the car for his hat and then rose to his full height of around six and a half feet. He turned and looked back through the arch as he placed the crumpled hat on his head. "Well, that was an adventure!" he said as if he had not heard her question.

Anna tried not to laugh hysterically, the hat made him look more like a vagabond than a wizard. It was badly shaped, as if it had been sat on for weeks then run over with a mower. It was also the color of puke. The sight of his full appearance made her forget her question.

Mistaking her laugh for joy, he clasped his hands on her shoulders and smiled. "Welcome home, Your Highness."

"Home?" she asked, sobering once more. Her heart skipped a beat when she thought about it. Then her eyes moved around the forest once more.

Behind the car, she saw two very large rocks, each over 100 feet tall. Spanning between them halfway up their length was a stone arch.

Glancing under the archway, she held her breath, waiting to see the full force of Jeeps and trucks rush through the same pathway the red sports car had just come. Instead, all she saw was more thick trees and the mushy forest floor.

Confused, she glanced around for the road and the ballpark. Maybe they had gone deeper into the park than she remembered? But somewhere in the back of her mind she knew she was no longer near the park. Or Boston. Or even the good old US of A.

The car sat against the tree near a clearing surrounded by large trees that reminded her of California's redwoods, minus the redness of the bark. Their large dark gray trunks spanned wider than the car, and they had deep grooves running up their lengths, right up to where their green branches spread out from their core in a beautiful display. She could smell the fresh air and the hint of pines needles.

"I didn't think Boston had trees this large." The sound of her voice echoed back at her in the small clearing, causing her to quickly glance around again.

She realized then what else was missing—the rain. She looked up to the sky and sighed. The thickness of the trees might be shielding them from the weather.

"Where have you taken me?" She grasped his arm with all the strength she could and looked into his blue eyes as if searching for the answers in their depths.

Looking confused, he gestured with his left arm, "Why, Genoa, of course."

Anna would have argued more, but her eyes followed the sweeping motion of the wizard's arm upward until she saw what sat above the large treetops, just beyond the archway. The moons. Three of them, to be exact.

The first moon, a crescent shape, was the color of summer grass. She blinked a few times and stared at it as it hung high in the blue sky in complete defiance of Anna's beliefs. She took a few steps closer to the archway and tilted her head to get a better view.

The second moon was smaller and to the left of the first one. It was as white as snow and round in its fullness.

The third moon was located above the other moons and was a little larger than Earth's own moon. This one was bright yellow, like a daisy, and had no craters to scar its pretty face.

She shook her head, worried once again that she was concussed, because there weren't three moons on Earth. Only one. She closed her eyes and took a deep cleansing breath, then opened them again and sighed. There were still three moons in the sky.

Maybe she should lay down for a while.

Rubbing her eyes now, she double-checked once more. The full sky wasn't visible, most of it was restricted by the trees, but what she could see were three moons, bigger and brighter than any moon she had ever seen on Earth.

"What are those?" she asked as she pointed up at the moons.

"What?" he asked, distracted as he looked closer at the car's damage. "Ah, yes, the moons, hmm...The yellow one is Blinske, the green one is Grenata, and the small one is Merria. She means good luck to travelers. There are nine to be exact, but only a few are visible this late in the day. Speaking of which," he continued as he walked around the car, "we should head out if we want to make the village by nightfall." The wizard walked to the right of the large rock formation, leaving Anna no choice but to follow him. She glanced once more up at the sky, then shook her head slightly in disbelief.

Leian bent down next to a bush and picked up what appeared to be a walking stick. He grabbed a leather satchel that had two straps, much like Anna's backpack, and threw it over his shoulder.

Then he faced the woods, placed his fingers on the edge of his mouth, and let out a long, loud whistle.

"Sam should be here soon; he tends to wander when left to his own devices." Leian glanced about, looking for Sam, whoever that was.

He pulled a water skin from his bag, removed a cork from the top, and took a long drink. When he was finished, he offered Anna some. Giving her head a shake, she turned and walked back to the car.

"I guess if we have to get out of here, it will be

up to me." Opening the passenger side door, she rummaged through the glove box. She considered herself lucky when she found a broken flashlight, sunglasses, and a pocketknife, which she quickly stuffed into her backpack. She also found a map of Boston, but wasn't sure it would do any good. Especially if she was indeed on another planet. Still, she grabbed it just in case.

Another planet! she thought in amazement. *No wonder I could never find any information on where I was from on Earth.* Doubts continued to whirl around inside her head. All the years of being in danger while searching for information. Now, it appeared that she would have never found any answers in any book on Earth.

Popping the trunk release, she moved to see what she could find there. "Great! A roadside kit! This should have some tools in it. You think you can get the car moving again? We may be able to maneuver it between these trees until we find a road," Anna said as she grabbed everything out of the trunk, including the tire iron, and placed it inside the black bag the roadside kit was in.

"We will not need the machine. Here comes Sam," Leian said.

Anna turned her head just as she heard rustling in the bushes between her and Leian.

She watched in amazement as the largest horse she had ever seen walked into the clearing and stepped towards her. The animal had to be ten feet tall from the top of its head down to its large hooves.

Shaking its massive head, it walked towards Leian. And that's when Anna noticed, not only was the beast huge, it was a dark purple and shimmered as if made of glass.

"What is that?" Anna whispered, not wanting to scare or anger the creature. She took a step back, ready to make a run for it if she felt threatened.

"*He*," Leian answered, as he continued to pet the nose of the horse, "is a crystal-haired horse from the Plains of Rith. Very rare to have a purple one. Most of them are yellow, blue, or green. Helps them blend in, you know." He glanced towards her. "Sam is somewhat of a runt too, but don't let that fool you." He turned back towards the horse. "He's as brave and willing as any horse you will ever find," Leian said with pride. "But a bit soft around the womenfolk if you ask me." He said and winked towards her.

Taking a deep breath, Anna watched as the animal butted its head against Leian's shoulder until the man pulled out what appeared to be a small eggplant from one of his bags and gave it to the horse. "Sam, do not be rude. Go say hello to Anna before she thinks you a savage or something."

By the time Anna could take two steps back towards the car, Sam was in front of her, using his large nose to smell the top of her head. His warm breath blew her hair about, and then he bent his neck and breathed in her face.

Not sure how it would be best to back away, she raised a hand to ward Sam off and found that the hair on his neck was soft as mink. Curiosity got the better of her and she took a step closer to take a better look at the totally translucent hair. Apparently, what gave the horse his purple color was the skin beneath the hair, not the hair itself.

Awed by this, she leaned closer and was so focused on looking at his skin that she didn't see him go in for a huge, wet kiss. Next thing she knew, the whole side of her head was wet with horse slobber.

"Yuck! Why did he do that?" She turned to Leian as she pulled Kleenex out of the pocket of her hoodie.

The wizard was laughing so hard it took him a minute before he could explain that Sam must be in love with her because horses rarely kissed.

By the time she cleaned off most of the horse goo, Leian was sitting astride Sam. Since Anna hadn't seen him jump, use a ladder, or fly up to the horse's back, she was not sure what to expect.

"Are we riding Sam?" she asked with uncertainty, slowly walking closer. "How do you expect me to get on his back? He's huge!" She threw her full backpack over her shoulder and looked up at Leian.

"Simple, just ask," Leian explained.

"Ask?" Anna walked to Sam. His head was

easily four feet above the top of her head. The animal didn't appear to be paying any attention to her as he gazed off into the woods, swinging his tail as if he had all the time in the world.

Deciding she had nothing to lose, she stepped closer to the animal and asked, "Sam, may I please ride you?" Surely, the animal would continue to stare off into space or even walk away. But she was shocked when Sam lowered his neck all the way to the ground. Anna was amazed to see that this brought his back to about her stomach height.

Leaning over to the side, she looked at Sam's legs and saw that he was bending all four of his knees to allow her access. Sam was not built exactly like horses on Earth and all his legs were bent in the same direction, giving him balance and the ability to lower to the ground without falling.

"Wild!" she said as she grabbed hold of the hair on Sam's mane and began to gently lift herself up onto his back. She was halfway on when Sam stood up to his full height.

Letting out a quick squeak, she tried to wiggle the rest of the way on his back and could have sworn she heard the animal laugh.

"Oh, I forgot to tell you, Sam has a great sense of humor. Sorry about that." Leian helped pull Anna the rest of the way up so she was sitting in front of him.

Once she was settled on the horse's back, Sam turned around and started off into the very bushes he had emerged from.

There were no stirrups, reins, or any kind of normal horse equipment. There was just Sam's long mane.

Anna, who had never ridden a horse before, found that riding a crystal-haired horse from the Plains of Rith was very pleasant. She was not thrown about and never felt like she was about to fall off. There was just a soft rocking sensation, as if you were sitting on a porch swing.

Leian was not holding onto Anna as expected, but was currently digging in his leather pouch and mumbling to himself.

"How far do we have to travel and where is it we are going again?" she asked, not sure how much the wizard was going to tell her.

"It will be sundown before we reach the outskirts of Tharian. According to the moons, I have only been gone one sun cycle, so Shiarra may not be expecting me yet." He proceeded to pull out a piece of parchment about the size of his palm.

Anna twisted her head and watched in amazement as he unfolded the item until it resembled a large poster. Leian held the paper between the two of them as he studied the item.

"What is that?" she asked, turning her head and trying to get a better look. Her fingers itched to grab the parchment.

"This? It is a map," he answered quickly.

"Don't you know where we're going?" she asked in a panic, not even a hundred percent sure he was the one steering and directing Sam.

"I know where we are going. However, I get the sinking feeling we are not the only ones who know where we are traveling." He bent his head and concentrated on the map once more.

Anna wasn't sure how wizards normally acted, since she only had known two in her life. However, she knew when someone was trying to avoid her questions.

What did Leian mean they weren't the only ones who knew where they were going? Why was he looking at a map if he knew where they were heading? He had said Shiarra was not expecting them, but who was Shiarra?

She felt once more like Alice down the rabbit hole. Her understanding of life was spinning around and all jumbled up. She knew nothing for fact, not even where in the universe she was. Her eyes moved once more to the three moons hanging overhead. What if the army and General Wilberg could make it through the archway?

Her thoughts mixed and jumbled for a time and then she started to worry about the unknown. Maybe it was time she did something about it.

Trying to act natural, she used the motion of the horse to bring her right hand back, resting it lightly against Leian's thigh. She brought her skills to the surface quickly. When nothing happened, she glanced down and confirmed she did have physical contact with his body and tried once more.

When nothing came to her, she tried harder. Confused, she glanced around and saw that Leian was staring at her over the top of his map.

His eyebrows raised in question and laughter filled his eyes.

"Whatever you are trying, it will not work against a wizard." He gave her a queer look, his smile falling away as sadness filled his eyes. "You should have known that." Lowering his map into his lap, he continued to study her, "Why do you not know this? How long ago did your wizard die?"

She felt sadness overwhelm her as tears stung behind her eyes. She sighed and turned back towards the front, wishing more than anything she could avoid his questions.

CHAPTER THREE

Seeking Direction

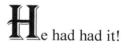e had had it!

Kriston's frustration and anger bounced inside him, boiling his blood and giving him a slight headache. The hatred that had been spawned by years of abuse could no longer be contained inside him. Yet hidden is where it had to remain in order for him to walk away alive.

Being summoned to the king's head chambers while he had his men in the middle of drills was one thing, but being escorted by his brother's secret guard, as if he were a prisoner, was another. He was being treated as if he couldn't be trusted to carry out the king's wishes when summoned.

Kriston glanced at the guards that surrounded him. His deep green eyes scanned the men and he realized he only knew one of the four that surrounded him. Their large bulk matched his, but if this meeting came to a fight, he would surely lose. At least he could count on someone to have his back in case he should have need. Dyne, his man, was good at deception and great at a fight. This was one reason he had been chosen in the secret guard. Kriston was thankful Dyne had not been discovered yet.

He was also grateful he was still dressed in his brown sparring leathers, which were wrapped around him and fastened by his dark weapons belt. If needed, he could move more easily in these clothes than his formal wear. Its stiff coat and high collar would have hampered him during a fight.

Facing the front once again, he walked further into the immense room. He barely noticed the elegant granite floors of the chamber, which gleamed in the afternoon light. The inlaid wood walls, which were over twenty feet tall, were lined with paintings that depicted some of the most famous battles Matera and her people had seen.

He didn't even look at the golden carved candle lanterns positioned around the cavernous room or the elegant tapestries hanging from the rafters. Instead, his eyes were directed at the man sitting on the royal throne in the middle of a raised platform.

Hate and anger filled him, so he squinted his eyes to shield his feelings as he looked at his brother sitting where their father once had been. If the throne was meant for a self-serving, lying murderer, then his brother was the man for the job.

Once standing in front of the king, he saluted as was tradition when meeting His Majesty. Even with Kriston's relationship to the king, his brother would not allow him to stray from tradition, which could make him look weak in front of his men.

"You summoned me, my lord?" Kriston said while trying to hold his contempt in check by lowering his eyes to the floor. This movement caused his jet-black hair to fall forward, giving him an unruly appearance.

"I have an errand for you, Captain, that requires your immediate attention," King Gillard said, addressing him by his formal title, as he always did. He moved down to stand in front of his younger brother. His lean frame did not reach the height of Kriston, yet this had never seemed to bother the king. Power was the only thing that had ever mattered to him and right now he held the power over Kriston.

An errand? Kriston's dark brows drew together as he contemplated the request. He had never been sent on an errand before. "What is it you require, my lord?"

"A trip must be made," Gillard said as he studied his brother. His light green eyes scanned Kriston as if looking at a pawn piece, instead of family. "A person of interest must be brought to me before the eve of the Moonvest." He reached up and laid one slim gloved hand on Kriston's massive shoulder, "I can trust no one but you to carry out my direct orders and my wishes, brother."

The unfamiliar word from his brother's lips made Kriston look quickly at his face. He did not miss the distinct hatred that was reflected in the king's eyes or the slight sneer on his thin lips. "With General Zobo out in the far south barrens fighting the Malics, it will be up to you to complete this urgent mission."

"I am at your service, my lord. Pray tell, who is this person of interest?" This was getting interesting, Kriston thought. Gillard never mentioned their relationship in private, let alone in the presence of the secret guard. He could tell the man was up to something and feared it would not go well for him or his people. Was that fear he saw behind the hatred in his brother's eyes? Very interesting.

"Leave us." The king dismissed his men, his tone striking close to anger. He was a man used to being obeyed, no matter what the order was.

Kriston watched the guards exit and saw only the slightest hesitation from his man when he looked back. Shaking his head once, he secretly informed Dyne to leave and was thankful the king was too busy pacing to notice the communication.

Once the doors were shut behind his men, Gillard walked back to his throne and sat once more, assuming the position of authority he preferred. He tilted his head to the side, causing his straight brown hair to fall about his thin face as he studied his younger half-brother.

Kriston knew what he would see. Kriston's hair was dark like his mothers had been, almost black, and thick with a slight wave to it. Gillard had their father's pale hair, straight and slightly thin. He wore it below his ears and kept it cut ruler straight. Kriston was built like the kings of old—tall, strong, and wide of shoulders. Gillard on the other hand was slight of build and shorter, much like his mother, or so he had heard. But both men were handsome in different ways.

Both brothers sported facial hair, as was the custom of the military. Kriston wore his in a fashionable short goatee while Gillard wore his chin hair in a point that extended beyond his collar. They both had green eyes, but Kriston's were dark like Grenata, the dragon moon, while Gillard's were the color of light moss and often full of hate or lies. Even now, hatred and deception flowed towards the young prince.

Kriston knew his brother despised him and had worried for many seasons where his older brother's deep hatred had come from. Currently, it appeared to be rooted in the fact that Kriston was one of the main captains of Matera's force and held the respect of most of the military men, something Gillard would never achieve.

Gillard required absolute loyalty in his men and when he could not obtain the whole force's allegiance, he'd had to create the order of his secret guard. This regiment was made up solely of men who would complete any task when paid handsomely and whose loyalty was always given to the one with the largest purse.

Kriston knew that his bold stare deeply angered Gillard but guessed that his brother required something from him badly enough that he was willing to overlook it, since he sat quietly. The king stroked his beard as if he was trying to decide on using a different tactic, then leaned forward, placing his hands on the arms of his throne, his eyes glued to Kriston's.

"Brother, we are at war." He spoke softly. "The Queen of Valorna has sent a spy into the lands in hopes of turning the people against us. She wants to deny us trading rights." As he leaned back in his throne, Gillard pressed his palms together as if considering a great choice. "Kriston, it is said this spy comes to take all magic from Matera."

Disbelief must have flashed behind Kriston's eyes, since Gillard leaned forward again. "I too did not believe this was possible. I have had Wizard Fulder search out the great books to see if this was a valid threat. He is concerned there may be an ancient magic about and has calculated that the spy is the key."

Kriston shook his head. "My lord, I have never heard of this being possible. When schooled, nothing was mentioned about the possibility of stealing magic." Kriston spoke of the education all royals received when their magic developed. "Why are we just now hearing about this?"

Anger crept into Gillard's face. "You doubt me!

I have told you what is!" He growled and once again showed Kriston his quickness to anger, much as he had been doing his whole life. "The Moonvest is the cause. It has been several seasons since the last phase of the red moon Enwar, but the next time will be unique. The wizard calculated that the traveler's good luck moon, Merria, will be aligned with Enwar. The small moon will travel in front of the red moon making Merria's good luck run red and a great eye will be in the sky for seven days until its time has passed."

As he spoke, he lunged towards Kriston. His eyes bulged and his thin face grew red. The prince didn't budge an inch when his brother bore down on him but instead continued to stand at attention.

"If this spy stands on our doorstep during this time, all magic in our land could be diminished, leaving us powerless against our enemies!" Once again, the king grasped Kriston's shoulder. "If this happens," he hissed, "all is lost."

Kriston thought about this. Could magic really be taken that easily? He knew from experience that his brother didn't always tell the truth, but he could only delay until more details were brought to light. "What would you bid of me, my lord?" He bowed his head for the first time since entering the chambers, in the hopes of appeasing his brother.

Smiling slightly, Gillard pulled a green parchment from his robe. "Take this seeking map and find the spy. She will be disguised as a young woman and will try to deceive all with her lies.

Bring her to me." After handing the parchment to Kriston, he turned and walked back up the steps. "Alive," he added. "I must find out the queen's plans." Turning back to Kriston from the throne dais, he added, "And Captain, do not fail me." With that, he exited out a side door behind the throne, leaving Kriston alone with his doubts.

Why didn't she know her powers wouldn't work on a wizard?

That was simple—because Orden had died before he had finished schooling her on her powers, back when she appeared to be in her teens, even though they had been on Earth for almost twenty years by that time. Old resentments rose in her as she thought back to her childhood. Orden had kept them moving around, most of the time living in the woods and always maintaining his use of magic.

During their seclusion, he had taught her all about his skills, teaching her things she was later never able to find in any of the books she had acquired knowledge from. Things about moons she never saw, trees she could not imagine, and even about dragons that flew in the warm sun. At least some of these items she had found in books on Earth, but they always called those fairy tales.

"How long ago did your wizard die?"

She remembered it like it was yesterday. They had stopped in a small town on the outskirts of

Texas when they saw General Wilberg.

By the time they realized he was no longer their friend, they were surrounded and it was too late.

If Orden's reactions had been any slower, they may have been finished that day. But escaping out of sheer luck and magic, they fled for their lives and headed to the northwest.

Anna had insisted that the wizard put away all magic, keeping it hidden from people near them so Wilberg could not find them. But old habits were hard to break. Two months later the wizard was dead and she was once again running for her life, constantly on the move, keeping to the back roads and forests, and to herself.

She was still burdened by Orden's death, struggling with the loss and loneliness because he was the only father or family she had ever known. The guilt and shame ate at her for years as she sought understanding of her powers and origins, always seeking knowledge that would lead her back home, even if she didn't know where that place was.

She had discovered her ability to gain knowledge from books with just a single touch and became a vagabond moving from library to library.

The first thing she had learned was self-defense. However, knowing it in one's mind was a lot different than knowing it with your body. So, she started training her body slowly and practiced the moves until they became almost second nature.

Her power extended to reading people.

Understanding came of how her powers had first shown itself when she had seen into Wilberg's past. She could obtain a person's knowledge, thoughts, and wishes just by touching them. She could also control their beliefs and force images into their minds by just thinking of what she wanted to convey.

She tried to keep attention from herself, yet always sought knowledge of any location on Earth that fit Orden's description of where they were from.

Searching every known library for clues to her origin and how to get back there was her number one priority. She tried to stay under Wilberg's radar but soon discovered he had a personal mission to capture her. He had started calling her "the alien."

Alien.

She used to scoff at the word, never realizing how true those words had been. Even now, she struggled with the fact that she appeared to be on another planet. One that, according to the man currently sitting behind her on a purple horse, she was from.

General Wilberg had been correct all along. She was indeed from an alien world.

"He died when I was small. A short time after my powers surfaced," she said and tried to shake off the despair. For a while she watched their progress through the woods as her mind whirled.

Several thoughts came to mind, things she had never understood but had always felt were off. For example, no matter what library she had snuck into, no matter how many books she gained knowledge from, none held any clues into her gifts. Her magic, if she were to believe the wizard's words.

She had looked in history books for any indication that there had been gifted humans on Earth. She had even begun to believe that Orden had been a family member, maybe a crazy one who had stolen her away.

Sometimes she dreamed that she had been from a royal family who had all been killed off, her lineage concealed away for many generations until it found her alone. Alone with no knowledge of who she really was, with no explanation of where the power inside her came from.

She had thoughts of mutation, experimentation, and even divinity. Never had it crossed her mind that she was from another world.

She felt Leian study her, then he shrugged his shoulders and went back to studying his map.

Anna's mind continued to swirl with thoughts and doubts. She studied the trees and saw pines and maples. She could even see some ferns and other plants in the underbrush that were familiar. However, the further Sam walked, the more she realized that not all the trees were familiar.

She started seeing bright spots amongst the foliage, reds and bright oranges peeking here and there. At first, she thought maybe this was the fall leaves getting hit with sunshine, then she noticed that some of the colors were not what you normally saw in fall. Purple was one of them. When they passed a small blue tree, she almost fell off Sam's back.

Straining her neck, she glanced at the blue tree with its very fine leaves. The closer they got to it, the more the leaves looked like fine thin feathers. Each stuck from black branches and hung in a pretty fashion down to the forest floor. Since the tree was not as tall as Sam, she tried to bend down to grab a branch with her hand. The horse shook his mane violently, causing Anna to quickly grab ahold in an attempt to prevent herself from falling off his back.

"Glad you did not grab the Stint tree. Stings like a Zent cat, and it would take a week for the swelling to go down," Leian said as he continued to contemplate his map.

After hearing this, she was convinced her hands were best left tucked into her lap where they were safe.

She continued to look about and was shocked to notice more differences between Earth and Genoa. She could hear birds singing high in the branches as they searched for food or love. There were high whistles and low hums from the trees. A few times she saw small animals as they scurried about, either moving in the tall grasses or climbing trees.

Her attention kept going back to the smaller trees, and when they passed a bright red tree shaped like a cone, she knew this was not a typical Earth forest.

All those years she had spent searching for home, and now here it was. Genoa.

This realization left her both excited and nervous. Would it live up to her expectations? More importantly, why did she have no memories of this place?

The wonder before her eyes had her longing for more details. Why had she been on Earth? Why had she been in the care of a wizard? But the most important one of all was, who was she really?

"Can I ask you a question?" She finally spoke up.

"What is it you wish to know, Your Highness?" Leian said as he folded the map back and placed it in his bag.

"Everything, but I'll start with why you keep calling me Highness."

Giving her his full attention, he gave her a small lopsided grin. "You, Anna, are the daughter of Lady Marybeth and his Highness King Edwin Collin Reginald the third, who had been supreme ruler of Valorna which sits in the center of Genoa. It is Genoa's crown jewel."

As his words sank in, she felt her breath whoosh out of her chest and her ears started buzzing.

CHAPTER FOUR

Which Way is Home?

After the initial shock came disbelief. After that came laughter.

"Wizard Leian, we really need to talk about your medication," she said with humor. Of one thing she was sure—she was not royalty.

When she thought of royalty, she thought of England's queen and royal family. Years of riches and breeding left no doubt of who they were.

One look at Anna and anyone would say vagabond, not princess.

But that was fine; her demeanor had kept her out of the General Wilberg's clutches for years. If she had pranced about Earth, she was sure she would have been dead long ago.

Shaking her head and pushing her bangs out of

her eyes, she forced this information to the back of her mind while she looked around again. While they had been talking, Sam had continued to walk along a narrow path through the woods. Anna could see the trees thinning up ahead as their journey continued.

"Tell me about Genoa. I assume it's a planet, but where? Is the planet located in the Milky Way?" she asked trying to get a better glance at where the sun was positioned in the sky to their left.

"Milky Way?" He thought for a moment with a frown on his face. "No, there is no milk in our sky, just stars and moons," Leian said just as Sam stepped beyond the trees.

The first thing she saw was rolling hills covered with tall waving grass. The colors varied from green to yellow to... was that purple? Here and there she saw cows dotting the hillsides, and they too were odd colors. No black and white or even a nice brown, here it seemed the cows ran towards a solid teal or a deep green. Even a pink one roamed lazily around as they all fed in the afternoon light, chewing grass or laying on the hills.

"Ah, we are almost there. These are the fields beyond my village, Tharian. See, I told you we would reach home before nightfall." He placed a hand on her arm and leaned forward. "Anna, for a time, we must keep your arrival secret. Your presence here will cause more trouble than we want at this time."

She turned and looked the wizard in the eyes.

She understood what he was asking, having been used to covering her appearance. She reached back and placed her hood over her head and covered her hair and skin once more.

"Thank you, Your Majesty," he said as he leaned back. "Sam, to the training house, please." And with that, Sam continued at a slow trot through the grass towards the hills beyond.

When they reached the fields, she noticed the grass was as high as Sam's belly, making it almost six feet tall. She saw patches of bright, multicolored flowers tucked into the grass. Their yellow and blue faces added cheer to the hills.

Beyond the fields, in the far distance, was the bluest ocean she had ever seen, the waves crashing on the distant shore of white sand. From this distance, she couldn't smell the sea air, and she wondered how many miles away the shore was.

As they neared the cows, she saw they were larger than Earth cows at well over six feet tall. She watched the nearest ones as they slowly chewed the grass. Each cow had at least two sets of horns sticking out above their ears, each over a foot long. They curved inward with spiral patterns along their lengths and were the same color as their hair.

As Sam continued their path through the fields, the sun dropped towards the sparkling water. Anna held her hand up sideways with her palm towards her face to help her calculate the time left before the sun set. She estimated they had about an hour before it disappeared below the horizon.

"Tell me about Genoa," Anna asked, turning back to watch the tall grass wave in the breeze and the cows meander around.

"Genoa is very old," Leian provided after a moment. "It is not recorded how old, but over two hundred generations have recorded their knowledge in the great libraries." He hesitated before continuing. "Currently her people are divided. In the south is Matera. Her people and king hold magic close and are secretive with their trading. To their north are the mining communities in the Cleveite Mountains. They don't fall under any monarch, but rather live under their own set rules. Their people's lives revolve around trading and they rarely leave their forges hidden deep in the mountains." The wizard pointed to their right. "To our southeast below the Deepen Forest are the Draydon tribes. Their existence has depended on their dragons and their territory for as long as anyone can remember. They too, live by their own rules as they have done for many generations. Valorna is located northwest and sits on the lake named Golden Enry whose waters are said to be liquid sunshine. Her people have a variety of trades and rare and valuable foods and medicines are grown in the fields beyond the lake. Then there is Tharian, my village, which mostly thrives on fishing, but wizard training has recently grown."

"Which way is north?" Anna asked, sure the wizard had pointed the wrong way based on the sun. If it was setting to their left, then north should be in front of them.

When he pointed behind them, Anna just shook her head and remembered she wasn't on Earth anymore. Trying a different tact, she asked, "What kind of trading goes on and did you say dragons?"

"Trading is key to a lot of villages—food, livestock, and other basic goods are the main things traded. The small towns are stopping points along the main roads. Most towns are maintained by the monarchs of that location, but the livelihoods of each town really depend on its people and their Sayer," Leian said with a shake of his head. "And yes, I did say dragons. They are very common here in Genoa. Most live south near the cliffs of Faro. They are the largest animals you will find in Genoa."

As they crested a small hill, Anna saw a quaint village in the valley below. A fat rolling river ran down its middle and separated the town into two halves. She could see yards between the houses that had gardens with tall green plants and flowers blooming behind fences.

The homes themselves were of wood and appeared to be well built. Each one had a tall chimney made of stone. She could see that hardly any of the chimneys had smoke billowing out, rising into the evening sky.

This got Anna thinking about the weather. Was this fall? It seemed rather warm, more like summer temperatures instead of fall, though it had been fall in Boston.

"Leian, what month is it here?" she asked, noticing that the flowers were in full bloom and marveled at the colors.

"Month? What does that mean?" he asked.

"The season, what season is it here in Genoa?"

"Ah, it is almost Mid-day, when we celebrate a new season," Leian said. "My favorite season—lots of sun and food, and the days are longer." He chuckled.

"Summer, it's summer here, correct?" Anna asked thinking about the difference in seasons, along with the sun's location.

"Sunner, yes, I believe that fits this season well. Here we call it the light season."

Anna did not want to correct the wizard's mistake and so she continued, "How many days are in a year here?"

"Year? What is it you are trying to ask?"

Trying not to get frustrated, she changed tactics once more. "How many days are there from one light season to the next?"

"Ah, you mean from one Mid-day to the next. There are nine hundred and twenty-two days from one Mid-day to the next. These are called cycles and are measured by the moon Lazerith and its new cycle. When the large moon is full, this is the start of a new cycle, which is called Mid-day. Each town and city celebrates Mid-day by spending the night watching the moon and drinking as much ale as they can find," he said with a chuckle. "Most do not remember actually seeing the full moon."

Shocked, Anna sat forward again and ran the numbers. So, on Genoa she would be almost twenty-one! "How long does a Genoan live? I mean, how many Mid-days?"

"Ah, the average person can live well past two hundred Mid-days. Why? How long did they live on Earth?" the wizard asked and curiosity could be read in his blue eyes. When Anna told him, he was shocked that the humans on Earth could accomplish anything in such a short time.

She wanted to ask further questions, but they were nearing the town. As they drew closer, she could see some people were lighting their lanterns. The lights glowed from the first few small houses, and she realized just how quickly the light was fading.

She saw people working in the yards. The women were dressed in cotton shirts with long sleeves and ankle-kissing skirts that were covered by long leather aprons in the front. Some had large straw hats on to keep the sun off their faces and were covered with thin ribbons or colorful flowers.

The men were dressed a lot like Leian, including the leather pants and the silly hats.

After they passed the first few houses, the news of Leian's return spread quickly. By the time they approached a bridge that spanned over the river, they had twenty or more people following them. Everyone was talking and asking Leian questions.

"Barion," Leian said, and all the people quieted down, giving him their attention, "please run and tell Shiarra to meet me in the training house." A small blond boy turned and took off like a rocket across the bridge.

"Wizard Leian, were you able to go through the Orick?" a woman with brown long hair asked.

"What was it like?" another woman with red curly hair pinned on top of her head asked.

"All your questions will be answered after I brief Shiarra and Sayer Phillip. Tamma, please tell the Sayer to meet us in the training house after he finishes his meal," Leian asked a blond woman who turned and walked off at a saunter to the left. Most of the people followed Tamma, however a few continued to walk beside Sam.

No one seemed to pay attention to Anna or attempted to peek under her hood, and none asked any more questions of the wizard.

As Sam walked over the stone bridge, Anna could see the clear water below in the failing light. Under the water, she saw large round rocks of various colors on the bottom of the river. They were red, orange, and even yellow, and they looked to Anna like a rainbow stuck at the bottom of the crystal-clear water.

After crossing the bridge, Sam turned to the right and stopped at a long two-story building with a large overhanging porch. Its wooden shutters were painted dark blue and the large doors held elaborately carved symbols that were surrounded by books.

After climbing off Sam's back, Leian led Anna

into the building and asked anyone remaining to wait outside. As he entered, he flicked his fingers to his sides and candles lit the length of the building all along the walls. Their soft glow reached the far corners of the large interior.

"Cool trick," Anna said. They were in a room with tables set about, all facing one wall. Leian entered and ignored her as he walked to the far side of the room.

"What is this place?" Anna asked, walking around one of the large wooden tables. The top was scarred and worn from years of use. She noticed each table had an unlit lantern in the middle and there were no windows on the walls. Then she saw that one wall was covered with books and almost lost control of her excitement.

"Leian. Books!" She walked towards them, her fingers already itching to touch and gain their knowledge.

"This is a wizard's school," Leian said as he walked to the bookcase and started searching their bindings. "These are some of the training guides needed to run this school."

He had just grabbed a large book when the door behind them flew open and a beautiful woman rushed inside. She came to a quick stop between two tables when she spotted Leian standing by the bookcase. She wore a long dress and a leather apron like the other townswomen. The only thing she was missing was the hat.

"Leian, you have returned." She breathed a

huge sigh as she twisted her apron between her thin hands. Her long dark hair was in a large braid that hung to one side of her soft oval face. She had full lips and round brown eyes that never moved from Leian's face as a small smile formed on her lips.

As he carried the book over to the nearest table, he casually looked over at her. "Of course, I have. I told you it would not take long." Setting the book down, he turned to Anna. "Shiarra is my apprentice and can be trusted. Shiarra, this is Her Supreme Highness Anna. Anna, my apprentice Shiarra."

As Anna slid her hood off her head, she noticed Shiarra's face paled as she glanced her way. The woman had a few freckles covering her small nose which seemed to stand out as her cheeks. She quickly turned and faced Anna, then folded her thin frame into a deep curtsy that brought her face inches from the floor. "Your Majesty. Tis a pleasure to have you home again." After straightening, she gave Anna one last look then rushed over to Leian's side. "You were successful!"

"Yes, everything was as it said in the Hinlen. The Orick took me to a planet called Earth and the map led me to Anna." Leian lit the lantern in the center of the table with a flick of his fingers and started searching in the massive book.

"So, then we must take her to Valorna next, correct?" Shiarra asked as she folded her skirt and sat next to Leian.

"What is a Hinlen and what map led you to me?" Anna asked with concern in her voice as she walked towards the pair. She was so used to hiding her identity and location that the thought of a map having her exact location on it caused her much anxiety.

"All in good time, Your Highness, all in good time. Right now, I need to check a fact about your arrival," Leian said as he turned the page again. "Shiarra, where is the scroll about the seeking map?"

The question was not fully asked before Shiarra was up and running towards the end of the bookcase, her long skirts billowing behind her.

"Ah, yes, I found the calculation regarding our arrival," he said as Anna turned to look down at the book. She noticed a language that was definitely not English, and other large symbols surrounding the pages. Curves and dots swiveled around in a pretty but obscure language.

"I have one more question," Anna asked as she set her bag down and placed her hands in the pockets of her jacket. She really wanted the knowledge in these books so she could try to make some sense of what was going on around her. But she was unsure if her powers would even work on these books, since her power didn't work on Leian.

"Yes, yes, what is it now, Your Highness?" he said as he moved the lamp closer to the pages and continued to read.

"I'm able to gain knowledge by touching books," Anna said as she took a step closer. "Would my power work with these books?"

Marching past his personal guards, each in full uniform and standing at attention as they lined the spectacularly decorated halls, Gillard spared no thought for them or his surroundings as he continued his walk with haste.

The king's robes dragged behind his thin form as his polished black boots ate up the distance. When he reached the small door at the end of the hall, he lifted the metal handle and shoved the wooden door open without knocking.

After giving the room a quick glance, he saw Wizard Fulder bent over his spices and solutions. The room was crowded with tubes and jars, each full of mysterious liquids in various colors. Where jars and tubes ended the books and clutter started. Each surface was covered in either papers or dust and any walking room was blocked by the apparatus of abandoned experiments and those still in progress. There was one small window in the far corner. The only real light was from the wall sconces and a rather large ceiling chandelier.

"I want assurance this will work!" Gillard demanded as Wizard Fulder straightened his short form to stare quietly at him. He was in the center of the room, bent over what looked like a large wicker basket. His thin face, void of any emotion, was covered in wrinkles and sporadic facial hair. Despite his small form, his movements always appeared agile when in motion, however at the moment his faded gray eyes only studied Gillard.

"The plan! If my fool of a brother is able to bring the wench here using your map, will I be able to use her?" he demanded, impatience seeping out of him as the wizard continued to look at him quietly. "I want assurances." He cracked the knuckles on his left hand one at a time while the wizard moved over to his wall of books and contraptions.

When the wizard started to rummage along his shelves, Gillard started pacing, moving from the door all the way to the small window and back again. Several times, he paused along the narrow walkway to study the old man, who was currently bent over a book. He waited, knowing better than to interrupt the wizard while he searched for the answers he sought. His mind began to wander.

He remembered the first time he had met Fulder. Gillard had been no more than fourteen seasons old. His father had returned from afar, meeting with the other lands regarding the trade passages and had brought the old wizard with him. Even then Fulder had seemed bent and wrinkled, yet the man's steps had been quick and he had appeared to move with purpose as he strode next to the king.

Gillard had hated the man on sight, but wizards yielded magic, and during that time of his life, he had sought out any help he could in freeing himself of the two people he hated the most.

Days had passed as the new wizard settled into the kingdom, keeping to himself while having constant meetings with the king in private.

Gillard remembered his father had been pleased with the wizard's suggested changes to the kingdom.

With the wizard's knowledge and magic behind him, the returned king had started his own crusade. No longer were the doors and gates left wide open, but immediately upon his return, they had been closed and guarded at all times. New rules came to be during this time, rules that Gillard had hoped would help in his own goal.

No longer were mixed races allowed to own land. In fact, the king had banished several prominent families who were said to have mixed with faeries. These actions created a small group of supporters of the king, but they also caused a huge uprising and soon threats were made on the king while unrest started in the kingdom.

Gleeful, Gillard waited each day to see if his fondest wish would come true, yet each day the bastard boy, Kriston, and his evil mix-raced mother continued to live in his home. Each day he had to endure training in the same room as the whelp and eat meals with them both.

Did his father not know of the woman's bloodline?

How was she allowed to continue living, let alone live in the dignified castle of his ancestors? Why could she walk along the marble corridors and eat from the golden plates?

Finally, one night, Gillard had had all he could stand and he sought the wizard out. He had climbed the high twisted towers and, reaching the center apex of the spirals, found Fulder already waiting for him.

"Welcome, great one," the wizard had spoken, even before Gillard had shown himself, having hidden upon arrival and kept to the dark shadows. "You have questions?" he continued as the young prince finally moved into the light.

Gillard was mindful of traps and thought through his first question carefully. He studied the wizard and his bent form. The man had white hair that was cut short past his ears but hung well over his forehead and a large mustache that drooped down below his lips. His large owlish eyes of pale gray studied the thin boy who in turn studied him with serious green eyes.

"What power do you hold over my father?" Gillard finally asked and watched the large eyes of the wizard fill with amusement.

"So..." The man backed away and turned to enter further into his room. "The young prince is perceptive."

Gillard followed, moving into the wizard's lair, and looked about with curiosity.

"I hold no power over your father," Fulder said with a wicked smile from the corner of the room and produced an object in his hands that glowed red, brighter than the sun and twice as

beautiful. Gillard moved forward without any thought. "The power is all your father's, but that can change." He held the globe up so the boy could get a better look.

"Here, Your Majesty," Fulder finally spoke, bringing the king out of his own personal memories. "The wizard books foretell of her return, yet see for yourself, they do not speak of what will befall her next." Fulder leaned over the enchanted books of great wizards who had passed many generations before. "See..." Using his crooked and arthritic fingers, he pointed at a rather long passage. "No mention of the extent of the power this one holds, just like the others. Yet..." The wizard rolled his thin mustache between his fingers, much like Gillard had seen him do countless times. "We can assume, knowing the strength of the power we currently have, that maybe she will hold as much, or more." He finished and watched the light of excitement glow in his young protégé's eyes.

Quickly meeting the wizard's eyes, the king gave a slow wicked smile as he imagined the power waiting for him. "I must have her!" Gillard straightened and cracked his knuckles again. As he continued to think, he paced back and forth once more. "Yes, I see it now, the others are weak. Was it not reported to us that no power was seen in either of them? But this one, she will be mine."

Gathering a force for his trip was one thing, but ensuring there weren't any of his brother's spies amongst them was a completely different matter.

The first order was to collect his most trusted men and have a meeting. Supplies had to be gathered and packed for the long journey and that meant work ahead. He also had to leave someone he trusted in charge of his troops and ensure the recruits were left in good hands while he was away.

After leaving the king's chambers, the first thing Kriston did was open the map. He noted that the map was indeed a seeking map and saw a small rip that was currently located in a village called Tharian. He proceeded to inspect every inch of the parchment to see where the person's personal object was that was required in helping locate them. However, he did not find any object as he continued to study the map closely.

The magic that made the map used deep colors and sharp lines, he was able to determine that the right edge of the map started at the great waters, based on the waves and shoreline. The map moved east and went past Mirror Lake. It ran east through the Helmand Mountains and over to the Highman Plains. Far to the north, it stopped at the great iceways above the Pintras Forest.

Genoa's rivers, mountains, and villages were all well-defined for his inspection. Close to the guide on the far-right side, just where the Deepen Forest started, was a white smudge like the artist had placed a finger over the spot before painting the

map.

Kriston held the map up against a light to see if any items were between the thin layers of parchment but still could not find anything.

Giving a shake of his dark head, he rolled the map back up and placed it in his cloak as he marched out of his family castle.

The dark gray stones of the walls shone in the afternoon light as the sun kissed the black metal twisted on top of the numerous spirals, hundreds of feet above his head. Bridges and walkways wound in and out of the castle.

The village, with its busy roads and clay-roof homes, continued down the hill towards the Maylin River where more homes and shops stood. Beyond that, the land opened into green farms and ranches.

Turning away from the view, he found and sent a runner to his man Jake and then entered the great library to see what his future may hold.

If the Wizard Fulder had located any mention of the ability to steal magic, he wanted to see this with his own eyes. The king would be furious with him, but he had to attempt to confirm some of the facts before he traveled well beyond Matera's borders and into another kingdom.

He spent until the evening meal looking through the ancient texts in hopes of finding any mention of the ability to steal powers. The closest he came was mention of a place high in the Helmand Mountains where a possible void of magic existed. However, when it came to the Moonvest, he found a whole book on its recurrence.

Knowing his time was limited, he took the book with him. It was now dark and he took a moment to study the night sky. The moons were out, shining bright upon the darker backdrop of the stars and galaxies. He saw a few bright stars. Their names and stories came easily to his mind as he took a deep breath of the warm air. In his mind, he could hear his mother's soothing voice as she taught him the constellations. She had taught him all there was to know about the sky above his homeland. Thoughts of her still made him ache for her so he turned his thoughts once more to his quest.

Taking a deep breath, he smelled the town, the buildings, and even the dust beneath his feet. He could also smell the river several clicks away, its clean fragrance rising up to where he stood. Was his home really in danger? Maybe even more danger than it currently faced?

After a moment of silence, he continued toward his office where he would meet with the men who would accompany him on this trip.

The group included his first in command, Jake Ryad. Kriston had known Jake his whole life; Jake had been in the old king's service well before Kriston had been born. When Kriston's father had died, Jake had been in charge of the young boy's education, taking him to his lessons for magic and battle drills. Even with Jake's short, stout build, he was one of the best fighters Kriston had the honor of knowing. However, his excessive hair growth was a trait that Kriston and his friends liked to tease him about.

Next was Captain Ray Fielder, who had recently returned from the far south. Ray, the oldest in the group, was the most experienced when it came to battle tactics. This fact would come in handy during this trip through enemy territory. Captain Ray was committed to Kriston as the prince had saved Ray's wife and young child as they attempted to escape from their home village, which had been under attack by marauders. Kriston had led his troops on a counterattack and saved the whole village. The war captain had made a life pledge that day to the young prince.

Brigdon Penn was the third man that Kriston would take. Brigdon had saved Kriston's life when Kriston was just a boy. The young prince had been attacked by would-be kidnappers in his father's country home. Brigdon had been a first-line guard at that time and had discovered his counterpart missing that night. He had immediately gone to the prince's rescue, giving no thought to his own safety. He had single-handedly killed three of the men involved in the attack and saved Kriston.

Brigdon had been promoted to security and eventually to weapons teacher in the king's army, a very high position. Kriston had never met Brigdon's equal when it came to the art of fighting. He was tall and bald and had little facial hair and many muscles. He was intimidating until you looked closer, and then his sense of humor gave him away.

Last was Kriston's personal security man, Doug Timmons II, who was also his best friend. The two boys had grown up together and their bond of friendship and loyalty went deep. When Kriston thought of the word *brother*, it was Timmons he immediately thought of. Timmons hated his first name, a name he had acquired from his father who had been killed the same time the old king had. So, to all his friends he was just Timmons. He had the same build as Kriston, but wore his hair shorter and had blue eyes that never let anything slip past their gaze.

Timmons was the best security man Kriston knew, which made him an asset on this trip.

They met in Kriston's command chambers in the outbuildings near the training fields well past the castle's walls. Gathering around a large wooden table with lamps lit to ward off the evening darkness, they pondered over the seeking map.

Kriston trusted these men with his life. Each had proven their loyalty to him and the people of this land.

After telling them of the quest his brother had demanded of him, he was anxious to gain their opinions regarding the matter. He updated them on his findings in the great library and the questions they asked were ones that Kriston had already asked himself.

Was the spy really trying to steal Matera's magic? Was this even possible, and did the Moonvest really hold the key to all the facts?

And most important, what was being kept from them?

His men started the process of creating a list of men they would need for the trip, each writing orders and then calling and sending their runners out to gather the required supplies. As they continued their planning and argued about their route, tracing the possibilities along the seeking map, a regiment of the king's secret guards entered the chambers unannounced.

The four guards wore black uniforms trimmed in blood red that had the secret guards' star insignia, but Kriston had never seen these particular men before.

Kriston and his men stood and faced the newcomers as was the custom. He quickly used this opportunity to gather the seeking map, making sure his men blocked the vision of the new guards. Unsure he would be able to trust these men, he felt caution was warranted and hid the magical map under his cloak.

All except the front man looked like they could break a Strenk tree with their bare hands. The sour expressions they had on their faces gave the impression they had chewed some of the Strenk bark for breakfast.

The small man in front only reached to Kriston's chest. His balding head had a few long streaks of hair combed over and it appeared he had more hair on his face than his whole head, as his chin whiskers were thick and touched the tips of the collar of his uniform.

"Captain Haddock, I am Sergeant Milton Bainst of the king's secret guard," the sergeant said while saluting the royal prince with the traditional right fist to the heart. As Kriston saluted back, the sergeant continued. "My men and I have been ordered to accompany you on your quest. We are to be at your disposal until the spy is brought before the king."

Studying the sergeant, Kriston understood what his true orders were—to control or spy on him. It appeared the sergeant and his four men were now part of the journey whether he wanted them or not.

"All are welcome on this trip. We prepare our small troop now and will leave by first light when the supplies will be fully gathered," Kriston said as he gestured towards the empty chair to his left.

"Captain, is it not wise to leave tonight while Merria is high? We could benefit from her good luck." The sergeant sat in an empty chair and looked around at Kriston's men, who still stood about the table.

Knowing every move and answer would be reported back to the king, Kriston held his temper in check. He glanced at each of his men, ending with Ray, whom he gave a silent message by nodding his head. He then turned back to the sergeant as Ray silently left the room unnoticed.

"We gather supplies and men for this mission and hope to cover much ground the first day. Most of the men we will be taking with us have just been pulled from active duty and will need a full night's rest to accomplish the many miles." Taking a normal map from his wall, he placed it on the table in front of the sergeant. "I aim for Blastro Station by tomorrow's dark." Kriston pointed to the small dot nestled between Matera and Peak Falls. "We cannot accomplish this trip by that time tonight even if we left now. If our men have not had a full night's rest and the time needed to prepare, then half a day will be lost when the men and horses need to catch up on their sleep." Kriston turned his attention back to Brigdon and started discussing the weapons they would need for the trip, thoroughly dismissing any further questions Sergeant Bainst may have voiced.

Before Tamil, the orange moon, had set behind the trees in its nightly route, Kriston's chambers were empty again. He was poring over the seeking map once again when there was a small knock. When it was followed by a scrape and another quick knock, Kriston stood to let Ray into the room.

"Ale?" Kriston asked.

"No, after this, I go to find my bed." Ray chose a large feathered chair next to the fire, propping his feet on the wooden stool before him.

"What news?" Kriston asked, knowing Ray had spent the whole time searching for the information that would aid him.

"Sergeant Milton Bainst has been in the king's company for ten seasons despite his young age, and his reputation is not clean. He has had several companies of men disappear and many more of them quit. There have been rumors that he seeks General Zobo's position no matter how he achieves it." Ray shifted to ease his tired back. "No family was mentioned. Next, we have Beal Franst, the large, dark, and hairy man, another great upstanding citizen." Ray said with a sneer on his lips. "Beal has been under the sergeant's command for two seasons and he too has no family. He is said to be of big muscle and little brain but follows orders to an extreme. Ali Standst was the blond with bushy eyebrows. His family was wiped out a few years ago under circumstances that appear to be unlisted. It was said Ali was placed under the Keeper's arrest for questions regarding their death but was then released on the sergeant's orders. This was just last season. Listed as dead were his mother, her new husband, and their two small children. It was said the bodies were not recognizable because some parts were missing. It's also said Ali carries a rather large ax that is not standard issue."

On this news, Ray stood and walked to the side table to pour himself a small metal cup full of ale. Turning, he stared back at Kriston with very old and tired eyes. After taking a deep drink, he started again. "The last is Sash Grant, the bald dark man. Of him, little is known. I found that he is from the north, a town called Pinewoods. Tis said the village is no longer there and no one knows what happened to its people. I was told the man does not speak, but has not been matched in his sword skills. Brigdon may even have troubles sparring him. I am sorry I could not give you better news, my captain."

Draining his ale in one long sip, Kriston too stood and walked over to his friend. Grasping Ray's shoulder with his right hand, Kriston stared deep into his eyes. "You have been a true friend since first we met all those seasons ago. If we are to find out the truth about this quest, we must be on our guard." Giving a little smile, Kriston turned back towards the fire. "We will just have to keep our eyes on the sergeant and his men."

"How many men will we be taking?" Ray asked, setting his glass down without finishing.

"Our men will number twenty. Add the four secret guards and we total my lucky number. I hope to travel fast and, when closer to the target, will nightly seek her out using other means." Kriston turned and gave Ray his full smile.

"You devil!" Ray said with a laugh. "Well, then, we cannot fail!"

"Go, give your wife a good night, then sleep. We leave before Ra Neth rises in the sky."

After Ray left, Kriston found he could not rest and settled in front of the fire. Picking up the Moonvest book, he scanned its pages once again.

CHAPTER FIVE

Power in Knowledge

As Shiarra bent to pick up the scrolls she had dropped, Leian studied Anna with a wary eye.

"Show me," was all he said as he slid the large book across the table towards her.

Giving him a guarded look, she sat at the table and held her hand an inch over the book as the candle light continued to flicker. "There's nothing to prevent me from this?" she asked, studying the young wizard.

Seeing him finally give his head a shake, she placed her hand on top of the book and collected its knowledge. When she was done, she sat back and contemplated the vast knowledge.

"Please, may I see your map again?" Anna said, holding her hand out across the table.

Reaching into his bag, he pulled the parchment

out and handed it over to Anna. As she unfolded it, he walked around to stand behind her. Neither noticed Shiarra walk over and join them.

Laying the map on the table, Anna pointed to the village labeled Tharian. "We are here, correct?" Anna asked and continued, "Where this rip is, which is caused by a spell you placed on this parchment to locate me."

"Correct, the Finders spell is what allows the parchment to show the location of a subject, no matter where they are located. I placed the spell on this parchment before I left Tharian two days ago, after my calculations were confirmed by the passing of Beannra, the queen's moon, with Merria. The two appeared to touch in the sky, which was foretold in the Hinlen book." Leian scratched his head. "This map allowed me to find you when I was on Earth also. It shows the subject while still using the elements of north, south, east, and west. Earth uses these directions also, so I was able to acquire an Earth map and located you in the days I was there."

"Wow, I don't know where to start." Anna sat back and thought for a moment. Here, finally, were answers she had been looking for her entire life. Now that she had some of the knowledge, she struggled with knowing what the questions were. One question popped into her mind. "What is the Hinlen book?"

Shiarra stepped forward. "I can answer that." The young woman grasped her hands in front of her as if giving a presentation. "When a wizard discovers magical spells, he creates a life book of his most useful skills or knowledge. Wizard Hinlen was a foreseer who lived about two generations before the Revan's war began. He foretold of the end of the war and had written down how the end would come about. There are other elements in this book of Genoa's current war." Turning to Leian, she waited for his approval before continuing. "Ten suns ago, Leian and I traveled to Byways and studied the Hinlen book in hopes of gaining knowledge about you, Your Highness..."

"Which brings us to your next question," Leian interrupted as he faced Anna.

Taking a deep breath, Anna thought about her next question. "So, you set the spell on this map. In theory, then, any wizard can cast this spell on a parchment and find me at any time, correct?" Anna turned around to face the wizard. Leian and Shiarra stood as a unit as they looked down at her.

"To do that, Your Highness, they must know of you and have something of your person," the young man answered and gave his head a scratch.

"Yes, so I'm assuming that you have something of mine, correct?" Anna asked, standing and facing the wizard.

"You are correct again, Your Highness." He opened his bag and pulled out something small and shiny. Holding his hand up, she saw a small leather string with a silver crescent shape hanging from it. Reaching out her hand, she stopped an inch from the object. "What is this?"

"This was left behind when you and your wizard escaped from Genoa almost sixteen seasons ago," Leian said as he lowered the necklace the rest of the way into Anna's outstretched hand.

As soon as the piece dropped into her hand, Anna's heart started a fast skip that had her holding her breath. She felt slightly dizzy until she released the breath she had been holding.

The crescent was small, no bigger than a quarter, and was warm to the touch. Anna could see the silver piece itself was not solid, but was of a woven design so intricate that it appeared to be a single piece of silver.

"This was mine when I was young?" she asked, grabbing the necklace by the leather strap and holding it up in the light from the lamp. "How old was I when I left?"

"You had not yet seen your fifth Mid-day." Leian turned to Anna, grabbed the necklace from her hand, and placed the leather string around her neck. Her short white hair fell over her face as she looked down at the piece. The crescent lay flat between her breasts, over her jacket.

Anna could feel the warmth seeping out of it to flow through her veins, out to the tips of her fingers and toes, causing her to smile slightly. It was a pleasant feeling.

"I had been on Earth so long, but could never figure out why I aged differently," she said as she touched the crescent.

"Unfortunately, I am not a calendar wizard and do not fathom why the two planets' times are very different," the wizard said as he stood back. "A good guess would be the suns are different and Genoa's sun has further to travel than Earth's."

"Actually, it's the other way around," Anna said with a smile. "But your guess may be close. It also appears the people on Genoa live longer lives." Turning again to the map, she placed her fingers on two other rips, one located by a mark named Valorna and another near the ocean to the south. "What are these two rips?"

"I have used this map before. Those are prior spells and nothing more." Leian waved a hand in dismissal.

Anna noticed that Shiarra cast a quick look at him during his answer but he quickly turned to his apprentice. "Shiarra, please find the history scrolls so we can help Anna with the holes in her memory."

Anna could tell that the wizard was not being completely truthful in his answers. He was acting as if he was keeping secrets, as if there was a hidden danger. But, for now, she had other questions and moved on.

She moved her finger to a burn mark she had seen. "According to this book, when a second spell is cast on the same person, a conflict is created and this creates a burn on the original map." As Leian leaned over to study the map, Shiarra walked back to the table carrying a multi-paged scroll that was rolled into a tight tube. The apprentice gasped when

113

she saw the location Anna was pointing to.

"Tell me about Matera," Anna whispered.

"To answer that question, Your Highness, I think it best to study the history scrolls first. Sayer Phillip will be here soon and I will only be giving him a part of your story." Grabbing the scroll from Shiarra, Leian placed it over the seeking map. "Please, for now, gather this scroll's knowledge and after our Sayer leaves, we will continue this conversation in private."

Leian turned and walked to the large front doors. Giving him one last glance, Anna placed her hands on the scrolls as its information passed to her quickly.

When she was finished, she looked up and discovered a small, elderly man with long frizzy hair staring at her from across the table. He stood in the light from the candles and held one of the silly hats in his aged hands.

"Welcome, Your Highness," he said as he bowed at the waist, "to our humble village of wizards." The man studied her with deep brown eyes and a smile spread on his face. Anna found him welcoming and warm and immediately liked the small man.

"Sayer, please have a glass of ale and I will tell you what has transpired since the last time we spoke," Leian said as he filled a metal cup from a large barrel next to the bookcases and walked towards the table.

"I see your trip was successful, but what is your next step?" The small man settled across from Anna.

"As you see, I was able to locate the exiled princess in the world known as Earth. Since bringing her back, some new information has come to my attention and at tomorrow's sunrise we will need to take a journey to Byways, to the Hinlen book to reevaluate its information." Placing the cup in front of Sayer Phillip, Leian sat next to him. Shiarra walked around and stood behind them both.

"Back to Byways? Was the information you gathered last time not enough?" the Sayer asked with concern in his voice.

"The journey is at its beginning, Sayer. We cannot afford any misdirection," Leian assured the man, successfully evading his question. "We have the first piece. We must trust in our skills and hope we gain all before the required time."

"The king's men draw ever closer. Most of the southern roads are already closed." Shaking his head, the Sayer turned to Shiarra. "What say you, daughter?"

"Father, I saw the same calculations that Wizard Leian did. Please, we must take these steps to assure peace in Genoa." Shiarra spoke with such strong conviction that Anna studied her more closely.

She did indeed bear small resemblance to Sayer

Phillip, especially in their eyes. Both had clear brown eyes but the shape also gave their heritage away. Shiarra was also slight of build, but her dark brown hair was wavy and thick, while the old man's was just plain frizzy.

The Sayer gave his head a shake, and Anna knew that he too saw the conviction in both the wizard and his daughter. "I will make sure your supplies are gathered." Turning back to Leian, he asked, "This time, will you take Shiarra on your quest?"

"I must. Her skills will be needed if we are to be successful." Leian's answer clearly weighed on the old man and the wizard placed a reassuring hand on his arm.

With a large sigh, the Sayer stood and faced them. Leian too stood and with Shiarra behind him gave the old man a deep and long bow. "With your blessing, we go to set Genoa's affairs in order."

"You have it. Be safe and return soon." With this, the old man turned and left the building.

"Well, that was fascinating, but what does all this mean?" Anna asked when the two turned and faced her once more.

"You collected the history scroll's knowledge?" Leian asked.

"Yes." Seeing her question was once again set aside, she took a deep breath and started to confirm the scroll's knowledge. "I know how Genoa was formed." She received a nod from Leian to continue. "Its people had been divided by the

Revans War. It speaks of how the old rulers tried to enslave all people without magic. How the wizards came forward, led by the great wizard named De Bransley. It states how the wizards combined their knowledge to stop and bind the kings who had limitless powers at that time." Anna stood as she continued to talk, pacing the length of the table. "It said they bound the kings each in their own stone where they could no longer work their magic. I know that after the war the wizards created a magical vow with the new kings of that time, and that each of these three kings was assigned a wizard to guard and guide them in ruling their lands. It's said this was beneficial to all, as the king's powers work against each other but not against wizards, whereas wizard's powers work for all the people." Here she stopped and gave Leian a hard look. "Does this mean that a king, or a royal person, could have their own powers held in check by a wizard?"

"No, it means that their power does not function against wizards, but they are not limited by a wizard. As I told you on the trail, your power will not work against me, however, it will work against any non-wizard." Standing, he placed a hand on Shiarra's shoulder. "For example, any power you wield would and could be used on Shiarra. As an apprentice, she has not yet taken the wizard's oath so her powers are not yet at full strength."

Anna thought this through for a moment, as several science fiction movies reeled around in her head. She finally came to the conclusion that a wizard's magic was stronger than her own and didn't appear to have limits, whereas her own magic could only be used to gain knowledge or temporarily control someone she touched. "So, it mentioned the three kings were King Cecil Edward Haddock, King Paddish Malicky, and King Edwin Collin Reginald. These three assisted the royals and Genoa's people in rising above the old kings during the Revan's war."

"Correct. It was key that the people were united during this time. And even though there were great heroes whose lives were lost, through their sacrifice, peace was won."

"So, what came next? Why are the people still divided if these kings were triumphant?" Anna asked, looking from Leian to Shiarra.

"Each of the kings realized one thing—to rule with peace, distance must be maintained. The Highman Plains were vacated and people were free to follow their chosen kings to each corner of Genoa." As he spoke, he took the scroll off the seeking map and grabbed three candles from the table behind him. Placing one candle at the bottom of the map he said, "King Malicky settled in the far south now known as Malic." Placing another candle in the north above a dot titled Valorna, he continued, "King Reginald settled in a new location chosen next to the Golden Enry for its healing abilities." Taking the final candle, he placed it over Matera on the map, "And last, King Haddock returned to his family's home, south, in Matera."

118

Once the candles were in place, he waved his hand and all three lit with flame. "These kings ruled for many seasons before new struggles started. He waved his hand again and the flame above Valorna blew out along with the one above Matera. "Two of the kings lost their lives during these battles. Their children rule in their stead now." With this he turned to Shiarra. "Please tell Pash we look for our meal now. We will be right behind you."

As she stood, Shiarra gave a small smile to Leian and turned to Anna with serious eyes. "The war was tremendous, many lives were lost, and the battles lasted many seasons, but know this, Your Highness, even though the land is now divided, its current wars are small compared to the Revan's war." And with that she turned to leave.

Watching her go, Anna turned back to Leian. "She speaks as if she saw the war firsthand. How long ago was this Ravans war?"

"Shiarra's mother was killed during the Ravans war and her home village destroyed in the process. It was not until her father brought her here to Tharian that they found peace under the good King Reginald, your father."

Considering all the information she had gained that day, along with the emotional turmoil of the trip from Earth to Genoa itself, by the time she had finished the evening meal, Anna was exhausted.

She found it interesting that their evening meal was so much like the standard dinners back home. They had meats with a side dish of roots that tasted like parsnips which had been mixed with potatoes. There was thick bread and plenty of ale to drink. Anna politely passed on that before discovering the water was not quite as clean as she was used to. She drank half the glass of ale before she realized the fruit-flavored drink, while very much to her liking, was quite potent.

After the meal, Shiarra led Anna out of the dining room while explaining that Anna would sleep in a room next to her own. They exited the wooden building and had cleared its covered porch when Anna stopped dead in her tracks. There above them in all its glory was the magnificent night sky of Genoa.

Anna had never seen anything so wonderful. Earth's Milky Way was spectacular, but even that didn't compare to the stars above Genoa.

First, you had the moons. Only a few were showing still, and she saw the one called Lazerith, its bright yellow crescent surface scarred with huge craters. Shiarra told her Lazerith marked the nightly time by its rising and setting. Then there was the smaller Blinske, straight above where they stood and apparently always visible, either day or night. It had a smooth surface as if the moon was made of yellow gas instead of hard rock. A large orange one called Tamil was setting behind her. Its odd shape gave her pause as it seemed more like a hunk of glass that was partially melted instead of a perfect circle. This moon marked time from sunset to deep night. The last moon was the small white one that was closest in shape and size to Earth's moon. Merria was currently full and hung in the eastern sky.

The moons were impressive, but the stars soon became the only thing she noticed.

Having only looked through a telescope on Earth once and having spent countless nights asleep under the stars, Anna found it amazing that with the naked eye in Genoa, you could see a galaxy. A large swirl of bright yellow and white could be seen far above them. The galaxy appeared to be the size of an apple held about four feet from her eyes, but it still took her breath away. Shiarra told her the Wolth spiral was named after the wizard who had discovered the use of air magic over four hundred seasons ago.

There was no Milky Way, just as Leian had said. Instead, beyond the Wolth galaxy, she could see two different star clusters. One had a green tint to it and covered a large portion of the sky in the west. The other was yellow and orange and was near the horizon to the far south.

"The green cluster is known as De Lorn. I was told it's named after the first dragon. The fire cluster is called Amber," Shiarra explained.

Anna explained that the spiral was actually a galaxy and it could contain hundreds of other stars or suns, and the clusters included hundreds of stars held in place by gravity.

Shiarra just shook her head as they both looked at the bright lights. An hour passed before Anna was willing to continue to the housing building. She made a pact with herself then and there to locate any astronomy books she could. No matter where she was, looking at the stars always made her problems seem small when compared to the vastness of space. Maybe tomorrow she would learn more about Genoa's night skies.

After being shown to her room, Anna washed using a large wooden bowl and an oddly shaped bucket that had been sitting on her dresser. She changed her clothes and, after rinsing her used ones, hung them up to dry on the back of the door, which she made a point to lock.

Leian had asked her to no longer wear the clothing from Earth and had instructed Shiarra to provide Anna with other clothes. Anna studied the dress she'd been given. The material was soft and appeared to be made of a woven fabric, but the undergarments would take some getting used to. She had never worn a corset before. At least it too was soft to the touch. They didn't have traditional buttons or zippers, but mostly used ties and flaps. When buttons were used, like the cuffs of the shirts, they were large and made of carved bones.

She checked the supplies in her backpack, which also included the emergency supplies from the sports car. She had always found that the Boy Scout's moto, 'always be prepared' had fit life and travels perfectly.

When she settled down in the single feather bed sleep eluded her and her mind whirled with questions and thoughts.

She knew it must be close to the middle of the night, but her system was still on Earth time, specifically, East Coast time. Leian's evening meal was really her lunch and this left her with plenty of energy to think.

She knew now that Leian was telling the truth. She was on another planet called Genoa and Orden was in fact a wizard. Which meant that both were originally from here.

Even though she didn't remember anything from before Earth, based on what Orden had told her, she felt this was the place she had come from.

Had she really been exiled?

Leian had used the term "exiled to Earth," and it appears she had been there for over forty Earth years, or around sixteen years on Genoa. It seemed that even when she was on Earth, her body was marking time based on Genoa's rotation around its sun. So, she was about twenty and not almost fifty. A part of her liked this fact, and a small smile formed on her lips in the dark. She calculated that this Revan's war could very well have started on Genoa around a hundred Earth years ago. She could also assume that she had been sent to Earth for a reason and worried over this fact for a while until her head started to hurt. Setting this subject and her questions about her reasons for exile aside until tomorrow, she finally moved onto the next fact.

If the history scrolls were true, which she couldn't doubt now given all the other facts she had faced today, then her father had been a man called King Edwin Collin Reginald. If that were fact, then she really was of royal blood here on Genoa.

"Still don't believe that fact yet. It may take some time to get used to this," she said as she stared at the wooden beams above her head.

She hadn't had any more private time with Leian or Shiarra to ask about their conversation with Sayer Phillip. What had Leian said about pieces? All these new questions swirled around her head until she felt dizzy.

What she needed was answers and lots of them. She finally came up with a plan of attack. She would start tomorrow and would hound Leian until she was satisfied.

When she did fall asleep that night, she dreamed of walking next to a small dark woman as they glided along a long marble corridor.

They arrived at a large carved wooden door lit by oil lamps set high in the walls.

She passed through the door alone, moving into a small circular room, and turned around to lock the door behind her.

Lifting her heavy skirts, she walked up to a large table made of smoke. When she moved her thin hand over the smoke, she was shocked to see an image of her own face reflecting back at her, floating amidst the smoke. She was further mystified when she saw worry in her own eyes.

Shiarra watched Leian as he paced once more in front of the small fireplace in her quarters.

She sat in her favorite horsehair chair, her skirts wrapped around her and her thin ankles crossed in a relaxed manner despite her emotional worries.

Her chambers were next to Anna's, a room Shiarra had been assigned since her first day as Leian's apprentice. She had made it her own by filling it with lots of color and different textures.

Leian once again ran his hands through his blond hair, leaving the locks disheveled around his handsome face. His actions were a sure sign he was agitated or worried.

"If he knows of her arrival, then we can expect trouble," the wizard told her. "Maybe you should stay." He finished and knelt before her to gaze into her brown eyes.

She knew he saw courage and determination in her eyes and was sure those traits had always attracted him to her, even before he had started training her.

She, however, saw worry in his blue eyes and realized his worry was not for himself, or even the trip they were expecting to take the next day. It was for her.

Giving him a small smile, she reached out and placed a thin hand on his cheek. She could feel

125

stubble growth from the day on his chin and watched as he too smiled. His blue eyes studied her and she felt heat warm her face. His gaze was steady and she held it for a long time.

"I cannot talk you out of this, can I?" he replied as she continued to smile at him.

"Why would you? You told my father my skills are needed and I know you believed it," she said as he raised his hand and covered hers.

"That is what worries me. We may face immense dangers and I cannot guarantee your safety." Gently he kissed her hand and then stood to pour himself some ale. "You studied while I was gone?" he asked, changing the subject to a more comfortable topic as he settled in the chair opposite of her.

Giving in to her laugh, she settled back in her own chair and wished her mentor was sometimes more direct when it came to speaking of his feelings. But it was better to cherish what you have than to wish for what you did not. She allowed the subject to wander away from their feelings, for now.

"You were gone all of two days, but yes, I studied the required material." She looked at him, suddenly serious. "I was not able to finish as fast as Her Highness could."

"We expected some magic in her, but how useful is Anna's!" He drank from his ale and then proceeded to study the liquid in his tumbler. "We will need to keep a close eye on her. Until she gathers more information and until we understand her more, she will be in danger of revealing herself too soon. We must guard her and keep our eyes watchful."

"So, it was not just me he was worried about," she thought. "Will he try for the others? Are they in danger too?" she asked as concern filled her dark eyes.

"I cannot tell," Leian said as he contemplated his ale. "He has let them be until now. I do not see that changing." But with his words, more fears blossomed.

Studying the small fire again as it popped and hissed, Shiarra thought about the princess in the next room for a time. "Leian, do you know what her life was like there? On Earth?" she clarified.

"I fear her life was hard. She seems to trust easily, yet I watch her eyes track me. She looks for every door and window and she keeps her small possessions with her at all times." He stopped, no doubt thinking about what her life had been like. "When I found her, she was surrounded by an enemy of great numbers." Leian turned to smile at Shiarra. "Yet she did not seem fearful. In fact, if I were to guess, I would say she would have escaped without my help."

Shiarra turned to look at him once more. "Do you think she holds more magic than she has told us?"

Leian gave another small smile. "That, dear apprentice, is a great question."

127

Stepping boldly into the room, he was pleased to see the man on duty was in fact guarding the objects and not sleeping or daydreaming.

Quickly dismissing the guard, he confirmed the man closed and locked the door behind him before turning and studying the room.

Its stone walls were dark and bare, and light from two oil lanterns filled the small chamber. This was one of many rooms he had special guards on. Other more secret rooms required magic guards, and only he knew of their whereabouts.

Turning to the large wooden shelves set in the far corner, he gave a small smile. It took only a moment for him to find the tool he needed for his next act.

Warming the stone, he waited impatiently, tapping his foot until a response came.

"Yes," was the only response he had ever received.

"I have a task for you," the king said as he leaned closer to the small blue stone. "There is a woman," he began and when his orders were relayed to his minion, he set the stone back onto the shelf.

His next order of business was to find another stone and warm another blue rock. This time the wait was longer but the welcome was warmer.

"Hello," came the breathless response.

"How is the queen?" he asked, dismissing the

disappointment in the voice when the response came.

"Nothing changes, except she visited the room tonight."

"Were you able to listen in on her conversation?" he demanded, even though he knew the response.

"No, nothing could be heard. There is still a strong spell protecting the room." After a moment of silence, confusion could be heard in the responding voice. "What are your orders?"

Gillard thought for a moment. Did she know? Somehow, he feared this meant they also knew what had recently happened. Had he made a big mistake many seasons ago by only sending spies to the north?

"Keep your eyes open and report if anything changes. I must know every detail." He thought for a moment of Wizard Fulder's words. "Report only to me," he finished and cut off before more could be said.

Placing the cold stone back into its drawer and turning back to the room, he thought of secrets long past kept. If they came to light, his personal power would be over, and possibly his life.

This would not happen, not if he could help it. Moving about the room, he started on his next undertaking.

He would never be brought down, especially by a woman.

Leian had not been kidding when he said they would start their journey at sunrise the next day.

When Shiarra woke Anna, it was still dark out the small window behind the thin cotton curtains of her room. She dressed quickly and was tying the small leather apron over the dress when Shiarra brought in some boots for her to try on. They discovered that none of the shoes fit, so Anna continued to wear her boots, hoping that the blue dress was long enough to cover them.

Once dressed, Shiarra led her back to the dining hall and they had a meal of eggs and roots that were grilled over an open fire. There were also some soft yeasty breads cooked by a man named Pash, who was rather large, but he smiled a lot and whistled while he cooked.

There was honey to coat the breads and big fat sausages on the side. The meal was like a feast, and Anna sampled everything but was unable to finish it all. As she always did with extra food, she tucked it into her backpack for later.

Before they left the building, Leian gave Anna a thin tan cloak with a hood. He informed her that a hat would not hide her features enough and for a while they would have to make do with a light cloak.

Leian rode Sam again, but Anna had been presented with a young yellow crystal-haired horse named Whinny who was half Sam's size. She was told Whinny was less than a cycle old and this was why she was so small.

Shiarra had her own crystal-haired horse, a large orange one named Bea. Bea had been with Shiarra for several seasons and since the horse was a female, she would not get any larger than her current size. She was only two feet taller than Sam and still considered small by Genoa standards.

As they mounted their horses, Anna made a quick comment about having a horse of a different color, but when Shiarra and Leian just stared at her, she shook her head and quickly asked Whinny if she would let her ride on her back.

They took a different road through the small village than the one they had used the day before. They started their journey south while the sun was peeking above the trees to the west. Anna could tell the pebbled road was well traveled. Bumps had been filled in or smoothed over and any large rocks had been cleared away.

The trees on the side had their branches cut well away from the path. The trees were much the same as the day before, the forest floor was covered with pine needles and reminded Anna of the Colorado forest she had visited often.

There were plenty of travelers and most pushed small handcarts full of goods that included foods, tools, and even leather saddles. Some travelers had horse-drawn wagons with large, colored canvas backs that reminded her of gypsy wagons.

She didn't mind keeping her hood up at first, as

the cloak was of a light material, but as the day wore on and the weather turned warmer, it became too hot. She was sure putting sunglasses on her face would draw attention, even with a hood to cover most of her face.

The travel time had allowed Anna to think about her current situation. How was she supposed to wrap her mind around all the answers she had been given in the last few hours? It seemed that when she started to understand something, more and more information was thrown at her. To the point of causing her mind to feel numb.

First it was the fact that she was an Alien from another planet, then the fact that she was royalty on top of that. It was obvious that she was on another planet, so maybe Leian was telling the truth about her heritage too? If he was telling the truth, what did this mean to her? How did this affect her? Did she have family here? That single thought got her heart racing as hope washed into her.

Family. Something she had lived a long time without. And if she had family, maybe she had a home too. Even as she thought of it, she told herself not to get ahead of herself. She had been wandering for so long that the thought of settling down in one place caused an uncomfortable feeling. She couldn't quite admit it to herself, but this new feeling was sheer panic.

It appeared that magic was common in this land, yet what Leian had said about wizards and royalty continued to swirl around in her mind.

Her magic had always been used for two purposes. Discovery and defense. Would she have to call on the defensive magic more here in Genoa? From what she gathered, it appeared that even here she would be hunted. Who was hunting her, had yet to be discussed.

She felt like she had discovered so many answers today, but still, she had even more questions than before. Yes, Leian had provided the where and who of her life, yet it seemed that all the 'in-between' was now popping up and demanding answers. She was very determined to get the rest of the answers with the help of Leian and Shiarra's.

Anna estimated their first break along the forest trail was about four hours outside of Tharian. Even though crystal-haired horses were easy to ride, her bottom needed the short break.

Each horse had been outfitted with packs set behind their rider, and when they stopped, Leian informed Anna that meals and ale along with fresh water could be located in the pack behind her.

After giving Whinny some water, she tied the horse's rope to the nearest branch and found a snack of berries in a metal tin. She tentatively tasted the first one. "Tastes like a blackberry," she said as she popped the flat, pink round fruit into her mouth.

"Black berry? No, they are pink not black," Shiarra said while drinking from a metal flask and smiling sweetly at Anna.

They had one more break another four hours later as they came out of the trees into wide-open plains, the hills covered with the tall grass she had seen the day before. Hues of blue, yellow, and purple brightened the ground before them and seemed to stretch for miles.

The air smelled of sea and, beyond the fields, she could see hints of a large ocean to her left, which was only visible when they crested small hills. The sky was a bright blue and she could see five moons, their light and colors faded a bit in the bright sunlight.

When asked, Leian told her one of the moons was Ra Neth, which she had already seen the day before. Anna thought it looked like a giant blueberry in the sky and it made her wonder when they would be eating again. There was also a pale silver moon just hovering above the horizon he called Beannra.

"That's the queen's moon," Anna said, glancing over to where the moon was just visible between two hills.

"Yes, but how did you know that?" Leian asked.

Shaking her head, she told him that Orden had informed her once of this special moon and she had always liked the idea of a queen owning her own moon.

They stopped a little after midday and let the horses graze while they ate a lunch of dried meat and more fruits. Anna was getting used to the ale and, sitting in the warm sun, she could feel some of her travel-sore muscles start to relax as she leaned against a rather large tree trunk.

Next thing she knew she was riding in a saddle on the back of a huge golden dragon. Its scales shimmered in the afternoon sunlight, each scale was the size of a dinner plate and overlapped the one behind it.

She could see the ocean below her and feel the wind against her exposed arms. Closing her eyes, she could smell the salty water and feel the cool air against her closed lids. The feeling of freedom was so great, tears formed in her eyes, so she opened them again and looked at the dragon. It had a long neck with bright blue tufts of ears on the top of its head and what looked like small leather fins behind its jaw. When it banked left, she could see its bright red eyes searching the green waters below. Its mouth was the same color as its eyes, and large whisker-like hairs were protruding from its nostrils.

She looked behind her perch on the leather saddle and saw its large wings open to the sea air, catching the breeze as it glided. Both wings were a thin material, stretched with air, and each had dark blue veins running down them, connecting to the large armed wing.

The dragon's body was longer and thinner than she expected and seemed to end in one giant wing. As she looked closer, she saw, in fact, two separate wings that appeared to act as rudders.

As the dragon dipped downward towards the water, she looked forward again and held tighter to what appeared to be reins. She glanced beyond the dragon. Ahead she could see a coastline white with waves and tall, jagged rocks where the water met the land. There were no beaches along this shore, only large cliffs and the sea. The cliffs were higher than any she had ever seen before, yet somehow reminded her of the formations along the northern Oregon coastline.

Each rock face was covered in tufts of grasses and vines, and when she looked closer, she could see more dragons nesting along the high cliffs, some black as night, some gray or white.

Hearing a loud scream, she glanced up and saw the most beautiful dragons above her, about twenty. Some of the beasts had iridescent wings, others looked like they had been painted by children, so colorful that she was mesmerized by them. Red, bright green, orange, and even a bright purple one with pink-tipped wings. All of them flew in a straight row above her. Each held a rider in front of their wings, strapped on in the same manner she appeared to be.

Then her dragon turned, spun its huge head around to face her, and said, "Time to wake up."

"What?" she asked blinking.

"I said, it is time to wake up," Leian said, giving her another shake.

Anna sat up and blinkingly looked around.

Gone were the dragons and the vast ocean and in their place, was Leian, standing above her with concern on his thin face. Shiarra stood behind him, the sun making her dark hair shine bright as she watched. Anna saw Sam poke his head around Shiarra's and quickly sneak a kiss, licking the apprentice's face and leaving a wet trail along her jaw.

As Shiarra scolded Sam for the wet endearment, Anna climbed to her feet and shook the dream off. "Must have dozed off."

"No wonder. The bright sun and ale probably helped with that," Leian said as he turned to load the lunch items back into Sam's pack.

"I was dreaming of talking dragons," she said as she dusted off her skirt.

"Talking!" Leian said. "No, I do not believe they talk, just squawk a lot during mating season."

Giving him a thoughtful look, she couldn't decide if he was joking or serious.

"Do they live along the coastline, next to very large cliffs?" She saw him pause, then he turned back to face her with an awed expression on his face.

"Your Highness is full of knowledge of Genoa. Yes, they roost along the cliffs of Faro, but I have already told you that," he said, shaking his head and climbing onto Sam's back.

That was it!

She remembered how he had told her about the dragons living along cliffs. That must be why she had dreamed of them. Shaking off the uneasy feeling, she walked over to Whinny to proceed with the rest of their day's journey.

After some time, Anna asked Leian when they

would arrive at Byways.

"We will be there by mid-meal tomorrow. There is a small inn along the way we will stop at for the night. You should find Byways quite likable. Their Sayer is named Otis and last time we were there he was quite helpful." Sam had slowed during his speech so Anna's own horse walked up next to him.

"You mentioned pieces last night to Sayer Phillip. What did you mean, pieces of what?" she asked.

Clearing his throat, he faced forward and was quiet for such a long time that she was sure he was not going to answer her question. After a peddler with a wagon full of pots and pans went by, Leian turned towards her once more. "Your necklace," he said, nodding his head towards her, "it is one of three. I have been told that to set Genoa back on a peaceful path, all three must be found and joined back together."

"Where are these pieces?" Anna glanced at Leian's side profile. Was he telling her the truth?

"I have an idea where they are, but for now we must gain knowledge about who is tracking you through another seeking map. This, I fear, is the more pressing matter at hand."

"Why? Would they be enemies or friends?" Anna asked with the first signs of panic in her voice. Her eyes tracked the fields surrounding them, half expecting General Wilberg and his men to jump out with their guns aimed at her heart.

"Friend or foe, I fear we will find out soon enough. But for now, we must be on our guard and keep your arrival a secret." He gave her a stern look.

"I don't know anyone here," Anna said with a wave of her hand. "Why would I already have enemies?" Yet she once again raised her hood to cover her head, all the time casting cautious glances about the fields as if an army would spring up to attack.

"Enemies of old, Your Highness, enemies of old," he said with a shake of his head.

JJ Anders

CHAPTER SIX

All is Not Lost

They had reached Blastro Station the first night, barely.

Kriston had a small command issue the following morning that delayed his travels, yet he was still able to start east before the sun had risen above the hills in the west.

Kriston and his company were well on their way to Peak Falls on the second day of their journey when they met their first real obstruction.

In an attempt to move more quickly towards their target, Kriston had left all wagons behind and opted for strong horses instead. Each crystal-haired horse was well over thirteen feet tall and able to ride a day's journey easily, along with carrying double its weight in supplies.

But horses needed fresh water regularly, and with the marshes ahead and the station behind, the only fresh water was what they carried.

The big oaf, Beal, had demanded that Kriston's supply man place all the water on a single horse. The horse in question was a rather large but young female who did not like the smell of the surrounding marshes. She became increasingly skittish each step they took towards the wetlands. At the first sign of a rather small Zent cat, the orange horse took off like a dart, ripping her lead out of her handler's hand and dragging her ropes behind her as she disappeared into the surrounding trees.

Jake was so furious that he ordered all the men to stop and reevaluate what each horse was carrying. He then sent his own man Bren and Beal to track the young horse and retrieve their supplies, ordering them to meet back up with the company at the falls before dark.

After taking time to ensure the supplies were evenly distributed and confirming each man had at least a days' worth of supplies on their own horse, they were off again.

During the day, the well-maintained road they were on was well secured and traveled by many diverse traders. Low brush surrounded the path on the far side and the marshes to the north were well away from the road. It was only the smell or an occasional wild animal that was an annoyance.

But they would not want to linger on the road after dark in this area. Kriston and his men hoped to reach the falls well before sunset to secure camp for that night.

"We are not even out of our homelands and these fools are already making me regret bringing them along," Jake said to Ray and Kriston as they rode beside each other along the wide trail.

"Timmons searched their supplies during our last break and found several non-standard weapons before he was interrupted. Personally, I do not trust any of them, and you can be sure I will be keeping one eye open at night while I sleep."

"I asked Brigdon to see if he can make friends with the sergeant. If anyone can do it, it would be him. It may help bring some information our way, if you know what I mean." Jake cast a glance back to where the large weapons master was riding his horse next to the sergeant. "We may not get much; the sergeant does not appear to like talking," he told Kriston, who glanced back and saw his large friend smiling and waving his hands about. He appeared to be telling a joke and after a moment proceeded to laugh at his own punch line while the small sergeant sat rod straight on the back of his horse with a dismissive expression on his face.

"Everyone loves Brigdon. He will wear the sour sergeant down," Kriston said with a laugh as Brigdon continued his loud laughter over his own joke.

"You think we will reach the falls before the sun sets tonight?" Jake turned to Ray with a sober expression on his hairy face.

"I hope so; we do not want to pitch any tents near the marshes." Ray's face reflected concern. "Safe enough during the day, but I would hate to have to sleep on the ground with all the Scarents slithering about in the dark."

"Heard tell you knew a man who got bit and survived once, is that right?" Jake asked.

Shivering in his armor, Ray turned to his friends. "He lasted a few days longer than most, but when the change started in him, he ended it himself. So no, he did not survive. That memory did not help me like this trip anymore."

They were quiet for a time, searching the low marshes for the solitary snakes that hid in the grasses along the lake and that would bite those who happened to wander near, changing them or killing them with one bite.

Kriston thought for a moment and after stealing another glance at the seeking map spoke up. "Our target is moving," he whispered. "It appears she is heading south along the coastline."

"Do we know any more about this mission?" Ray asked, giving his beard another scratch.

"It is said that traveling that far north into the queen's territory can be dangerous," Jake added, casting a glance around as if the hairy man expected the queen herself to come charging out of the forest.

"I think the northern army has other urgent matters than a small garrison traveling through the Helmand Mountains. Before I left, it was said her forces were marching to hold the south road near the Cleveite Mountains," Ray informed the two men.

"Neither the queen nor her men can stop me from discovering the truth about this quest my brother has sent me on. I studied the Moonvest book last night and discovered some very upsetting information." Noting that the sergeant's man Sash had quietly nudged his horse closer, Kriston shook his head and moved his own horse, Rath, away from his men. The news would have to wait until their conversation was more private.

They had just passed the last of the marsh inlets as the blue moon, Ra Neth, started disappearing for the day behind the hills on the other side of the Tentril Lake. Each man was taking a deep breath of fresh air and thankful they would soon be out of the marsh area when they heard the first noise from the Scarent people.

Calming the spooked horses, Kriston's men moved into formation as he saw the first of the snake people.

They came out of the tall grasses surrounding the lakeshore and some even came out of the waters of the Tentril itself.

They walked on solid legs as they formed a line across the path leading forward. Each snake person was well over seven feet tall, and each had long dart guns strapped around their scaled frames. The weapons were worn over tattered clothing, which was covered in mud and marsh foliage.

Timmons glanced backwards and noticed there

were more Scarents covering the path behind, he quickly called warnings to the others.

One of the first darts bounced off Kriston's leather arm shield and embedded itself in his horse's back, making Rath rear up. Kriston was able to grab hold of Rath's dark blue mane before he fell off.

As the horse settled back to the ground, Kriston grabbed his sword and saw that his men were already fighting the closest of the Scarent people. He grabbed the dart and pulled it out of Rath's skin with his shield hand and then raced towards the nearest enemy.

He had heard of the Scarents, but he had never seen one this close before.

As he defended himself and his horse, he saw that some of the stories he had heard were true. The Scarent people were said to be survivors of a bite from a Scarent. Once the venom gets into a human's bloodstream, they usually go mad or die.

If they survive, they begin to change—their skin turns brown and scales grow to cover them. Their eyes change to resemble the serpent's. Deep vertical black slits with blood red irises now stared out at him. He could see their limbs were longer and thicker than normal and they moved their arms as if there were no bones in them.

When the nearest Scarent attacked him, it slid right past his first sword swing and did a quick slither, trying to get underneath his defenses.

After three more attempts, he discovered the trick was to aim for their bodies and not their arms.

Out of the corner of his eye, Kriston saw Jake take two of the serpent people down with his sword, but then his friend was pulled from his horse by a third as it wrapped a large arm around Jake's body. Kriston raced Rath towards him and counted at least twenty more coming out of the water to charge the old man.

His other men were still back on the trail fighting a smaller number of Scarents, so Kriston yelled for Brigdon and Timmons. He urged them to form ranks as he headed to Jake, who was now standing knee deep in the waters of the lake as he hacked at anything that got close to him.

Slicing with his sword, Kriston cut the head clean off one creature and was shocked to see a snake slide from the dead body and head back towards the water. Turning back, he was in time to fight another reptilian who was now clinging to Rath's neck, trying to dislodge him from the horse's back. He smacked the snake person between its slanted eyes with the butt of his sword, and it fell backwards, landing in the water. However, it soon scrambled back up and attached itself to Rath's neck again.

Turning his horse, he saw more Scarents come out of the water and head towards him. They were outnumbered now. Some were firing their poisoned darts and others were dragging his men down into the water. If they stayed, the whole company would be lost.

He shouted to his men to race towards the falls,

knowing the Scarents were territorially bound. They might be able to elude the snakes if they moved beyond their boundaries.

He headed Rath back to where Jake was still struggling with two rather large Scarents and saw one of the reptilians land a hard blow to Jake's temple.

He grabbed Jake by his collar as the man went limp. Kriston had enough time to haul Jake up on the back of Rath sideways before more reptilians were on them.

Fighting through a small handful of the enemy, he turned the horse towards the falls and had Rath at a fast run when he felt the dart dig into his thigh above his armor. The poison took effect quickly, and he wasn't able to feel his hands or hold onto Rath's leads anymore.

"Rath, take Jake to the falls and find Timmons," he said as his body went numb. He was unable to stop himself from sliding from the horse.

He landed on the hard rock of the ground and saw the scaled feet of one of the Scarents approach him before he blacked out completely.

Byways had more people than Tharian and stretched out for miles. The town and its homes started in the fields and went right up to the shores of the ocean.

Anna had found last night's inn, a log cabin, to

be quite fantastic. The old couple who ran the establishment prided themselves on their home and the three smaller cabins they rented out to travelers. Shiarra and Anna had slept in one small bungalow while Leian had made do with the cot in the stables.

They had been sent off with a large breakfast of breads and dried meats along with fresh ale, the latter of which Anna refrained from until after she had her fill of food.

Wizard Leian once again asked Anna to place her hood on to keep her hair hidden while in the city. As she covered her hair and followed them beyond the city gates, Leian asked if it was acceptable if they called her just Anna.

"What else would you call me?" she asked.

"Your Highness, without permission, no one may call royalty by their first name." He turned to Shiarra. "We must get her a book on Genoa etiquette. Quite unheard of for royalty to not know what is acceptable," he said with a shake of his head.

Anna felt quite ashamed until she remembered she had just found out she was royalty. On Earth, she had never studied up on any royal's behavior. She had been far too busy trying to find out her origins and staying alive. Dismissing this, she turned her attention to the city.

There was a large stone gate that led to the homes and cobble streets beyond. The houses themselves were made of large stones and had wooden doors and small gardens. Each yard held beautiful flowers that were larger and more colorful than any she had ever seen. Some were as big as her face, while other's twice the size. Most of them were one color, while some of the biggest ones held more than a dozen colors melted together. She wished she could stop and smell each and every last one. There was so much to see she couldn't possibly take in everything.

"Byways prides itself on the garden shows they hold once a season. Each house is judged and the finest home wins a ribbon and the honor of free trade for a day," Shiarra said as she rode Bea past Anna.

Young kids ran past them and women working in their gardens stood and waved as they passed. Men pushing carts full of foods or tools stopped and shouted a hello to Leian and Shiarra, some even waving their hats.

Everyone seemed happy and content in their daily business giving Anna a warm and welcoming feeling. Something she wasn't quite used to, but enjoyed the feeling nonetheless.

The city appeared to be on a circle grid and soon they came into a large courtyard where a huge farmers market was taking place. She saw everything from furniture down to delicate teapots lined up for sale.

People of all ages walked or raced along the roads, some with small handcarts, others with large baskets over their backs.

The colors and sounds were enticing and so

were the smells of roasted nuts, popcorn, and caramel that came from the vendors' tents. Anna once again realized how hungry she was.

"It is trading day; shall we grab a bite of food over here at this pub while I send word to Sayer Otis?" Leian led them to the south road and a block away they were able to find stables for their horses for the night. "The pub also has rooms to lend and we will be quite comfortable there tonight." Looking at Shiarra he said, "We have stayed here before."

Anna could have sworn she saw the apprentice blush.

"What is taking him so long?" Shiarra asked Anna for the third time.

The young apprentice sat on the small wooden chair in the corner of the room with her arms crossed over her chest as she tapped her foot impatiently.

If the wizard didn't show soon, Anna was sure he'd receive more than just a welcome; he might end up with large chunks of Shiarra's mind along with it.

"He said the meeting was across town, right? Maybe he just hit traffic," Anna said as she leaned back on her bed fully dressed, the picture of ease as she contemplated her next question.

Shiarra, on the other hand, seemed full of

energy. She had been pacing back and forth since Leian had left them in the small room they had rented for the night.

After their meal, a runner had come and told Leian that Sayer Otis would meet with him before the sun set that day. Leian had rushed off immediately, informing Shiarra they were to stay in the room until his return.

Anna estimated it had been about two hours, and the sky outside the windows had turned dark. With each passing minute, Shiarra's nerves sizzled and popped with impatience.

"I want to know more about the war. Leian said your family moved to Tharian. Where did you live before?" Anna asked.

Shiarra sat forward in the chair as if preparing to answer.

"Wait!" Anna said sitting up. "I have an idea." She turned and looked at Shiarra with interest. The woman had been answering her questions regarding Genoa truthfully, and up to this point Anna had not wanted to use her powers on the apprentice, worried this could cause misgivings with her. She could see Shiarra was distracted by the wizard's absence. Maybe this would be the best way to get answers quickly. "I wonder; would you be interested in an experiment?"

Shiarra closed her mouth and stared at Anna with open curiosity. "Experiment?"

"Yes, come here and sit on the other bed. I have a secret I want to tell you." Anna patted the soft cover on the bed opposite her.

As the small woman sat on the empty bed to face Anna, Anna saw the hesitation in her oval eyes. "Shiarra, you know how I am able to gain a book's knowledge by touch?" Seeing Shiarra nod her head, she continued. "I can do the same with people." She watched as first shock then amazement crossed the woman's face.

"You, you have done this?" she asked with hesitation.

"Lots, but always to save my own life. I never used it to cross the line into a person's personal business, and I would never use it this way with you. But I was hoping you would allow me to gain Genoa's data from you, and only that." She folded her hands in her lap to wait while the apprentice thought about this new information.

"So, my knowledge only, not my thoughts or wishes?" Shiarra asked a few seconds later, trying to understand more before making her decision. "I would keep my personal thoughts to myself?"

"I would not dive into any of your personal thoughts. I would give you control over what you share."

"I? I would have control? How...how is this done?" Shiarra asked, leaning forward with curiosity and a little excitement.

"We would be in communication; you would let me know what it is you wish to share. Only that information is what I would gain," Anna reassured the apprentice. "I wish to learn more about the workings and history of Genoa, not your personal love life with Leian." Shiarra blushed again and gave her a small smile.

"We have no love life," Shiarra said quickly and brushed hair out of her face to shield her eyes.

"Again, not really interested in that. I'm just looking for history," Anna said with a small smile. "Will you let me try?"

Shiarra sat back with her arms crossed close about her thin frame and thought for a time. She had spent her whole life scared of the invaders from the south. Having lost her mother during an attack when she was young, she remembered how she and her father had been some of the only survivors.

Did she want Anna to know what she had seen that day? How she and her father had hidden in the garbage piles until found by their savior? How they had fled north knowing that only in the north they would be safe? Originally, they had headed to Valorna, but word had gotten to her father that Tharian was seeking a new Sayer, having lost theirs to an illness.

If she was really in control of what Anna saw, then she was honor bound to provide information that would benefit Anna in the years of training to come.

Looking into Anna's pale eyes, she realized if she did not trust the woman sitting across from her, then her whole world was lost.

"Yes, Your Highness, I will allow this. And am at your service." She bowed her head.

Anna was pleased and awed by the bravery she saw in the apprentice. She knew courage when she saw it and always appreciated its presence in another.

"Okay, relax. When I touch you, you will hear my voice in your head. Try not to fight it. Think of it as a little visit between friends where time stands still. If you don't want me to dig further into a memory, just tell me so. If you want me to stop entirely, just say stop." Anna stared deeply into the woman's eyes. "Do you understand?"

Shiarra nodded her head.

Anna held her hand an inch above the apprentice's. "You know you don't have to do this."

"It will be fine," Shiarra said as she reached up and grabbed Anna's hand herself.

His head was killing him. Had he drunk too much ale?

Kriston was having a hard time remembering what had happened to him. Maybe he was sick. He didn't remember going to bed, but maybe one of his

JJ Anders

men had carried him here. His legs felt as if they were asleep, but when he tried to move them, he heard a rustling sound, so they must be moving.

He tried opening his right eye and quickly shut it again. The pain was almost unbearable. Taking a deep breath, he tried again. Not so bad this time, he was able to keep it open for a bit. There didn't appear to be any light through his windows, so maybe it was night still.

He remembered being somewhere, but where?

He tried to open the other eye but his eyelash's movement made dust fly up and into his mouth. He must be laying on the ground. This meant he was not in his quarters. Coughing, he quickly closed his eyes and turned his head to the right. Pain shot from the top of his head into his neck. He took another deep breath, hoping he didn't pass out.

Where was he and was he injured?

He mentally checked his body. He could feel his arms, but they seemed to be at odd angles. When he tried to wiggle his fingers, he found his left arm was underneath him and his right arm was well above his head. He moved both so they lay on his chest and heard the rustling noise again. He quickly reached for his weapon but found his sword was missing, this fact caused instant panic.

He was unable to move his ankle to feel if his small knife was there or if it too was missing.

Trying again, he opened both eyes but still couldn't see anything. He cleared his throat and tried to speak but his mouth was so dry he couldn't muster enough saliva to call for help.

"You are ssafe. Pleasse lay sstill until the dizziness passess," a voice said from the dark.

Shocked the voice sounded so close to him, Kriston quickly asked, "Who are you?"

"We are many, but right now we are called Colab the Meshi."

"Where am I?" Kriston asked and tried to swallow again.

"You, Captain Kriston Haddock, are in the nesst of the great Mero the Pussh Tu." With this news, a small lantern was lit and Kriston saw a rather large Scarent kneeling beside him.

Kriston's memory came rushing back to him. The fight, the blood, being hit with a poisoned dart. Its poison must have knocked him out and left him paralyzed for the Scarents to bring him here. But where was here, what did they want with him, and why was he not already dead.

"Why am I here?" he asked while he slowly lifted his head and looked around.

He was in what appeared to be a cave with water dripping down the sides in dark green trails. Dark rocks glistened in the lamplight. Every few feet he could see bright crystals poking out from the walls. Overhead, he could see pointed rocks and he smelled musk and dirt.

"That iss for Pussh Tu to tell you," the Scarent said with a hiss. "When you are ready, we will take you to him."

Kriston's head still felt like it had been hacked

off and stuck back on, but he was sure there was only one Scarent next to him. "We?" he asked, casting about for another hidden body in the dark.

"Yes, we are Colab and Meshi." He pulled his shirt away from his body, and Kriston saw a small Scarent snake wrapped around the man's neck. "We live together after the choossing and ssurviving the change. Now we are a unit." The reptile peeled his small scaly lips back in what Kriston could only assume was a smile.

Shaking his head, he tried to stand or move away. When Colab reached a snaky arm out to assist, Kriston shrank from the cold touch.

"We do not hurt; we are here to assists you," came the hissed voice.

When Kriston managed to partially stand, he allowed Colab to assist him the rest of the way. "No offense, but when your people attacked my men, I did not feel you were trying to help."

"That was Jurat the Euxien. That Scarent and person have a high sense of stupid," he said with a shrug of his shoulders. Kriston noticed the hissing was gone from Colab's voice. "But the Scarents follow him when leaving our nests. He is a great fisher and hunter, which makes the snakes feel safe."

"The Scarents?" Kriston asked. "I thought you were a Scarent."

"We are, but I was speaking of the snakes," Colab explained and Kriston noticed the hissing had not returned

"Why does your voice keep changing?" he asked.

"When the human speakss there is no hissing. When the ssnakess sspeak, we have the distinct hiss to our voice," supplied Meshi.

"This is how we know who speaks. It causes less confusion," continued Colab.

The Scarent helped Kriston as they walked over the flat but rocky ground. Kriston couldn't tell if they were heading further in or out of the cave. Without Colab's lantern, he wouldn't have been able to see a foot in front of his face.

As they moved along the cave, he could feel the Scarent's cold scales against his skin. He wasn't sure if he was extra hot from his body trying to fight the poison or if the reptilian was truly that cold.

He could only manage a few small steps at a time, but the dizziness had passed and now he was left with a foul taste in his mouth. "Tell me Colab the Meshi, you mentioned the choosing. What is that?"

"Choosing, it is when Meshi heard the water speak to him and told him where to find me. I was younger then and had wandered into the marshes. When I came upon Meshi, we bonded and together we survived the changing." Again, the reptilian peeled his lips back in a smile. "Simple, yes?"

"Bonded, you mean when the person is bit by a Scarent snake?" Kriston said as he felt the strength come back into his arms. His legs still felt like he was walking in mud.

"Yess, the biting musst happen to bond uss," came the hissed reply from Meshi.

Kriston was worried he already knew the answer but had to ask. "What happens if the human kills the snake right after they are bit?"

"The human will die in pain." The Scarent hung its head. "The ssnake is what keepss the pain away during the change."

Kriston could hear rushing water ahead and was worried they were nearing the one Colab called Mero the Push Tu. He had a few more questions and felt he was running out of time to get valuable answers. "What if the human does not want to be a Scarent? Can he choose?"

"Everything in this world has a choice. If the bonding is not pleasing, then the two can part. But usually after the bonding, when they separate, they find only loneliness." Colab stopped and looked at Kriston. "I can tell you I would not wish to be parted. I know I would be very sad."

The reptilian's eyes blinked, and pale tan lids covered the bright red irises briefly. However weird the eyes were, he could see the seriousness behind their color and shape. "Is that the human talking or the snake?"

"Both, Captain Kriston Haddock." With this, they reached the opening at the end of the cold cave.

Kriston looked around and found they had come out from the dark cavern and into the open air of the evening.

The light from the lantern stretched out and showed him the dark waters of the Tentril. To his right, he could see the river, which he assumed was Maylin, but Colab the Meshi told him in fact it was the river Vi Porta, which flows out of the great Cleveite Mountains to the west.

"The great Mero the Pussh Tu iss our leader. Colab thinkss of him like the chief, but uss ssnakess know him by the name of Pussh Tu. He iss the oldesst ssnake and hass kept uss ssafe and well cared for," said Meshi.

When they came fully out of the cave, Kriston noticed his legs were easier to move. He kept this advantage to himself in case he needed it.

Colab took him around to the left, away from the river and deeper into the soft high grass that surrounded the lake. They hadn't gone far when he started to see other Scarents walking along in the grass next to them. Everyone was dressed much like Colab in rough clothing covered in grass or moss. None of them carried any weapons and he couldn't see any women or children.

"Do you have females?" Kriston asked, glancing around. If he was going to die, he wanted to know as much about his enemies as possible.

"We do, they are about. They are the gray scaled Scarents, while the males are brown or black," Colab said matter-of-factly, leaving Kriston to wonder if he meant the snakes or the transformed humans.

Before Kriston could ask another question, they

came into a large clearing in the grass. In its center were some tall, thin trees. The small grove was about fifty feet across and all the treetops were gathered and bounded into one grouping about twenty feet above their heads, making a makeshift room below with an opening in its center.

Moving under the tree's protection, he could see several Scarents gathered already, kneeling on the ground in tight small circles around small, glowing rocks. Smoke billowed from them, its small white mass moved upward towards the branches far above. When they passed, he could smell pine and something sweet in the smoke.

The only bright light was from the lantern Colab held, which cast all else into dark shadows.

Turning back to Colab, he saw the reptilian watching him with dark eyes. "This is the Mobius hut. It is where we come to be one with the Lady and hear her wishes."

Colab the Meshi led him further into the structure. They moved to the far side, past all the watching reptilians and their small glowing rocks. When they got to the other end of the Mobius hut, they stood in front of a small row of Scarents that sat elevated on a pile of straw only a foot higher than the ground.

The Scarent sitting in the middle was unlike the others he had seen. This Scarent had the snake wrapped about its head and had eyes of cool blue with the vertical black slit staring straight at him.

Colab the Meshi let go of Kriston's arm, placed

his free hand high on top of his head, and gave his head a quick bow.

"Mero the Pussh Tu, I bring you Captain Krisston Haddockss of Matera from up the great Maylin River." He hissed and took a step back, leaving Kriston staring at the chief of the reptilian people. Unsure if he was going to die or be turned into one of them, he stood his ground.

"Welcome to our nesst Captain Krisston Haddock," Mero said. Kriston hid his shock when he realized it was a woman who was speaking. "I want to apologize to you about Jurat the Euxien'ss behavior earlier. Our orderss to them were to requesst your attendance in thiss reading, not causse harm. He wass not to usse any force on you or your men."

Since he could hear the hissing in the voice, he knew he was speaking with Push Tu. Colab and Meshi had both called Push Tu a male, but he was clearly bonded with a female who had yet to speak.

"Why have you brought me here?"

"Two reasons but only one is my own and will not be spoken yet," Mero said, and with this the Scarents surrounding them started to murmur, causing Kriston to quickly glance about.

When Mero spoke again, all went quiet. "Push Tu has read the waters and the Scarents all agree; the planet says you are the man who must take on a great task." Mero rose and walked slowly towards him, her tall form swaying as she neared.

She was smaller than the other Scarents, about

Kriston's height and very slender in body. She wore a dress made of leather, which strapped about her. It had only one large strap over her left shoulder and a belt of woven grass around her thin waist. But like the others, she had no shoes or boots on her feet.

She placed a hand on his shoulder and looked him straight in the eyes. "This task is important to all who call Genoa home. If it fails, we fear there may not be much left after the next great war to come."

CHAPTER SEVEN

Great Minds

Shiarra could feel Anna slowly enter her mind.

It was not a strange feeling to have her enter her thoughts. Instead it felt comfortable, she realized she was standing in the warm sun and was glancing at the clouds above her.

She turned and saw Anna next to her. They were both wearing their clothing from the journey and they were still holding hands.

"Not so bad?" Anna asked.

Giving her a smile, Shiarra told her no. "What is next?"

Anna glanced over her shoulder and when Shiarra turned around, she was shocked to see they were now standing in the house she had shared with her mother and father in Pinewoods many seasons ago.

Her father sat in front of the fire smoking his pipe, a small content smile on his lips. Shiarra let out a quick gasp when her mother walked into the room carrying a lovely small child in her arms.

Shiarra guessed the image was from when she was three or four seasons old. Though she herself did not remember the house, her father had described it along with Shiarra's mother so many times that she knew this was a true image she saw now.

"You look like her," Anna said as she tilted her head to study the image.

Shiarra looked and saw that Anna was right, she did look like her mother. They both had dark hair, soft oval faces, and full lips. Her mother wore her hair long, its dark locks currently piled high in an intricate braid on her head.

Shiarra turned towards Anna with tears in her eyes.

"I started our visit of your past here because I am unable to remember my own family," Anna said. Shiarra could see tears in her pale eyes. "I wanted to give you something special and thought this would bring you joy."

"It does, Your Highness, it brings me great joy to visit a loved one that is gone." She turned back to watch her mother place the young child into her father's waiting arms. "I did not know I remembered my mother. It is good to see her,"

Shiarra said with a huge sigh as feelings of longing and sadness continued to wage war inside her.

After a time, she turned back to Anna. "Thank you for this gift. But I fear you did not come into my mind for family time. You came for knowledge and I am ready to move on."

Anna nodded. She saw the strength and resolve in the apprentice's stance, and after a moment they both turned and the image changed.

Shiarra and her father were walking along the bottoms of some high mountains with only the clothes on their backs. Both were blacked with ash and her father had a small limp in his right leg.

The image changed again and the two entered a trading station. Gone was the dirty clothing and the limp was no longer apparent in her father's walk.

She saw her father buy her a small doll made of straw and cloth and hand it to the small child Shiarra had been.

Smiling, Shiarra thought this was not so bad. It felt like visiting herself, or stages of her life.

Again, the image changed, and Shiarra saw her father teaching her how to read and write, about all the moons and their phases, and about the seasons and their effects on Genoa. The image passed so fast before her eyes, she was sure Anna couldn't understand all the information.

Before she could ask, the image again changed. This time she was older and getting tested to become a wizard.

She saw the shame in her face when she didn't

pass the last intense test. She felt some of the sadness that she had felt that day, but then the vision shifted to when Leian had come to her days after the testing and said that failure was part of the test and she had passed into service.

He had asked her if she would become his personal apprentice as they had stood in the doorway to her father's home.

The visions started coming even faster after this. They ran past her eyes now with great speed, showing her studies and classes with such detail that she heard some things she had forgotten.

Some of the visions were of Leian showing her how to complete magic, guiding her in his knowledge.

One vision was of them standing on the banks of the Pontella River. Leian was standing behind her, guiding her arms so she could use her magic to pluck stones from the rivers bottom to form rock castles in the air. The sun was setting and the sky was alight with golden colors, making the rocks sparkle. Shiarra felt the same emotions she had felt that day. Hearing a sigh next to her, she remembered that Anna was watching these visions too.

Feeling her cheeks redden, she asked Anna to move to another vision.

As soon as she asked, the vision changed back to the classroom. Shiarra could see the other wizards and their apprentices around her. Each was studying their own book while the old wizard Wyne stood in front and talked about the importance of a good wizard's book. He was explaining how to maintain it and keep its spells and histories alive.

The visions passed and Shiarra saw herself grow while learning all the knowledge it took to be a wizard. She saw all the fieldwork and studies, the nights out in the open sky where they studied the moons and stars themselves. As each vision passed, another took its place.

When the vision showed the start of her prior trip with Leian to Byways, Shiarra shook her head and turned to Anna and said stop.

Next thing she knew, they were back in the small room of the inn, sitting across from each other on the feathered beds.

"Wow, you did a lot of schooling!" Anna said as she sat back.

Shiarra was sure Anna would say something about her request to change visions or about her feelings towards Leian. When she didn't, she asked instead, "Is schooling different here than where you were?"

Anna considered for a minute. "I wouldn't know firsthand. I've had no formal education. But I do know Earth's schools are different. Less hands on and more books and numbers." Anna gave Shiarra a smile. "However, I now feel like I have gone to school, thanks to you."

"No education?" Shiarra was shocked but then her curiosity overtook her and she asked, "What was this Earth like?"

"Would you like to know?" Anna once again leaned forward. "Really?"

Shiarra understood and with excitement she nodded her head. "Yes, if you don't mind."

They grabbed hands again and this time it was Anna's visions that rushed before Shiarra's eyes.

She saw Anna's memory of the wizard Orden as he spun a pale little girl above his head while both laughed. Her pink dress twirled around her as her long pale hair whipped back and forth around her pretty face.

The wizard was large, his big hands waving in the air as he cast the loft spell that kept the little Anna floating gently in the air.

Next, she saw Anna alone at such a young age, walking through a forest where large red trunked trees rose high above her. Their green leaves spread and blotted out the sky. She could see huge ferns spread on the ground around them, blowing gently in the soft breeze. With excitement, she watched as a small brown woodland creature darted in front of their feet and scurried up the nearest trunk. Turning she saw there were small red deer nibbling on low grass in a field beyond the trees and watched as they lifted their heads while they chewed their lunch.

Next, she saw Anna wander a huge building with so many bookcases that Shiarra could not count. Each case was filled with books of all sizes and colors, the cases lifted well above their heads with ladders set about the room. Turning, Shiarra could see even more behind them lined up in neat tall rows. Looking up, she saw a glassed window of many colors way above their heads with sun shining down, making it appear they were in the middle of a rainbow.

Then they were on a mountain looking down at a vast city. Shiarra had never seen one so large. It appeared to span for miles and miles, as far as the eye could see. At its center, the buildings piled high into the sky as if in defiance of gravity itself.

"Turn around, the view is even better back here," Anna said and tugged on Shiarra's hand.

Turning, Shiarra's breath was taken away. Mountains taller than any she had ever seen lay in front of her, their snow-covered peaks spearing up to touch the very clouds themselves. The mountains further back took on a deep purple hue and their white-capped tips shined as the sun sent its light amongst their peaks.

"Where are we?" Shiarra said in awe.

"The Rocky Mountains," Anna said with a grin, but then she turned sober. "But Earth was not all fun and beautiful scenery." Choosing carefully, she picked her memory.

Shiarra saw a small dark room with horizontal wooden walls. She could smell hay and something else that made her want to hold her breath. She looked around and saw a small girl in the corner shaking with cold. Then Shiarra noticed the whole room was shaking.

"We are on a train," Anna explained. "This was the day after my wizard died. I was running for my life and had no one to help me." The train stopped with a jerk. "Or so I thought."

After a few minutes, one side of the room slid open and revealed a winter sky with snow falling all about.

A man climbed up into the room and, spotting Anna, walked over and crouched in front of her. His blond hair was cut short, and his clothing was different than Genoa's style. He wore pants of a blue material that had pockets in the back. His shirt was soft looking and had no clasps, and it had a picture on its front that Shiarra had never seen before, one of a wooden pole with another pole across its top. He studied Anna for a moment and then his face lit up with a small smile that reached his pale blue eyes.

"How long have you been here?" he asked.

The smaller Anna glanced up and Shiarra could see shock and despair in the young lady's eyes.

"You must be freezing." Holding his hand out palm up, he waited. "I have warm blankets and hot food."

When Anna made no move towards the help, he glanced back at the door. "No harm will come to you. I come here to help people who need it. That's all." He continued. "If you want, I'll be waiting outside on the platform. There are others here who want to help too. We have a place where you can be safe and warm for as long as you need." And with this, he stood and went back out of the train box.

After a few seconds, Anna stood and climbed

out after him.

Shiarra and Anna returned to the inn's room.

"His name was David. He and his wife ran a home for runaways. He was right, I was safe and warm and had plenty of food while I stayed there." Anna stared at Shiarra. "But more important, I learned that not all people are bad."

War.

Kriston didn't understand; sure, there were rumblings from the south. The Malic's had stopped trading and recently kept closing roads and turning Matera's traders away.

Battles were happening between Matera and several towns to the south, and to the north it was not much better. If his brother's words were correct, soon Matera could be an island surrounded by enemies, with no way to gain supplies from either location. Yet what did the Scarents know of these unsettling events? Where they affected too by Genoa's upsetting?

"What task would you ask of me?" he whispered.

"Come, sit with me while we complete the reading. You may get some of your answers from the Lady." Mero the Push Tu held her arm out and something in her manner made Kriston look twice at the leader of the Scarents. She had a grace about the way she talked and held herself that made him wonder about her origins.

After he took her arm, she led him back to the raised area and faced away from the crowd. As she folded herself comfortably on the straw, he hesitated only a moment and then sat next to her.

It was then that he noticed two Scarents on either side of the rising. They came forward and placed large wooden bowls in front of them.

"This is the cold clean water of the Vi Porta. When they are combined with the clean waters of the Maylin River, we are able to communicate briefly with the Lady of Tentril," Mero said as she lifted her bowl and drank deeply. When she was finished, she motioned for Kriston to do the same.

Glancing at the wooden bowl, he saw the clear liquid and hesitated. Was this really just water? What did she mean communicate with a Lady in Tentril? Tentril was a lake, right?

"Please, all will be clear," Mero said, and once again motioned with her hands towards the bowl.

He lifted the bowl and took a quick sniff. Since it smelled like water, he proceeded to take a quick drink. Finding it some of the cleanest water he had ever had, he took a second larger drink.

Once his bowl was placed back on the ground in front of him, Mero raised her arms and all the Scarents started hissing.

Kriston was so intrigued by their behavior that it took him a few seconds to realize the room was moving.

Glancing up, he saw the thin trees that had

made the Mobius hut were separating, creating an opening as they curved away from each other to expose the clear night sky above.

Colab, who stood to the right, extinguished the lantern, plunging the hut into complete darkness. Only the faint glowing rocks lit the darkness now, their yellow glow mixing with the twinkle of the stars and the soft luminescence of the moons.

Kriston blinked a few times to help his eyes adjust and saw the night was clear with no clouds blocking the heavens. The moons and stars reflected in the lakes, but it was soon the lake itself that held his full attention.

He saw the stars' reflections winking and pulsating, yet when he looked up, they appeared normal, with only one or two twinkling.

Glancing back to the water, he saw the stars' reflections move in slow circles. He lowered his gaze and rubbed at his eyes. Looking back up, he noticed that the moons were now moving too in the waters reflection.

"Must be something in the water," Kriston said under his breath, only to receive a quick hiss from Mero.

When the moons and stars stopped moving, he noticed that all the Scarents had become quiet.

"Children." A loud female voice spoke as all the stars in the lake vibrated.

"We listen, Lady," Mero the Push Tu said from next to him.

"Listen, all will be revealed," came the voice

again. "Kriston of Matera, I require your help."

What trick was this? he thought.

The stars vibrated each time the voice spoke, but surely one of the Scarents was doing the speaking. Maybe he was still drugged?

"Show yourself," he said. "If I am to help I must know who you are!"

This earned him some angry hisses from the Scarents surrounding him, but soon they fell silent again.

"I have chosen well," came the voice. "I do not ask for blind obedience. I need a warrior who will seek out the truth. You are him." With these words, the stars started moving again, forming a face in the waters next to the hut. Kriston worried that he had gone mad.

"Who... who are you?"

"I am the Lady of Tentril."

"Tentril is a lake. Made of drops of water, not the stars above. Who are you really?"

"Can you not feel me? I am formed by the magic of this place, an ethereal, set here by Genoa to keep these waters and lands clear. They are my charge."

"Why have I never heard of lakes talking before?" Kriston was positive he had never heard tell of any woman in the lake before.

"I talk to those who listen. The Scarents have always done so, and now they have helped you to understand and see with your eyes and hear with your ears."

"How?" he asked, still not quite believing.

"They have shown you where to look, child." The stars in the water winked. "I require your assistance. Will you help?"

Taking a deep breath, he contemplated his options. If this was a trick, no harm could come in finding out what was requested. If this really was a lady in the lake, set here by the planet, he had a duty that ran deep and any task asked must be attempted.

"Help? How can I help?" he said, trying to make sense of this vision.

"Will you help me and your fellow races in keeping lives from falling during war?"

"What war?" Kriston asked and saw the stars move again.

"War that may come if all is not set right." With this, the stars dimmed and Kriston could see smoke settle before his eyes.

When he blinked again he saw a large open field. On one side stood an army of gray. The men in armor carried red flags with a black star, indicating Matera's army. On the other side was an army made of wild creatures, some Kriston had never seen before.

He saw dragons and Scarents amongst the creatures and was shocked when he saw Valorna's banner of gold and blue riding high above the massive army.

As Kriston watched, both armies launched themselves forward as battle cries filled the air. Before the two armies met, the vision dimmed and he saw the plains again. Not a single blade of grass was left on the scorched ground. Bodies from both sides littered the soil. He saw death and destruction before him and smelled raw magic mixed with the decay of rotting flesh.

Closing his eyes, he realized this vision could be possible. Not too long ago, the Highman Plains had looked like this and many lives had been lost then too.

"If this war comes to pass, all life on Genoa will be wiped out by one flash of magic," the Lady said.

Shocked to hear this, Kriston stood. "Not all! You cannot mean all life!"

"All, child. I do not wish to be alone and poisoned. You must help stop this atrocity."

"What can I do to prevent this war?" he asked, flailing his arm around. "I'm just a man."

"What four men started, one must complete. To stop the war, you must start at the beginning and undo what has been done," she said while the stars winked.

Kriston stood with the Scarents behind him as he faced the lake. "The beginning? What does that mean?" he asked, his deep voice rising above the hut and mixing with the sounds of the now silent night.

"Find the girl," the Lady urged as the stars started to swirl once more. "But I give you a warning. She must be brought to me by the finish of the Moonvest."

"You want the spy?" he asked, astonished that she knew of his mission.

"She is the key. Keep her safe or all life is lost." With this the stars spun around in the waters of the lake and fell still once again, leaving just the reflection of the normal night sky above.

"Then he said we would be only allowed to look at the book once," Leian explained to both women as they sat in the rented room at the inn.

"Did you explain that all wizard books are to be kept available to any wizard when requested?" Shiarra argued as she sat next to Leian with a shocked expression on her face. "He cannot restrict us from reading it. This goes against the laws! I've never heard of a Sayer restricting any of the magical books before and cannot fathom why Sayer Otis would put this limit on the Hinlen book now."

"I did explain that to him, and he said there were too many requests lately, and he is concerned the book is getting worn and might be damaged. Since this is the only wizard book they hold in this city, he is taking his charge very seriously."

"All I need is one touch." Anna spoke up as she studied the two across the room from her.

"We know this, but I am worried we will be questioned if we leave too early after being allowed to see the book," Leian said. "We do not want to reveal your gift too early and even here, this far north, there may be spies."

Shiarra sat up straighter and Anna glanced at the two. "Spies? Spies of whom?" Anna asked.

Taking a deep breath, Leian looked at Shiarra. He must have seen something in her expression that confirmed his own thoughts because he nodded slightly.

"Tell her. It is better for her to be on guard now than to be blind and walk into trouble later," she added before he could speak.

Nodding his head, his blue eyes turned back to Anna. "Your Highness, we told you that Genoa is at war. That is not quite true, it is more like on the edge of war." Leian leaned forward on the bed, his blond hair falling forward over his brows. "When the three kings went to their corners in peace, that peace did not last long. One king, it appeared, was not happy with just his magic, so he sought out more." Leian stood and walked over to the dresser and poured himself a glass of ale. "He found a scroll hidden deep in an ancient library that explained a way to steal another royal's magic."

"Steal magic? Like from one person to another?" Anna asked and panic set in. Her magic kept her safe. She didn't want to imagine a life without her abilities.

"Yes, it is said he immediately set his evil plan in place and went after King Malicky, thinking he was the least protected." After taking a deep drink of the ale, Leian continued. "King Malicky's wizard was stronger than thought, but during the battle the wizard was wounded badly and the evil king fled with his life, injured from the attempt."

"Did King Malicky's wizard die?" Anna asked.

"Eventually, but not until he finished his own book and gave it to his king for protection." Leian sat next to Shiarra with a sad expression on his face. The silence hung in the room for a moment and then he continued. "When the evil king recovered, he was convinced he could only obtain power from a weaker person. Knowing the King and Queen of Valorna had a young child, he made her his new target." Both Leian and Shiarra stared at her.

Rising from the bed as fear ate at her, Anna poured her own glass of ale. Turning back, she saw both the wizard and his apprentice still looking at her with sorrow in their eyes. "So, am I to assume that I am that child?"

Taking another deep breath, Leian continued. "When the good king heard rumors that his daughter was in danger, he had her surrounded by wizards for protection. They were charged with her safety, but even they could not stop what came next." He walked to Anna and placed both of his hands on her shoulders.

"The royal family went into hiding for a time. It was not clear where they hid, but eventually the wizards and the young princess ended up at the magical stones, where they fought a great battle with the evil king and lost."

Shaking her head, she let his words sink in. "But I'm not... They couldn't have lost!"

"Most of the wizards were destroyed. It is said a few survived. Your wizard Orden was one of the survivors."

Anna took a step back from Leian in shock and placed the glass of ale back on the dresser, untouched.

"Wizard Orden took you to the one place he knew you would be safe. Earth."

Sitting down hard in the small corner chair, she stared at her hands as she thought about the story she'd just heard. If she was the princess, then what became of her parents? Did she have any family left here in Genoa?

"Where are my parents?" she whispered without looking up.

Standing, Shiarra answered the question, "It is known the king died in Pinewoods, my home village." Shiarra grasped her hands in front of her. "Your mother was taken by armed forces and has not been seen since. But since she contained no magic, it is believed she was murdered years ago." Going to Anna, she knelt in front of her. "I am sorry, my friend, but they were your only family here in Genoa."

Anna felt the loss of a family she had never known ripple through her soul. The hurt went deep and her eyes burned with tears she couldn't stop from falling. How unfair to learn of your family only to lose them seconds later, never knowing their faces or hearing their voices.

"What of the evil king?" she asked with a weak

184

voice. "It was King Haddock, wasn't it?"

"Yes. King Haddock went back to his own domain and then perished sometime in the next season. Now his oldest son sits on his throne and rules with the intent to finish his father's quest. To obtain all the magic and power." Leian sat once more on the edge of the bed and placed his head in his hands as if in defeat. "Here is where our troubles start."

"I don't understand," Anna said, grasping Shiarra's hand as the apprentice knelt in front of her.

"We fear he knows of your return," Shiarra whispered.

Lazerith had reached its peak in the night sky above Byways when a shadow detached itself from a doorway and raced across the empty street. Its form was neither animal nor man, but something in between. As it crept down the road towards its goal, it could smell the townsfolk and the foods that had been consumed earlier that night in the square.

Not wanting to be seen, it kept to the darker, less-used streets, well away from the lanterns that were set high on poles at each street corner.

The summons had been expected, but not this early. It meant the enemy was moving faster than anticipated.

But plans were flexible and so was he.

He smelled the town's peace-keeper before he

could hear or see the man. The creature rushed to the nearest alley and took to the walls as a large man walked by his hiding spot, whistling as he strolled well within the lantern light and only a few feet from a creature who could kill him with one swipe.

Once the Keeper passed, the creature traveled on, using the roofs of the buildings. He was almost to his destination and hoped the fool had left the window open as promised.

He now knew why the king had kept this man around. Having a spy this far east, and in the queen's territory, was well worth dealing with his incompetence and nagging.

As he reached his destination, he could taste the sweat and fear emanating from the man, along with a large amount of ale he had consumed, well before he even climbed through the open window. He hated that a light had been left burning but guessed it gave the man sitting behind the desk a sense of security.

As he entered the room, the small man stood quickly and started to shake from his very polished boots to the top of his dark head.

"Tell me the news!" the creature demanded in its mechanical voice, making sure to stay well away from the circle of light.

"The Wizard Leian was here tonight," the man said as he shook with fear and no doubt a little of the cold that the creature had brought into the room.

The weather was still warm and harvest season

was a long time away, but this cold was deeper and more primitive and purely from the creature standing before him in the large black robes, its face buried deep in its hood.

"Was a woman with him?" he asked.

"He said he travels with two apprentices; he did not bring them tonight."

"Fool!" the creature growled in his low voice. "If they have left town, we have missed our chance." It took a large step towards the cowering man.

"I did not let them see the book tonight. I put the wizard off until tomorrow morn. I told him the book was old and his time would be limited." Sweat was visibly pouring down the man's bald head now, onto his neck and past the fancy collar of his shirt.

"The wizard did not suspect anything?" he asked.

"No," the man said, falling back down behind his desk as if his legs would no longer hold him up.

"Did you find out where they were staying? I can go for them now," he said as he took another step towards the panicked man.

"No, the wizard would not say. They could be in any inn or home. I do know they will be here tomorrow and he intends to bring the women with him. He had an apprentice last time he was here, Shiarra was her name, but the other I know nothing about."

"Very well, I will wait here until then." The creature turned away from the man.

"H... here?" the man stammered.

"Do you have a problem with my presence?" he asked, glancing back towards the man.

"No, no," he said with more conviction. "It is just that to keep me in the service of the king, it may be better to capture the woman outside of the city."

The creature was on him before the man could react. He had the small man by his fancy collar and lifted him so high his bald, dark head hit the ceiling. Sweat poured from his skin and his dark eyes grew wide with terror.

"You dare to tell me how to do my job!" he growled.

"No!" the tiny man said and tried hard not to empty his bladder of the ale he had drunk while waiting for the king's messenger. "I just meant that if the king wishes to keep using my service, we may want to keep my involvement quiet a bit longer," he squeaked out.

Giving the man one good shake, he set him back down and grinned with sharp, yellowed teeth from below his dark black cloak.

"Maybe you are smarter than I thought," he whispered. "I will consider this and tell the king you have done well." The creature turned back towards the window and disappeared the same way it had come.

After a brief time, the man sank back into his chair and reached once more for his ale with shaking hands. He paused as his fingers brushed the small painting that sat on the corner of his desk. Picking it up instead, he studied the portrait and forgot all about his ale.

JJ Anders

CHAPTER EIGHT
Traveler's Woe

Kriston and the other captured men emerged from the Scarent's nest along the Tentril. Mero the Push Tu had ordered Jurat the Euxien to bring Kriston and his men safely back to his soldiers, explaining that Jurat needed to make amends with his people and this was the start of his punishment. Though no human life had been lost during the initial scuffle, two Scarent people were dead, and Jurat needed to answer for their lives. Once a Scarent person was killed, the snake was left to find another match and the risk to their lives was great during the bonding process.

Early that morning while it was still dark, they had been led along hidden trails beside the lake. They had continued down steep cliff walls that had led to hidden falls and had then traveled through a small cave. At the mouth of the cave, Jurat the Euxien had told them they would find their men located just below the falls. He said that he and his fellow reptilians would travel no further.

Kriston left them behind and easily caught up with his men below the falls just as the sun was rising behind them.

When they walked into the small camp along the water's edge where his men had set up to heal after the battle, Kriston's men and Sergeant Bainst were shocked to see him and the other captured men alive.

Kriston took a few minutes to explain to them that the Scarents meant no harm, and they were simply trying to ask for Kriston's help. He made a point to not explain too much detail while the sergeant was around. He would tell his friends later that night if he had the time. But for right now, there were more pressing matters.

Since they were still short for time and most of the men had rested at the falls that night, they pressed on, hoping to make the Deepen Forest before noon that day.

Once Kriston was on his own horse, his tired mind had time to think about his private conversation with the Scarent leader after they had met with the Lady.

"We have some of your men and will lead you back to your company, but I ask to speak with you alone first."

She stood and led him out of the hut. Kriston

glanced over his shoulder and noticed the trees once again were closed over the tops of the hut.

They had then headed towards the waters' edge. The tall grass gave way to soft sands that moved beneath his boots. When Mero's feet touched the edge of the water, she stopped and looked out at the calm waters for a time.

"Have you had the joy of parenthood?" the Scarent finally asked.

Kriston was shocked by the question and unsure of her reasons for asking it. He turned and looked at the reptilian now. He saw her worry her fingers, twisting and rubbing her thin digits while the rest of her remained calm.

"No, I have spent my life in battle. I have not yet found the one to share my life," he said, trying to get a full view of her face. "Why do you ask?"

"It was my greatest joy and has been one of my biggest sorrows." Turning, she faced him. "You speak with just Mero now, Kriston. Push Tu gives me privacy for what I must tell you."

Taking a step towards her, Kriston grasped her hand. "Is that possible? Colab told me of the bond, but I assumed it had to be maintained full time."

"No, and yes. I do not wish for Push Tu to leave my body; the feeling of loneliness would be too great. But sometimes, when I sleep, he goes and completes work and leaves me to a night of rest. He is always there when I wake."

Shaking his head, he asked what was still on his mind. "Do you like being a Scarent?"

He could tell the question both shocked and confused her. He watched her eyes as they searched inward for a time, then she refocused on him. "I have been here almost as long as I was at my old life, and find happiness and peace here with my fellow people." Giving a small shake of her head, she continued. "But that is not why I brought you here. I need a personal favor from you. I do not ask with a light heart." Taking a deep breath, she lifted a hand, and her slender fingers shook before they grasped his shoulder. "You are a warrior, and I fear Genoa will need your fighting skills before peace is found, but for now I must know of your heart."

Kriston could see the conflict in her blue eyes and was concerned for this soft-spoken leader. "You brought me here so I could understand the dangers that our planet is in. The Lady's charge leaves me heavyhearted. What more could you ask?"

"Just a small thing," she said and grabbed both his hands. Her strength both shocked him and convinced him of her passion. "But, I would pay dearly for this one favor if you ask."

Stepping back from her, he turned and watched the water as small waves started to hit the shore now. If he was charged with stopping a war, bringing the spy back to Matera and his brother, what was one more task. He could not promise he would succeed in any of these tasks he had been given so far, but all his skills and training would allow him to try.

"What is it you ask of me?" he asked without

194

turning back towards Mero.

"A chance for revenge," she said.

When Kriston turned and looked at her, she continued. "No, I do not ask you to complete my revenge." She walked the few steps to him and once more grasped his hands. "I want what was taken from me."

She needed a shower.

It was the one thought that kept running through Anna's head as she sat next to Shiarra in a small wooden entryway in Sayer Otis' offices.

She was still wearing the clothes she had been given in Tharian, along with Shiarra's overcoat. She had, once again, tucked her hair into its big hood.

She hadn't slept well the night before, since she'd had more dreams of dragons and cold circular rooms. She felt more exhausted when she'd woken up than when she'd gone to bed.

Shiarra seemed to be deep in thought and sat quietly with her small hands folded neatly in her lap as they waited for Leian to return. Yet Anna felt restless and wanted action. She was anxious to see the Hinlen book and gain its knowledge, but felt shut up in this small room. She hated the trapped feeling it gave her. There was only one outside door and one other door, but she didn't know where the second one led. She never would have walked into such a small space on Earth.

Maybe her restless night was finally catching up with her? She was on edge after thinking about all the lessons she'd seen from Shiarra's past. Stories of wizards being trapped, evil kings, and whole villages being destroyed did something to a girl's mojo.

The teachings of a wizard in the making had helped fill large gaps in her understanding of Genoa, but she had so much more to learn and felt like they had been waiting for hours in the foyer of the small offices. Waiting for Sayer Otis to show up so he would allow them to view the book caused her anxiety to grow.

Just when she turned to ask Shiarra how much longer it would be, the door opened and Leian walked in followed by a short dark man.

"Sayer Otis, my apprentices. You remember Shiarra from our last trip, and Anna has just joined the following. I have taken on her training as well. With your permission, they will accompany me when we inspect the Hinlen book." Both Anna and Shiarra stood.

Anna watched as Shiarra touched her forehead, with her right hand and moved it down to brush her heart. Anna repeated the motion knowing from Shiarra's memories that this was the traditional greeting wizards and apprentices used.

"Good to see you again, Shiarra," the little man said with a very thick roll of his r's in Shiarra's name. Turning back to Leian, the man didn't even give the cloaked Anna a glance. "I have never heard of a wizard taking on two apprentices."

Clearing his throat first, Leian informed the Sayer that he had been assigned two apprentices because there were numerous students this season and Shiarra was nearing her oath time. Otis seemed to believe this and turned to open the door for them to enter his office.

"I am sorry about the short time I can permit you to study the book. There have been too many requests to see it lately and I am concerned for its condition." He led them into an office room with only two lit lanterns hanging on the sparse walls.

He walked past a desk to another set of double wooden doors. Placing his hand on the oval knobs, he turned his face once more to Leian. "You will place a protection spell on the book for Byways?"

"It is very simple, as it appears the book's previous spell may have worn off. The new spell should help with its current condition and prevent any more damage the sea air may have on the pages," the wizard responded.

While Leian continued to talk to the Sayer about the protection spell, Anna glanced around the room and spotted a small framed portrait of a dark-haired young woman sitting on the corner of the desk. Anna had the odd feeling she knew the woman but was unsure of where she would have seen her before.

She hadn't met many people here, so she quickly glanced back at the Sayer and noticed that he was watching her. Since she had her hood pulled tight over her hair, and her face should've still been in the shadows of the dark room, she wasn't sure the small man could even see her eyes.

She dismissed her uneasiness when Otis turned back to Leian as the wizard finished his description of the spell he would cast on the book.

"I thank you, and Byways thanks you too. Please, I can grant you till noon." And with this, he opened the double doors and stood back to allow them entry.

Once they were alone in the room with the doors securely shut, Anna pulled off her hood and turned to Leian. "What now?" she glanced around the windowless room and saw a small table and one cabinet on the far side. A rush of uneasiness returned as she looked around, and her flight-or-fight instincts kicked in.

The room was small, but with its high ceilings it didn't feel too closed in. There were no chairs in the room, just a small round table made of dark wood and a large matching cabinet. Her panic took hold once more when she didn't see another exit.

Unaware of her panic, Leian opened the drawer to the cabinet and pulled out a large leather covered package. He placed the package on the table and began to unfold it to reveal the Hinlen book.

Suddenly, her concern fled and was quickly replaced with wonder.

Anna was shocked at how small the book was. The bindings were of leather and wire, and its pages were yellow with age and were worn and slightly torn on the edges.

"Before we begin, I will place the protection spell." With this, the wizard placed his hands above the bindings and bowed his head. Anna saw a small amount of light glow around the book's edges and thought she saw the book itself shiver.

Turning to Shiarra, she asked, "Can we trust Sayer Otis?"

Shiarra considered the question and after a time informed Anna that he had proven useful the last time they were in Byways.

"I could swear I know the woman in the portrait on his desk. I just don't know where from," Anna said thoughtfully.

When Leian looked up into Anna's eyes, she saw the toll his magic had taken on him. His eyes were glazed slightly and she could see worry lines around his mouth. His distress caused her to forget about the picture on Otis' desk.

"What was that?" she asked.

"A protection spell that leaves a coat around an object. It can take a lot of the wizard's energy, but since this book is old, I placed an extra healing spell along with a protection. This should allow the book to last several more seasons without damage." He turned to Shiarra. "Please make sure the door is secure."

As Shiarra walked to the door, he placed a finger over his lips, indicating he wanted Anna to be silent.

Once Shiarra returned to them, he spoke,

"Now, if you could collect the knowledge of the book, then I will ask my questions of you. We will not need to open the book."

Taking a deep breath, Anna reached out her right hand and placed it on the bindings. As the knowledge flowed into her, Leian glanced into Shiarra's eyes.

When Anna was finished, she stood and looked at both the wizard and his apprentice.

"Wow, Wizard Hinlen led a full life. I don't know how he fit so much into such a small book." She reached under her cloak for her backpack and took out a granola bar.

"Tell me, the seeking map, can more than one wizard place a spell on the same person?"

Chewing, she pondered his question and finally answered. "It's unclear. Wizard Hinlen thought that even spells would have a limit." She paused as she chewed on her granola bar and thought for a minute. "For example, we just saw you place a new spell on the book, but Hinlen states that he had placed a similar spell over it when he created it. It appears limits with time and space do actually apply." Taking another bite, she considered her own answer.

"Time and space," Leian began. "So, it appears a wizard did place another seeking spell on you. But could a third?"

Looking hard at Leian, she shook her head yes. "I fear your question, or more to the point, the reason why you ask it. But yes, Hinlen was unsure of restrictions in casting of this spell. So, if there is another wizard out there who wanted to find me, they could, as long as they had something of mine." She felt a shiver rush down her back.

Shiarra placed a comforting hand on Anna's arm.

Anna smiled and continued. "He speculated that there may be a counter-spell to block yourself from the seeking map. It may not prevent the spell from being cast, but it could place a shadow over you for a time." A shocked expression crossed Leian's face. "I don't like being tracked," Anna said with conviction in her voice.

Something was wrong.

He felt it as soon as they left the Sayer's building. Otis had barely talked to them at their departure and had made excuses again for not allowing them a longer time with the book. The little man had looked visibly ill and when Leian questioned him, he only said he was not feeling well, but had more appointments that day and would be fine by the evening meal.

But something was wrong.

Leian could feel a shift in the weather, as if the air itself was holding its breath.

As they headed back to the inn, he kept glancing over his shoulder. When that didn't satisfy his anxiety, he sent his magic out to discover what was amiss. As he did this, Shiarra asked quietly what was wrong.

"Take Anna and meet me at the bench." He whispered so only she could hear. "I will be along, but if not, take the map and find the others." He thrust the parchment in her hand and swung off towards the left. His long leather-clad legs ate up the ground as he headed down a side road, away from the inn and the women.

As Leian veered off, Anna slowed and turned towards Shiarra to ask what was happening. Her friend grasped her arm firmly and shook her head. Dragging Anna behind her, they headed towards a side street, one that would lead them towards the ocean.

After a few steps, Shiarra brought her own magic forward, releasing it out into the streets and shops that surrounded them. When she sensed the creature shadowing them, she felt panic rise in her. She hoped their slow pace would allow Leian time to get into position as they wove their way in and out of the crowd, heading towards the bench as instructed.

She didn't have time to think about the bench to their right, or the memory of her and Leian sitting close while the light faded so many days ago, she only had time to think of the danger they were currently in.

When she felt a shift in the danger, she slowed

and entered a small shop at the end of the block.

"I assume you have a reason for dragging me around?" Anna whispered so no one could hear them.

"We are being followed and are in danger. Leian is trying to track the thing that is behind us, but it got too close to us, so I ducked in here." She spotted a back door to the pottery store they had entered. "Follow me and when I tell you, run."

"Thing? Run? Run where? I don't know where I am and have no clue how to get back to the inn," Anna informed her.

"Just run towards the ocean. Not the inn," Shiarra responded.

As they exited the building, she looked around and, seeing only the villagers, headed towards the empty path at the curve of the street that led to the ocean.

The path they were on came close to the edge of the cliffs that Byways was settled on.

Glancing around, she noticed no one had ventured out this far today, leaving them alone. With market day currently underway, she hoped it remained empty enough to prevent people from getting hurt.

To the right, she saw the copse of trees that hid the bench where she and Leian had sat and talked past sundown that first night in Byways on their last trip.

Sensing a presence behind them, she whispered instructions to Anna, hoping she would follow them.

Turning, she met the danger with her magic already flowing around her body, praying she was skilled enough to hold the cloaked figure at bay until Leian could get in position.

Leian had gone no further than twenty feet when he backtracked to get behind the creature he sensed that had been following them since leaving the Sayer's office. Turning back, he saw the cloaked figure twenty paces behind the women and felt his heart kick. It was gaining on them quickly.

The wizard bolted back down a side street in time to watch Shiarra and Anna disappear into a shop. Knowing where her destination was, he skimmed past two more streets and caught up with the women as they exited the back of the shop. He couldn't see the cloaked figure but still felt its evil presence close by.

Following the women at a distance, he rushed towards the open pathway leading to the bench on the right. As they neared this, he caught his first sight of the creature. His magic told him this was not a man, but his eyes saw a dark cloaked human wearing a hood pulled closely about its face. Lengthening his strides, he caught up to the group just as the women took the small path towards the cliffs.

When he was mere feet behind the cloaked

figure, it disappeared in front of him. Leian was so shocked, he stopped walking for a second. When he realized what had happened, he started running towards the women.

Seconds had been wasted. He hoped he would get to the outlook in time to save them all.

What stood before them was not human. Both women could see that clearly now. The cloak was shaped like a man; however, the creature underneath was something else completely.

Anna could see the slits of the green glowing eyes staring back at them as if they were its next meal. Dull gray skin hid under the cloak. It reminded Anna of a sheet of diamond-plated metal with deep slashes cut across it.

She watched as a bright yellow glow surrounded Shiarra and was amazed when the apprentice spoke to the creature with a calm voice.

"You have no business here, creature. Turn and leave before you feel my magic!"

"Give me the girl, and I will let you live," it growled in a metallic voice as it took a menacing step towards the women.

As the creature moved forward, Shiarra's magic turned red around her. "Take another step! My wizard and I are ready!" she screamed as she saw Leian run onto the path behind the creature, his magic already glowing red around his body.

"It is a shadow!" Leian yelled over the creature towards Shiarra, Anna watched the apprentice pale with this news.

A shadow! Anna's new knowledge flooded her. A creature who could move without moving. It could end up behind them before she knew what had happened. It could also project itself in another place. How did they know if the creature they were facing was there? Or in fact, somewhere else? Maybe attacking them from behind.

Upon hearing the wizard's voice, the creature turned sideways and kept both wizard and apprentice in his sight as it smiled from beneath its cloak.

This action encouraged Shiarra that this really was the creature and not an illusion.

Anna stood a step behind Shiarra and watched helplessly. The only power she held was through touch and even the small knowledge she had gained from the two magic books was not helpful. Even if she knew how to practice magic, she didn't think she could work any of the wizard spells.

Much like learning Earth's Tai Chi, she had a feeling that magic had to be practiced before you could be successful at it.

The creature's lips peeled back and its sharp yellow teeth glimmered in the afternoon light before it launched itself at Shiarra.

Screaming, the apprentice released her red magic at the creature at the same time Leian's magic flew into the cloaked figure from the back.

Anna watched in amazement as both beams of red magic flew around the creature, twisting and slicing at its outer cloak.

At first the creature stopped in its tracks, but when it took one large step towards the two women with the red magic swirling around its body, Anna knew even magic would not stop it.

It gave a low growl and broke free from the wizard's magic, just as it shoved past Shiarra. The apprentice took the blow on her left shoulder and flew backwards to land ten feet away in a large heap of brown clothing.

Anna turned back to the creature and had taken two steps back, towards the cliffs when she saw Leian launch himself onto the creature's broad back.

The wizard was screaming and ramming his fists full of red glowing magic into the robes of the creature around its head. The creature faltered and took an unsteady step towards the cliffs, as it reached into its own robe with one massive hand. When it took its claw out of the robe, Anna saw a smooth blue rock grasped in its clutches. She watched as the creature raise the stone above his head.

She noticed when Leian realized what the creature held above its head near his face. Leian pointed a hand at Anna and she felt a hot wind pick her up off her feet and push her more than twenty feet away. She landed hard on the ground as the creature slammed the rock into the ground, breaking it into a million pieces as it released a scream that shattered the silence.

Her long robes were twisted and wrapped around her legs and arms but she broke free, ready to run. She raised her head in time to see the wizard and creature engulfed in a blue haze that seemed to come from the rock's broken pieces. As the haze settled back to the ground, both the creature and the wizard had vanished.

Kriston had halted his men well before sundown and ordered camp. They were settled well prior to the evening meal at the very edge of the small road leading into the Deepen Forest.

By then, he was so exhausted that once the meal had been consumed and his tent set up, he only wanted his cot. But he had responsibilities, and one of those was to inform his men of his previous night's adventures.

The hardest part was keeping the sergeant's men from knowing. He spoke with his own men privately and asked Timmons to be near the tent opening so he could keep an eye out for any eavesdroppers.

"What have you found out from the sergeant or his men?" Kriston asked Brigdon first as he settled his long-tired body on his cot.

"Nothing," the weapons teacher said as he lit a pipe. "What I have found out is only through observations."

"Tell us."

"The sergeant is not respected by these men, nor does he care as long as they fill out his orders. He is not patient and isn't skilled with either weapons or military science. I do not think he knows much about this trip other than what pertains to the spy. It is my belief that Beal and Ali know nothing about the nature of the trip at all. They have been given only one order, to cause us trouble and report everything to the sergeant." Brigdon sucked on his pipe for a moment and thought. When he continued, a small smile graced his lips. "When we met up with Beal and Bren after the lost water horse was located, the huge oaf had the nerve to demand we fire Bren for insubordination." Here, a chuckle escaped his lips as he turned to look down at Kriston, who was trying hard to stay awake. "It was then that Ray explained to him that Bren was a higher-ranking officer than him. The man tried to tell him all secret guards were to be obeyed and that he would see that Bren was discharged when we returned home."

Kriston heard a laugh and turned to Jake, who explained what Bren had told him of his adventure with the giant man named Beal. "Turns out Beal has no knowledge of tracking, so Bren took point in their adventure. When they came to a small path leading away from the marshes and heading into the plains, the man tried to tell Bren that he had gotten them lost and they should just continue the road to the falls. Bren continued to track the mare through

209

the brush and when he was only about a hundred paces through the thicket, he heard Beal scream like a girl. He turned back to check on the man and do you know what the oaf said? He said a tree tried to eat him." Jake chuckled, but then turned sober. "Bren said the man tried to strong-arm him after that. He said Beal tried to wrestle him off his horse and leave him for dead. If he had not been faster on his horse, he would not have made it to the falls at all. It was pure luck that the lost mare had stopped only a few feet away for a sample of the soft grass, allowing the two to capture her and head towards the falls. But our man said he will not be turning his back on the big fellow again."

"He had a lump on his head the size of a Rine melon," Timmons said, shaking his head with disgust. "Imagine, attacking your own men!"

Kriston thought for a while. It was better to deal with idiots than smart soldiers. But the stupid ones usually got someone else killed, never themselves. "What of the other, Sash? Do we know anymore of him?" he asked.

"Nothing," Brigdon said, shaking his head as he leaned back in the small space. "I have not even seen him lift his weapon, so I cannot gauge his skills." He paused and thought. "I have seen the way he treats his horse though. He shows the animal respect and cares for it, unlike the other men, who leave it up to our men to care for their creatures. I have also seen that he does not communicate with any of his regiment, including the sergeant."

"I see the same," Timmons added, leaning closer. "I have tried to talk to him, but he only listens. He does not turn away, just listens. But I see intelligence in his eyes." He rolled his shoulders. "I also see great anger but do not know who that is directed towards."

Gauging the time, Kriston slowly stood, stretching his sore muscles as he walked to the back of the tent. Once there, he turned and looked back at his men. All these men were his soldiers. He had learned, worked, and sweated next to them. He had even fought beside them. Foremost, they were his friends.

"Before we continue, I need everyone to keep an open mind," Kriston said as he again looked around the room with a yawn.

"What are you up to, Kriston?" Jake asked.

"I need your word that what you hear next stays in this tent." When Kriston got nods from each of his men, he raised a small corner of the tent canvas and all five men watched in amazement as a thin figure slid in to stand in the darkened corner.

CHAPTER NINE

Finding Lost

He heard his men gasp as the Scarent, Colab the Meshi crouched before them. Hidden in the darkness of the corner, his dark brown scaly skin blended into the tent's canvas while his red slit eyes shined from the lantern's light.

"What is that doing here?" Timmons said as Brigdon rose next to him while pulling his short sword from its sheath. Jake stood too, and as he bumped into the small table, he had to make a quick grab before the lantern fell and caught the whole tent on fire. The only one to stay sitting and calm was Ray. His dark eyes showed no fear or anger at having a known attacking species amongst them in the tent.

"Well, invite him in the rest of the way and get

on with your story," the captain said as he took another sip from his cup as if nothing were amiss.

Slowly, the men settled in around Kriston as he sat back down on his cot. Colab the Meshi sat cross-legged in the very corner he had entered, keeping to the darkness, but able to see all in the tent.

Since the tent was small, all six of them were well within arm's reach. The small lantern had been quickly turned down low so their shadows would not be cast against the sides of the tent.

Kriston then informed them of his travels, about the Scarents and their way of life. How the snakes choose a host and the two lived in peace and apparently do not like separation after the change is complete.

He explained how he had met Colab the Meshi and about the Lady of Tentril's visit with him and her charge to keep the spy safe. He kept only one part of his visit with the snake people a secret, their leader's private request. He only did this because he had promised Mero that he would not tell anyone of their discussion.

"But we are already on a quest to track down this spy. Why would they ask you this same task?" Jake asked.

Brigdon, who had folded his tall frame next to Kriston, stood and tried to pace. "Maybe this spy is more dangerous than we first thought," he said as he turned to pace again, but when he bumped into Timmons and then Ray, he took his place next to Kriston again and rubbed his short goatee.

"I have my doubts about what my brother said. Part of me thinks he is the one not telling the truth," Kriston said as his green eyes glanced from one friend to the next and then back at Colab.

"Why would he send you on this trip if the spy is not a threat to Matera?" Ray asked.

"Why would the Lady need this spy safe is the real question," Timmons piped in. "The ethereal is the one whose quest we should respect. If she is fearful that all life will be extinguished, this, truthfully, has me worried." He checked out the tent opening again to ensure no one was near.

"The Lady asked that I keep the spy safe for her. When she spoke of this, I got the feeling I was to guard the spy, not arrest her," Kriston said as he stared off into the small flame of the lantern as it flickered back and forth. He could feel his body drifting towards sleep.

"We know we must find the spy, whether she is a danger or not, we just do not understand yet," Brigdon said to all as he adjusted his weapons to fit more comfortably in the confined space.

Ray turned to Colab. "Do you know anything about this?"

Colab lifted his face and stared at the canvas on top of the tent. "We know little, but Meshi knows more than I."

Ray leaned forward with doubt in his dark eyes. "Meshi?"

As Colab opened his shirt to reveal the Scarent snake, the men closest to him scooted farther away,

215

all except Ray. "What does Meshi know?" he asked instead.

"We knowss a lot. What Captainss Krisston wantss revealed iss up to him," the snake explained and fell silent.

"These are my friends and family; I think they should know what we know," Kriston informed the Scarent, crossing his booted feet and tucking his arms behind his head.

"The sspy, you call her. Sshe is mosst important to the peacess of the peopless on Genoa. Sshe iss in great dangerss and musst be protected sso sshe can fulfill her desstiny."

"Who is she?" Jake asked as he crossed his short arms in front of his wide chest.

"Sshe iss part of a plan that went wrong. Sshe wass exiled from Genoa and hass returned after many sseassonsss," the snake told them. "Thiss iss all I have learned sso far. The Lady keepss the resst hidden to protect uss."

"An exile?" Ray said out loud. "Where was she exiled to?"

"We do not know," Colab responded.

After several more questions that Colab and Meshi were unable to answer, Colab the Meshi returned to the dark woods where he promised to continue following the company at a distance.

He promised to reveal himself only to Kriston or his men after dark if something was needed. It took several more minutes for Kriston's men to wear down their discussion and file out of his tent, heading for their own cots.

Kriston had told his men that Colab was not a fighter, and that the Scarent and human were both used as a messenger. When Mero the Push Tu had asked Kriston to take the Scarent with him, he had asked her the reasoning behind her request.

"We need an ambassador on your quest. I fear that before your quest is over, you may have need of our people, and Colab the Meshi can get word to us if we are needed." Kriston felt something was still missing from this explanation but did not pursue this hidden reason any more with the leader.

When Kriston finally settled in for sleep, he found the air in the tent too hot, his cot too hard, or some other nonsense. After tossing and turning for several minutes, he decided that taking a quick peek at the seeking map to check on the spy's location would help settle his nerves. If he could assure himself that finding and capturing the spy was possible, he could then get rest.

He checked the map, but it took him a while to locate the spy. When he did locate the rip, he was shocked to see it was moving. She was moving at a fast pace right towards them.

There were days in between them, and the Helmand Mountains stood in their way, but she now traveled on the same road he was on. And it looked like she was in a hurry.

Having witnessed the Wizard Leian disappear, along with the creature that had attacked them, Anna was sure of only one thing. She had been found and betrayed.

She had a pretty good idea who had informed the creature of her whereabouts, but she didn't know enough to make a solid accusation and had no clue how to even proceed with this speculation. What good would it do?

Thankfully, Shiarra had not been seriously injured in their battle with the creature. After relaying what had happened to Shiarra, the apprentice had informed her the magic used to disappear the wizard and creature had been a trans rock.

The apprentice's dark hair was knotted and her once neat braid lay in ruins around her pretty face. Anna feared she looked no better. Her short hair stood at every angle, and both women were covered in dirt along with burned black patches.

"Trans rock?" Anna asked, fearing the wizard was blown to pieces and no longer able to assist her. "Is, is he dead?" she whispered.

"No, but I fear for him just the same. I am not familiar with the creature that attacked us, but the rock I know of. Magic makes them, and they are always made as a pair. Two can take a rock, and it allows them to communicate, but throw the rock down, smashing it, and magic transports those standing nearest the first rock to the location of the second rock. No matter how far the rocks are apart."

Anna watched as Shiarra's head cleared. They both realized the danger Leian was now in, and that they were still in danger too. Standing, Shiarra grasped Anna's arms. "Your Highness, we must leave Byways immediately!"

"The creature is gone," Anna said, looking around as if she expected another to leap out at them any moment.

"If the creature relayed our location by using the rock, there may be more enemy nearby. We must leave now!" The apprentice gathered her cloak about her and headed back in the direction of town, wiping dirt off her as she moved.

"Where do you expect us to go?" Anna said as she picked up her skirts and followed. "What of Leian? If he's captured, we have to rescue him!"

"His rescue will take time. I fear he is now beyond our borders and down in Matera with the king. As to where we will head, Leian gave me instructions and I intend to follow them." She continued to walk as she pulled a small metal tin from her robes and rubbed some Winnept sap on her arm where a small gash was. She wiped the blood and sap from her hands with a cloth after the cuts had been healed.

Stopping in the middle of a street, Shiarra turned to Anna. "Were you harmed?" After Anna shook her head, she quickly placed her hood back on and they continued, heading towards the inn.

When they were a block away, Shiarra changed her mind. "Did you leave anything in the rooms that you must have, Your Hi... I mean Anna?"

"I have everything I need in my bag here. How about you or Leian?" she asked.

"No, we took everything. What we have is with us or with the horses. We will leave the city tonight. I fear the inn may be compromised and it would be dangerous if we returned."

"Agreed, but where are we going now?" Anna asked as they headed towards the stables.

"I will tell you once we are out of the city. For now, keep your eyes open as we gather the horses."

Once they could see the stables, Shiarra had Anna stay back and hide in an alley as she continued to the stables to get the horses.

As Anna crouched in the alley, she realized that her journey had started in a street much like this one, but so different. Worlds apart, she thought with a laugh. Literally. She glanced down at her new clothes and sighed at the dirt-stained leather. They were so different than her worn jeans and hoodie.

Just like her clothing, the two cities were different, both alleys she hid in held trash containers and each city was near water. She could smell the ocean a few yards away, just like she could smell the rivers when she had been in Boston.

She just hoped, like Boston, she would escape this adventure unharmed.

As she watched, Shiarra came out with Sam and Bea. As she crossed the street, both women kept their eyes open, looking for danger. When everything looked clear, Shiarra continued across the street towards Anna's hiding-place.

After they had settled on their horses, they headed out of the city, keeping a slow pace so they wouldn't raise suspicion.

"I asked that they send Whinny back to Tharian. I fear we will need to travel light and fast once we hit the city borders," Shiarra said as she continued to glance behind them to make sure no one was following them.

Anna found Shiarra was right. Once they hit the outskirts of the city, they picked up their pace. Both women bent low over the large horses. Anna was shocked at how fast the animals could move and held on tight to Sam's mane for fear of falling off. His long legs ate up the distance, putting miles between them and the city.

They stayed on the road at a full run for more than an hour, at which time Shiarra called a halt and slowed the horses to a walk once again. Luckily, the road was smooth and the forest closed in on either side. The trees loomed above them, blocking out the evening light. Anna could hear small insects buzzing as evening started to settle around them.

"This road is not well traveled; I feel we are safe for a time. However, after tonight we will want to take a few back trails I have heard of."

"Shiarra, where are we going?" Anna feared the apprentice had no clue where they were heading. She worried they were heading back towards the wizard's village and feared it was no longer safe after their betrayal.

"Leian gave me the seeking map and told me to locate help by heading to one of the others he had previously used the spell on."

"You mean the other rips?" Anna asked. "Do you know who these people are?"

Shiarra turned and looked at Anna. Both of their hoods had fallen off their heads during their race along the road, and the wind had blown Anna's short hair around her head. Shiarra's hair was still a tangled mess, most had slipped out of the large braid and fell around her face. "I know, but I'm not sure if help or more danger can be found with them."

"Which one are we going to first?" Anna asked, placing her hood back on her head and pulling her cloak closer around her neck as the sun began to set behind them.

"We go to Valorna," Shiarra said as she too pulled her cloak tight and tucked her long hair inside her hood. "The horses can take us far tonight, but must rest between running. How long do you think you can ride?"

"I'm good for a few more hours." She studied the forest around them. The fading light was behind them, confirming that they were still heading due west.

"Good," was Shiarra's only response as she glanced around.

The horses moved at a slower pace for a while, but then Shiarra sighed as if remembering something and kicked her horse into a run again.

When they finally reached the end of the forest, the temperature had dropped, making the night a little more comfortable. When Anna spotted Lazerith straight above them, she guessed that it meant it was somewhere near the middle of the night.

After a time, Shiarra took them off the main road so they would not be spotted easily.

They set up camp in a clearing near a small stream of cold water. Anna helped tie the horses to low branches with enough rope that they could easily eat the tall grass and drink from the stream.

Shiarra and Anna both pulled sleeping blankets off the horses' packs and Shiarra produced a small tent. After a few minutes of struggling, they had the tent up and their bedrolls laid out on the ground just like avid campers.

Shiarra provided some water for them and they ate a meal of dried meats and fruit. They didn't make a fire since the night was warm and the stars and moons provided enough light. Plus, Shiarra had said that she didn't want to take any chances that they would be spotted from the road a few yards away.

"Tomorrow we will have to travel slower. We will be traveling on the back trails that go up into the hills surrounding the Helmand Mountains," she informed Anna as she stretched her sore back.

"Those are the ones we saw today?" Anna asked as she remembered the jagged mountains she had spotted before the sun had set. They were a deep brown with little spots of green tucked between huge cliff faces. None of her views of the mountains gave her hope that tomorrow's travel would be easy.

"Yes, the mountains travel far to the south all the way to the Maylin River. We are lucky we will not have to go into the mountains themselves for they are dangerous when not traveling on the main road. Tomorrow, we only go to their feet. The Mirror Lake would be a great spot to camp tomorrow night. The day after, we turn north and spend two more days to get to the crossroads. We can resupply there and another day or two might see us in Valorna and a soft bed. I hope to find help in trying to rescue Leian from a friend of his in the queen's city."

"Help? You think we can help Leian?" Anna asked as she remembered the wizard's face as he disappeared in a puff of smoke, still clinging to the back of the metal creature.

"I know Leian's friend can. He is the queen's wizard," Shiarra said with a huge yawn.

"Queen?" Anna asked in surprise, sitting up slightly. "Shiarra, is there a queen in Genoa?"

Being disturbed during his meal was enough to set his anger blasting out at the messenger. After the boy's message was delivered, the king had the lad sent to the mines to work while Gillard's anger simmered and boiled around him like a tangible cloud.

"Failed!" he exclaimed to Wizard Fulder from his throne room. "The creature only retrieved a wizard, not the girl!" The angry king marched back and forth in front of his chair as the old wizard stood bent before him.

"What would you have me do, my king?" the man asked in anticipation. He hungered for action, death, and magic more than anything, something he only revealed in the king's presence. Though they looked entirely different, deep down both men had the same hunger for power. Hunger that could only be fulfilled with magic.

Fulder had been right to trap Gillard's father many seasons ago. Getting the king addicted to the use of other's magic was simple, but keeping the king's conscience at bay had been another trick. But Fulder had found a kindred spirit in the king's oldest boy, Gillard. That day many seasons ago when a young Gillard had looked upon the wizard with curiosity and hunger, Fulder had known their futures were twined together.

Each day, each hour of his life, the king gave the wizard what he needed-power and magic to feed from. He took everything he could like a leech, each day growing stronger and more addicted while hidden within a shroud of age to hide his true form. While seeping power from the young fool, he also made sure the king got what he needed. He had learned many seasons ago that his prey must be strong for the feeding to continue.

"I need that woman!" the impatient king shouted. "Bring her to me!"

Giving his head a great bow, Fulder placed his old bony hands inside his cloak pouch, retrieving a large white crystal ball he held it high above his head.

Gillard's eyes grew large as the crystal started to glow from within. The bright white faded and turned gray and then inky black, dark as night.

"The spy will come to you before Moonvest is finished," Fulder exclaimed in a high voice. His own eyes now mirrored the black from the ball as he looked into the future. "She will bring your downfall if she is not killed before that time."

Gillard stomped closer to the wizard, his outrage showing on his face. "How do I stop this?" he demanded.

"Take another. Bring her here to deflate the spy's intentions."

"Who!" Gillard screamed again.

"Weaken her by capturing the queen."

Gillard turned from the entranced wizard with an evil smile on his youthful face.

"Get me Zobo!" he shouted and was pleased when the runner's footsteps could be heard echoing throughout the halls of his home.

He traveled far that night. Not in body, but as

his alter spirit shape.

He didn't need days to get to his destination; once he set his mind, it only took minutes. But even then, it took him a while to locate what he was looking for.

As he crept closer to the small clearing that held a single-man tent, he made sure to stay on the far side of the creek so he was not seen.

Sliding closer, he passed in and out of the shadows. His feet made no noise as he crept nearer. If he could just get one glimpse, then maybe his curiosity would be satisfied.

When he was a yard away from the tent, he heard a noise to his left. Baring his teeth, he watched as the object of his search stepped out of the shadows. The woman whom he had been sent to track, capture, and deliver to his brother, walked slowly towards him from the other side of the water.

She had not yet spotted him, so he completed a quick study of her.

The first thing he saw was her hair. Despite it being wet, it glowed white in the many moons' light, like a short halo around her oval face. What he could see of her skin was pale and translucent and looked very soft.

His enhanced eyesight saw that she wore a simple full-length slip made of light wool that hung down to the top of her bare feet. She appeared to have narrow, small feet, like those of a child. He paused a moment when he realized her toenails were painted a deep red. He had never seen a woman's toes colored like this before so he studied them for a while as she dried her hair with a clean cloth.

His eyes traveled up to her dress collar, which was untied and hung open, leaving her neck exposed. He watched in amazement as her pulse softly pounded along her slim throat. Her face was soft and he liked the look of her full lips, which were currently tilted up in a small smile.

She reminded him of a fairy, so delicate and beautiful that he was afraid if he blinked she would vanish, as if she had never been there at all.

He let out a low growl and watched as her body froze. She turned her head towards him, and their eyes met, dark green ones to very pale blue. Her tongue darted out to lick her top lip and then he heard her swallow nervously.

Glancing back to her large pale eyes, he was mesmerized as they held him captive, giving him a quick look into her soul. These were not the eyes of evil and they did not hold any deceit. These eyes held wonder and compassion, and at the moment a little fear.

Lowering his head and walking further out of the shadows, he allowed her to see him fully for the first time. She inhaled sharply and a small smile formed on her round lips.

"Hello, you frightened me." She glanced around the small clearing then returned her eyes to him, "Are you lost? Where have you come from?"

He walked closer to the edge of the water and

she took a small step forward.

Even from this distance, he could hear her heart beating in a fast rhythm. Her skirt rustled against the forest floor as she moved through the soft grasses.

As he got closer he could smell her, a scent of flowers freshly picked with a hint of lemon, mixed together with the scent of the water from the stream. He breathed deeply while he stood there boldly returning her gaze.

As she raised the cloth to the wet ends of her short hair, she continued speaking to him. "Glad you didn't catch me while I was washing. I think that would've scared the both of us." She chuckled softly and he liked the sound very much. "Boy, another day without a shower and I think even the horses would've complained," she said with a small laugh that filled his head with images of a fast running brook.

He sat down along the creek bank and tilted his head as he continued to study her. She didn't appear to be in any danger, but what was she doing here?

"You hungry?" she asked as she reached in her bag and pulled out a small rectangle item. "I've been trying to save these, but I guess a small midnight snack won't hurt." She continued talking as she peeled the cover off the item and took a large bite.

Once she finished chewing, she broke a piece off and tossed it across the creek towards him. The item landed at his feet. He kept his eyes on her as he slowly bent and smelled it. It smelled like fruit and honey.

Deciding to show some trust, he ate the item and was shocked at how good the small bite was.

As he lifted his head again, one of the horses behind her shuffled, and she glanced towards the noise.

When Anna turned around again, she was disappointed that the large black dog was no longer across the creek.

He had sat there watching her with the deepest green eyes she'd ever seen on an animal. She'd felt joy at seeing a familiar creature in this land.

Giving a quick glance around, she saw no signs of disturbance as the brook continued its slow travel through the clearing.

"Bye...thanks for the visit," she whispered, turning back to the camping spot with a shrug. She was pleased that there were friendly animals around to keep them company, unlike the wolves and coyotes of northern America.

As she finished drying her hair, she thought back to Shiarra's words.

"Yes, Genoa does have a queen. She is ill and you may be able to provide her help."

"How can I help a queen?" Anna had asked. *"Doesn't she have a wizard like Leian?"*

"What ails the queen is from magic and only

the right kind of magic can help her." With this Shiarra stood and took her boots off, making sure to tuck her long stockings into the tops to keep creatures out during the night. Then she lay down in her bed. "I only know this much. Leian is the expert and we must rescue him before we attempt to help anyone else."

"If the Queen is ill, how am I to help?" she thought as she climbed into her own bedroll while Shiarra slept lightly next to her.

Anna knew her powers were only good for gathering knowledge and tricking people. Maybe the queen was under a spell that kept her mind trapped in a maze. She remembered seeing something like that in a movie once.

Maybe she needed Anna to help her find herself.

Could Anna assist with that?

She continued to think about the queen until her mind settled and she finally drifted off to sleep.

"She is coming."

"I know."

She was back in the circular room, again facing a mirror with only her reflection as company.

"Will she understand? Will she believe?

"Did you?"

"I still have problems understanding, but yes, I believe."

231

"*When she comes, we need to complete the next step. We must!*"

"*I know.*"

"*Are you scared?*"

The following pause was so long it was unsure if the reflection would answer. When it did, it was very quiet, like a whisper.

"*Petrified.*"

JJ Anders

CHAPTER TEN

Up a Creek

They were lost.

She knew for sure right after their last stop and should have admitted it to Anna, yet something kept her from uttering those words to her new friend. She had been charged with leading Anna to safety and now they were lost in the woods that nestled along the Helmand Mountains.

What would Leian think of her if he knew she couldn't even go a day without him. She had been training for years with the wizard about survival and magic and now she couldn't even find the road leading to safety?

Would she find help in her search for her friend and mentor?

She could only guess the wizard was now deep

in the enemy city of Matera and hoped he was still alive for her to find.

After waking that morning, both women had picked up camp and eaten a small and quiet meal. Shiarra estimated they had three days of supplies left so both women settled for smaller portions of the dried meat and berries that remained. Shiarra was good at foraging for food and was not too worried about their supplies. It was clean water that had her concerned. She knew the water from the Mirror Lake was good for a swim, but didn't think fresh, safe drinking water would be available until they reached the trade station two and a half days away.

After mid-morning, they had stopped along the back trails and had eaten some more food. She had been unsure of which trail they were on at that time, but had been sure they were heading in the right direction. She did not remember the trail being so steep and rocky last time she had traveled it, but it had been well over ten seasons ago that she had laid eyes on this side of the mountains while traveling with her father.

They had gone to visit the neighboring villages and meet with their Sayers. For most of the trip, she had been entertained by her father and had paid no attention to the road they had taken.

Now, she had made sure to keep to the left of the main road, knowing that if they strayed too far they would end up near the feet of the Helmand Mountains and could always follow the mountains north until they reached the lake.

She remembered that the smaller path she and her father had taken had been well worn. It had dipped along the smaller rolling hills and she remembered there had been a meadow or two along its path. She thought they were on the right route until she noticed this trail led closer to the mountains than she remembered.

They appeared to be gaining in altitude too, climbing higher than they should into the mountains. There were also more rocks here and, as the horses kept a slower pace to prevent tripping, she saw that some rocks had large airy holes on their surfaces.

"We may need to find a path to the north. I think the trail is heading too close to the mountains and we want to veer to the right more," she said over her shoulder to Anna, trying to keep the concern from her voice.

"Sure. What are those pink flowers there? They smell so pretty and I don't remember seeing them yesterday," Anna asked, looking like she enjoyed riding on Sam's back, as if she took long trips into unknown territory all the time.

Then Shiarra realized that, with Anna's exile in Earth, maybe she did have more experience in this kind of travel than Shiarra did herself.

"They are called Purfla. They are great for perfumes or to hang in homes." Shiarra thought about the time Leian had given her a bunch of the flowers and was distracted by that thought when they passed a small trail leading off to the left into the trees. Since it was the wrong direction, she kept going on the main rocky path. "Anna, did you do much traveling on a horse in Earth?"

"I didn't really ride horses much, but I did a lot of hiking. My favorite hiking was along the Rockies." Anna stared off to the left and contemplated the mountains. "These mountains are sharper and more rugged. The Rockies are massive and breathtaking, but you know that. You saw them in my vision the other night. There was always something welcoming and awe inspiring about them. Course, I did most of the traveling in the summertime. No way I would've survived a winter with the cold and snow."

The Helmand Mountains had no snow on them. Their rough peaks were jagged and tipped at odd angles, as if an angry giant had slammed the rocks about. Every once in a while, they would see a fresh slab of rock laying near the bottom, as if part of the mountain itself had fallen at the hands of time or nature.

Small pale yellow grasses and spindly gray trees grew in between the rocks where their roots could take hold and find some nourishment. The wind had bent most of the trees on the higher peaks, but down where they were riding, the trees grew straight and tall.

"These remind me a little more of the mountains in Utah. These might be volcanic rocks here with the holes, though they look too sharp."

She pointed to a rather large rock. "It kind of looks like cheese that a cartoon mouse was always trying to steal." She chuckled.

Shiarra thought she heard regret in her friend's voice when she talked about her travels on Earth. "Do you miss Earth?" she asked after a moment.

"No, at least not very much. I was always on the run. Course, we've been on the run or moving since I got here too." Anna sighed.

Shiarra saw the trail ahead take a sharp right turn and was encouraged by this. "Were you lonely much?" she asked as Bea walked carefully over the loose rocks on the narrow pathway.

"I never felt alone. I had a mission," Anna said as Sam picked his way over the trail. "I didn't know where I was from. I had no memory of how I got to Earth. Most of my time was spent searching for information about magic or a place that held magic." Anna gestured her arm to encompass the foreign world she was in, moons and all. "The rest of the time was spent trying to stay under the radar of the general."

Shiarra was about to ask what this meant when her horse crested a small rocky rise and her eyes fell on the vision in the valley below her. Pulling tight on Bea's reins, she studied the tall rock columns.

She saw over fifty pillars rising from the flat ground, each one reaching over a hundred feet in the air. The formations were smooth and their tops speared into the sky, then bent into a sharp cone which ended in a point, like giant fingers raised into the air.

"What are those?" Anna whispered.

"Your Highness," Shiarra said and turned to her friend, "RUN!" She screamed as she yanked hard on Bea's reins to turn her around.

When Anna came up next to Shiarra, she noticed the apprentice had gone deathly white, causing Anna to turn once more to stare at the formations.

Shiarra brought her red magic forward and Anna knew from the last time that this couldn't be good. She tugged on Sam's lead to turn him back the way they had come, down towards the rise, away from the valley of pillars.

She only spared a quick glance backwards as Shiarra threw her red magic outward into the valley and attempted to lead Bea at the same time. She must have hit something because Anna could hear a deep rumbling after each strike.

She felt Sam tense each time they came to a rocky area on the path, and she kept looking over her shoulders to see where the danger was coming from.

At first, she couldn't see anything, but then she noticed movement to her right and caught a quick glance at the things surrounding them. No wonder she hadn't spotted them—the creatures were mere feet from the ground. They jumped like kangaroos but were the same color as the sharp rocks surrounding the area. In fact, it appeared they were made from the very rocks that surrounded them. She spotted one ahead and could see that its head was pointed and sharp just like the stones.

As she spared another look behind her, Shiarra came up fast on Bea with her magic slicing out around her. Anna had just turned back around when Sam lost his footing on the uneven ground.

As her body flew through the air, she had a quick wish that she was back in the Rocky Mountains on a nice hike in the fall as the aspen changed colors. Where the rocks didn't chase you down and attack you.

"If I hear the sergeant complain one more time, I will not be responsible for what happens," Timmons thought. He was known for his patience but, for king's sake, this was too much.

They had set out well before sun up and had traveled at a quick pace amongst the towering trees of the Deepen Forest. Timmons had seen the unusual trees of this region before, but he was sure most of their group had never seen the white and black trees. As far as he knew, this was the only place the Austera trees grew. Their dark black trunks had a sinister look and feel about them, and even now in the warmer seasons with the bright white leaves swaying in the breeze, they gave off an eerie feeling.

However, these trees were just that—trees—
and Timmons knew not all of Genoa's trees were as
tame as these. They didn't have any special powers
and as far as he knew, the animals in this forest
were known to be timid and scared of humans.

No, the trees did not bother him, it was the
mountains ahead that caused him concern.

Their current path led through a wide valley
and missed most of the jagged peaks, far away from
the sheer cliffs and trails that led high into danger.
Many travelers had been lost in these mountains and
he didn't want to be one of those to never return
home again.

Kriston had told them he felt an urgent need to
get to the Mirror Lake by midday tomorrow, telling
his men their quarry would only be half a day ahead
of them if he guessed her direction correctly.

And though the sergeant was riding a horse, the
man complained as if he were the one trotting
through the murky forest floor instead of the
animal. Yes, there were bugs. Yes, there were vines
that tried to snag you at every corner, but for king's
sake, they were on a road.

"The king would never approve. Marching
through the wilderness at this unruly speed will only
get our necks broken, is what it will do!" Sergeant
Bainst said to no one. "It is clear to me that the
captain has no idea where we are!"

As Timmons rode his large orange mare next to
the sergeant's horse, he could see the small man

holding a cloth over his nose and mouth, no doubt to keep the musty smell of an old growth forest from his sensitive sinuses. Timmons thought this was quite funny but knew that laughing would enrage the man, so he decided avoidance was his best plan. He urged his horse on and rode up next to Kriston's.

"Brother, I do not mind the pace we set, but politics are in play here. Do we really have to keep this man and his goons around?" he whispered to Kriston.

"Remember Pesha?" Kriston said as he looked at Timmons. When he saw Timmons nod his head, he knew his friend understood.

Pesha. Timmons remembered.

He thought back to when he and Kriston were young men, their lives ahead of them like a great valley full of adventures.

They had recently gotten out of first-line training and were sent to ride the borders with a small brigade under the command of a man named Captain Crain. The captain was a small built man but didn't let that stop him in his large actions. He prided himself on training men in the art of living off the land, teaching them how important it was to know your surroundings and understand the local peoples of the forests. He was also one of the best trackers Kriston and Timmons had ever known.

Unfortunately, his second in command, a man named Sergeant Banner, thought that teamwork was giving orders then taking all the credit.

One day, Crain, Timmons, Kriston, and another young trainee named Dryna had spent the whole day out in the rain, tracking a rather large gray buck.

After their hunt, they had headed back to the village with the hopes of a warm dinner and dry clothes.

What they found instead was an empty village and more than half the huts burned to the ground.

Searching the village, they discovered Sergeant Banner hidden under a hayloft. When questioned, he stated he had been taken from behind and hit over the head and had remained where he was until being discovered by the small group.

Sergeant Banner had voiced his belief that the attacking goblins had killed every trainee and villager, and they should leave right away for Matera.

However, Captain Crain called for them to gather weapons and supplies so they could start the tracking and rescue of their friends. "We must not assume all is lost. We will track these creatures and see for ourselves what has become of our people."

It wasn't until the second day of tracking that Sergeant Banner attempted to kill Crain. Luckily, Kriston had stopped the attempt and subdued the sergeant before any damage could be done.

So, fierce was Banner's anger at Crain that they knew he would make another attempt on the captain's life. They decided to leave him tied to a rather large oak and continued with the rescue.

When they caught up with the goblins that night, the captain sent Timmons and Dryna into the surrounding upper hills surrounding the goblin camp.

With some deception, a few flaming arrows, and one rather large ox horn blown by the captain himself, they were able to scare the guarding goblins enough that most left the prisoners unattended. Those remaining were easily dispatched.

When they returned to Matera several days later, the sergeant had boasted and bragged of how he had single-handedly initiated the rescue of the town's people.

When Kriston asked Captain Crain why he allowed the sergeant to lie about these deeds, the captain told them, "We know what we did and how we did it, and in our hearts, we know we did right." He placed a hand on each of their shoulders. "We do not need any praise to feel good that our friends are alive and well."

The king had promptly promoted Sergeant Banner and had given the man a combat medal along with his own battalion of men. Then the king had sent Banner to the front lines of a Malic battle.

The only man under Banner's command that survived the trip was Kriston's friend, a quiet man named Dryna. When he alone had reached the king's army on the front lines, he informed the commanding general that Captain Banner had marched his men into the middle of a Harpies nest.

Prior to reaching the nest, Dryna, who was acting as scout, had attempted to warn the new captain of the pending danger. The captain had not taken the warning seriously and had abandoned Dryna and tied him to a small willow tree to be left behind.

"Remember, it is always better to keep a close eye on your enemies," Kriston said with a small smile. "For now, brother, we will wait until a time comes when there is no doubt of ill intent."

When Anna woke, her head was the first thing she felt.

Sharp, stabbing pain moved from her skull into her neck and then shot outwards towards her fingers and toes.

Giving a small moan and turning her head, she tried to open her eyes. What she saw was confusing. The rock kangaroos were gathered around her, and she could see their sharp little feet jumping around. When she tried to sit up, she realized her hands and legs were bound by rough scratchy ropes.

Panic set in. Quickly looking around, she made out Shiarra's form laying across from her on the hard dirt. She appeared to be tied up as well and unconscious at the moment.

Great, no help from there. She thought and started to imagine crazy things, which she blamed on all the horror movies she'd watched over the years. Things like being roasted alive or sacrificed to a pagan god flashed in her mind.

"Don't panic, they haven't eaten you yet," she told herself.

As she raised her head slightly, the creatures saw her movement and started making noises at her. It sounded like they were clanging their teeth together, and this gave her the unpleasant feeling that she was about to be dinner after all. However, as she glanced up into their faces, she realized they didn't have lips; their faces were made entirely of stone. She watched a couple of them talking and realized the banging and grinding sounds were the creature's stone jaws hitting the bottom of a blunt nose that sat in the middle of their faces.

One of the small creatures pulled on her bindings and helped her sit up. Her hands were tied in front of her, and the bindings were not tight, just wrapped around her torso a few times to ensure her movements were restricted to slow any attempts of escape.

Once she was sitting upright, she noticed that she must be several feet taller than her captors. The tallest creature hit right below her chin as she sat there in the dirt making them only two to three feet tall. Total.

They appeared to be in a perfectly round cave-like room. There were slabs of stone spiraling up the walls at intervals. It took her a moment to realize these stones were steps leading to another floor above her head.

There was one door to her right and several

windows on each level of the room, including along the steps.

"Great, I've been captured by the munchkins," she said and settled more comfortably in the dirt.

"Munchkins?" came a weak voice from across the room, causing her to glance quickly at her friend.

"Shiarra!" she exclaimed. "What are these creatures?" Anna asked as the rock kangaroos helped her friend sit up.

"Well, they are not munchkins, they are rock trolls. Something I should have been able to avoid," the apprentice said as she brushed the nearest troll away from her with her tied hands.

Anna noticed her friend had a deep gash on the side of her face and many scratches along her arms, which were tied just like hers were.

"Trolls?" Anna looked again at the hopping rock things. "Are you sure? I thought trolls were large and hairy."

"These are indeed trolls, Your Highness. Though, where they came from is beyond my understanding. Last time I was here, there was no sign of trolls." A rather small troll hopped up to her carrying a water skin. Shiarra took it with her bound hands and drank deeply.

"Are you sure that's safe?"

"Trolls are a territorial creature and will always fight for their land, but poison is not their typical punishment. We must think of a way to get out of their capture or this will delay our trip. They do not take kindly to those who walk right up to their city gates as we have done." She handed the water skin back to the small troll who proceeded to hop over to Anna and repeat his offer of water.

After Anna had finished drinking and had returned the water skin to the troll, it hopped off and a slightly larger troll bounced into view. After a few grinding noises from him, Shiarra clacked her teeth together three times and grunted once.

The troll walked over to her and patted her on the head as if she were a child. It then hopped out of the door, leaving its friends and the prisoners behind.

"Shiarra? What is going on?" Anna asked, trying to keep the concern from her voice but failing.

Shaking her head, she replied, "I am not sure."

The rock trolls hopped about and banged their jaws together in discussion for a few minutes. Then another troll came in and, next thing Anna knew, they were being helped to stand up and marched out the small door.

"Now where are we going?" Anna asked and wondered to herself if trolls ate women. Kind of like the three goats from an Earth story she had once heard.

"I think we are meeting their king," Shiarra said from in front of Anna. Each woman had two trolls holding on to ropes tied to their hands and at least five trolls hopping about in circles around them. If she wasn't so unsure of their situation,

Anna may have found the whole thing funny.

Once they had left the troll building, they were once again out in the fresh air. After taking a deep breath, Anna noticed that it appeared to be the same day. Maybe only a few minutes had passed since their struggles with the trolls. She spotted both horses in a fenced area and felt a rush of relief.

"Okay, we still have our rides," she thought.

The group of trolls led them away from the fenced horses and towards another of the large stone cones that Anna now assumed were houses. Once there, they were led inside and asked to sit on the floor again.

After her eyes adjusted to the dim interior, she watched as most of the trolls left until only a handful remained.

Anna tried to think of different ways to escape, but Shiarra sat tall, looking at the large troll in front of them. His gray stone skin showed more cracks than the few she had seen. He stood still and looked from one woman to the next. When he spoke with the typical clacking and grinding, Anna's hopes dropped.

Maybe she should try her magic on one of the trolls. Or she could try the old dodge and misdirect trick she had done on Earth several times. That was always a sure way of escape. But she had Shiarra to think of too. Could she pull it off without explaining to the apprentice first? Also, how would they get their bonds and ropes off?

As she contemplated her options for escape, the

king troll continued to clack as if Anna and Shiarra understood his every word.

When he fell silent, Anna was interested to hear Shiarra clack her teeth and grunt several times.

"You speak their language?" Anna exclaimed.

"Quiet, Your Majesty!" Shiarra hissed and then she continued to communicate with the troll at the front of the room.

Anna's attention waned as Shiarra and the troll continued to communicate. She was thinking of her stomach when it appeared the two came to an understanding.

"King Clagk will grant us our freedom after the sun rises tomorrow," Shiarra told Anna as she stood. Anna's hopes rose and she started to speak but was interrupted before she could, "However, tonight we must travel with him to the oracles, as is their custom." Shiarra turned to Anna. "Do not ask. I know nothing of these oracles. They were not here last time I traveled this road."

Anna stood with the help of the trolls around her and faced the apprentice. "What is an oracle?"

Taking a deep breath, Shiarra just shook her head and at the urging of the trolls walked out of the room with the king in lead.

Wherever they were heading, it appeared they would travel by foot. And the whole troll village would be joining them.

As the little creatures hopped alongside or behind the women, who were still bound by the ropes, Anna tried once more to find out what the oracles were.

"On Earth, the word oracle was used for an entity who could tell the future. Oftentimes, they foretold of doom," she said and faced her friend. "Is this word the same here in Genoa?"

Shiarra stared straight ahead and whispered, "I have never had the pleasure of meeting an oracle, so I do not know. But if rumors are correct, then yes, Anna, we may soon know more than we care to."

When they got to the edge of the troll village, the trolls started to hop and climb the surrounding steep rocks, as if they were the little mountain goats Anna had seen on Earth.

Reaching the first abrupt rocks, the women noticed a small path leading straight up into the hills. The red rocks were still filled with holes. Little shrubs and sand filled many cracks and the path was smooth, showing them the way forward. They slowly picked their way up the carved steps. At times the trolls had to show the women where to place their feet.

After a while the only sound was the soft crunch of rocks and sand beneath their feet, along with labored breathing.

After about thirty minutes of climbing, both women were freely sweating and very short of breath, but they took courage when they noticed they were reaching a rise.

It took a few more minutes to crest the peak. The land flattened out and she saw there was a path that took a southern route right between two rather large mountains.

They reached the shadow of these mountains within minutes and the way forward was swallowed by darkness.

The trolls seemed to know their way easily, but the women had a harder time, as their eyes didn't adjust quickly to the dim light.

Their guides tugged and pulled on the ropes in the hopes that the women would travel faster. It wasn't until the path opened ahead and the evening sun came shining through the darkness up ahead that both women felt confident with their footing again. The way had just widened when it abruptly ended in a large box canyon and it appeared the only way out was the route they had just taken. The only other opening was a very small crack, no larger than three or four inches wide, that ran vertical on the cliff's face straight ahead.

All the trolls entered the canyon and stood looking at a crack in the cliff as if their life depended upon the rock surface. After a moment, they settled on the ground and continued to study the crack.

Anna saw that the sun was sinking slowly towards the crevice, its light shining directly on those below the rocks.

When the sun hit the top of the crevice, all the trolls made a loud crack with their mouths and thumped their rears on the ground, as if an exciting movie was just starting and they didn't want to miss anything.

She glanced back at the sun and almost fell to her knees when a large voice boomed out from the cliffs themselves. The sound shook the ground she was standing on, as the noise echoed around them.

"One who is not whole, we welcome you."

Anna felt every word inside her body and with her ears still ringing from the noise, she glanced around again.

"You may ask your question of us," came the voice.

This time Anna did fall on her knees as she tried desperately to find the speakers. The voices sounded neither masculine nor feminine, but with the loud volume it was hard to tell.

"Who are you?" Shiarra yelled but no answer came.

The king of the trolls clacked at her and then pointed to Anna. "The oracles speak to you Anna; you must address them."

"Me?" Anna asked of Shiarra, but it was not the wizard's apprentice who responded.

"Yes," came the thundering voices.

Anna faced the setting sun again and noticed what she had missed before. Two disfigured faces were roughly carved into the cliffs walls, each faced the other with the crack or crevice in the middle which ran from the sky down to the sand. The faces appeared to have feminine features.

Unsure of her first question, she asked the one Shiarra had already voiced. "Who are you?"

"We are the sisters. Formed to be here in this

time and space, determined by our mother. Placed, so we can guide you on your journey to right past wrongs."

Anna saw that the sun had sunk lower and was now near the oracles' stone eyes. She had the sudden feeling she was running out of time.

"What wrongs would you have me right?" Anna asked.

"Evil has stolen, good was split, lives now lay in destruction's path. Find what is hidden deep at the base, bring light to people who have none, and hold strong when royal blood flows from its veins."

"What? Where do I start?"

"Where all stories start. At the beginning."

"Helpful," Anna mumbled. She thought about her next question, gave Shiarra a quick glance, and asked, "Who is your mother? Who set you here to guide me?"

"Genoa."

Confused by this answer, she set it aside until later as the feeling of urgency rushed through her again. "What guidance do you have for my journey," she asked as the sun sank further and touched the oracles' lips.

"The walking dead must be placed to rest. Enemies must be won with the truth, and the rocks must be broken for pieces to reign."

With this last statement, there was a large cracking noise and Anna saw a huge line form in the forehead of one of the oracles.

"What is happening?" she screamed as the

trolls hopped up and jumped around in every direction.

"Our mission is complete; our knowledge has been passed," the oracles boomed as a chunk of rock fell off the cliff face. *"We go to join our mother. Take heed, Your Highness, danger lies in your path."* Large rocks fell from the oracles' faces and smaller rocks and sand rained down on the ground several feet away from the two women. This last blast scattered the remaining trolls, who fled into the trail behind them.

"Welcome home," were the last words from the oracles as they disappeared into dust. Anna and Shiarra stood on the shaking ground and watched what was left of the carved faces vanish into rubble.

CHAPTER ELEVEN

Strangers

This was taking forever! She thought once more as she looked about.

It appeared to Anna that the trolls only moved fast when trespassers were in their village.

As Anna rode on Sam's large back, she looked back to see the rock trolls bouncing behind her in rows. You really couldn't call it marching, even though they were lined up like little hopping soldiers.

However slow they traveled now, they sure had made up their minds quickly. After the oracles had crumbled, King Clagk had apologized to Shiarra and Anna for his people's actions. And had demanded that Shiarra translate all his words to Anna, which slowed down the process even more.

The king apparently had a lot to say to her now.

He told them that the oracles had appeared in the hills behind their village over a season ago with a request that his people bring all travelers to them.

Since no one else had ever entered their village, and the oracles had no further communication with the trolls, they had no idea why the oracles wanted the travelers or what they intended to do with them.

"It is now clear we must help you," he exclaimed to Shiarra after he had given orders to several of his trolls, who proceeded to bounce around doing his bidding.

He had ordered his people to collect supplies and make ready to follow the women wherever they were heading, in high hopes of assisting them on their journey.

"We cannot ask you to follow us, Your Majesty," Shiarra said, but she was quickly dismissed.

Anna asked Shiarra to translate her words for the king. "We're going to Valorna and don't know exactly when we'll be traveling back this way."

The king had paid little attention when she spoke, as if the sisters had quantified her importance.

"We go. That is what is needed. The ladies said you will bring courage to peoples, and we are peoples. Yes?" the king said with a clack.

That had been late last night and after spending a very uncomfortable night sleeping on rocks, the women, along with well over a hundred rock trolls, were now on their way to Valorna.

Anna wasn't sure what the trolls could do to help, but she remembered how quickly they had dispatched her and Shiarra, who had magic. All because they had been trespassing. Maybe they would need bouncing rocks. After all, if they met any more monsters along the way, the trolls could be helpful.

Shiarra told her they would pass Mirror Lake by midday and hoped to camp somewhere past the mountains along the road at the edge of the Highman Plains. She had voiced her hope to get back on schedule.

Anna could tell that Shiarra hadn't given up hope of finding Wizard Leian again, but she could see desperation building in her eyes.

She could also see she was worried about something else. Maybe it was finding the help they needed in rescuing the wizard or maybe it was that a troll village now marched behind them which caused her some unease.

Glancing up, she realized how dark the sky had gotten just as the first raindrop fell onto her raised cheek. Pulling her hood up, she looked around and saw that the high mountains were giving way to smoother ground and that they were heading downhill now. Maybe they'd get to the lake by lunchtime, but Anna just bet they were going to be soaked by the time they got there.

When they finally did reach the lake, she was shocked to see they weren't the only picnickers.

Two men had set up a large open tent near the shore in an attempt to keep dry during the rain. She could see two horses, one a dark blue and the other a burnt orange. Both horses were tied near the small tent as they nibbled on the short grass found on the banks of the lake.

Glancing at Shiarra quickly, she followed the apprentice as they aimed their horses a small distance from the tent. Anna kept casting glances towards the men from under her hood.

When she dismounted, she found Shiarra right behind her. "Remember, keep your hood on, no matter what. We leave right after we rest," she said before walking over to the rock troll king.

Shrugging her shoulders, she took her backpack down and glanced around, but she found no trees near the shore. Instead she headed towards a flat round rock positioned in between Sam and the two men.

Sitting on the wet surface, she kept her hood up and her cloak tight around her to keep the rain off her while she ate. Pulling a granola bar from her pack, she unwrapped it and started eating. She didn't mind the dried fruits and meats that Shiarra had provided, but she was missing a hot meal. An Earth meal.

She had just started thinking of a nice juicy steak with a heaping side of garlic potatoes when a heavenly smell drifted her way from the tent.

"We have plenty." The deep voice was so close by, she jerked her body around in shock. She hadn't

260

heard him approaching, maybe because she was fantasizing about food. When her body twisted, the wet material she was sitting on slid on the slick rocks, and she landed hard on her butt in the soft mud. To add insult to matters, her skirt was now riding high, bunched around her knees.

She thought she heard a soft chuckle, but then he cleared his throat and continued. "We do not mind sharing with you and your friend if you are in need of a hot meal."

"What?" she said and glanced up into the rain at the tall figure standing above her. She couldn't see him clearly and only managed to get a face full of cold rainwater as her hood fell off her head.

"Pardon." He chuckled again. "I did not mean to startle you." The man reached his large hands down, and placing one under each of her arms, picked her up and placed her back on her feet as if she weighed nothing.

She quickly pulled the hood back on and tried once again to look at the man. Her eyes traveled up past his wide chest, clad in black leather to see his face. However, quickly realizing he was standing only a breath away, she attempted to move back a step and almost ended up in the mud once more when she bumped into the very rock she'd been perched on before.

"Hold on," he said and reached for her arm to steady her. His large fingers wrapped around her thin arm, making her feel small. "I mean you no harm." He said as she finally got her first glance at his face, hidden beneath his own cloak.

He flashed white teeth in a friendly-enough smile but was still too hidden from her view to see much more than a dark goatee and the white teeth. "My brother and I were just enjoying our midday meal when you and your troops came into view." He turned to look towards Shiarra as she came marching quickly over to where the two were talking. "We do not have enough for your whole army but can share with you and your friend here."

When he turned the rest of the way towards Shiarra, Anna took some more time to assess him.

He was well over a foot taller than her and was very broad shouldered, from what she could tell under the long cloak that covered most of him. The hood that was covering his head and keeping the rain off him also hid most of his features. She could just make out a strong jaw and thin lips surrounded by a dark goatee. She remembered the smile he'd given her moments ago, and wondered if he was harmless.

"Anna, are you well?" Shiarra asked as she stopped in front of her, blocking the man's view of her friend and shielding her at the same time.

"I'm fine," she said, noticing then that her friend appeared to be very tense. "I just slipped off the rock. That's all."

"Kriston Timmons at your service, my ladies," the man said with a rather large bow of his upper body.

"Shiarra, the wizard's apprentice, and this is my

sister Anna." Anna tried not to show her shock at Shiarra's blunt lie. She hoped her cloak hid most of her face since she knew humor reflected in her eyes. The two women looked nothing alike, let alone like sisters.

"Ah, sisters," Kriston said with another smile. "It happens that my *brother* and I are enjoying a hot meal under our canvas. We have food to share if you are interested. We apologize we will not have enough to feed your army." He glanced quickly over to where the army of rock trolls sat.

"Thank you, the rock trolls just happened to be traveling on the same pathway. We are not with them, and have just made their acquaintance," Shiarra said and turned to look over Kriston's shoulder. "We would be happy to join you if you have enough for two hungry women."

Once they were under the canvas, Kriston took his hood off and introduced the women to the other man whom he called Doug.

The other man was built like Kriston, however he had much lighter hair than his brother. The two looked as much alike as she and Shiarra did, and Anna instantly got the idea that no one in the small group was going to tell the truth.

Even though they both had friendly smiles on their faces, she doubted she would get far if they chose to run for it. Besides, the food smelled delicious, which made her realize that she was okay with letting the lies go unchallenged.

As Anna took a seat, she noticed that Kriston's

thick hair was jet black and hung just past his shoulders. He'd tied it all back with a thin leather strap and was unsettled once more when his bold green eyes kept zeroing in on her.

When she glanced at his brother, she noticed that Doug's eyes were a pale brown, and his light brown hair was worn short. The man handed a tin bowl to both women and proceeded to eat out of his own steaming bowl like he'd been starved.

Anna waited until Shiarra had taken her first bite before she started in on the warm meal. It looked like beef stew and smelled like it too, and after taking a small bite, she realized it even tasted like it. She didn't want to appear like a foreigner, so she decided she would ask Shiarra later what it was they were eating.

"We travel back to the trade station," Kriston informed them. "We were down to the Draydon tribes for their trade fair and are now making our way back home." Kriston took a small bite of his meal then once again studied Anna. "And where are you fair maidens traveling?"

Anna gave a quiet snort upon being called a fair maiden. Images of old fairytales she'd read as a child jumped into her mind. Shaking her head, she decided she was just the opposite of a fair maiden.

"We are going to visit our uncle in Valorna," Shiarra answered after giving Anna a stern glance. She gave no further information and continued to eat as she stood next to Anna.

Giving Shiarra a quick glance, Kriston asked,

"Are you two not worried about traveling alone?"

"I am half a season from my oath," Shiarra added, as if this explained everything.

"Ah, my apologies," Kriston said with another bow of his head. At the same time, Anna heard the first booming sound of thunder. The sound seemed to echo around in her head, which had started to feel very light. "You are quite dry under our cover, my lady. Feel free to remove your hood." He said and turned towards Anna.

"My sister has a cold and should keep her cover," Shiarra said. Anna realized that Shiarra had lowered her hood when they entered under the tent. Her long dark hair flowed around her shoulders freely.

"Ah, nasty things." Kriston turned to Anna and attempted to gaze under her hood. "You are warm?" he asked.

"Feeling dandy," she said with a giggle as she covered her mouth quickly. She felt like she'd drunk two full glasses of ale and was struggling to remember why she had to keep her cloak on. She was getting warm standing there so she walked towards the edge of the tent for some fresh air. Blowing a big breath, she turned and smiled at Shiarra, who gave her a concerned look.

"Anna? Are you well?" Shiarra asked, stepping towards her.

Before Anna could answer, a second loud boom sounded so close that she wondered if it was thunder at all she heard. When her body vibrated with the sound she noticed, through her fading vision, a sharp flash of light shine brightly from behind her. Then she was shocked as everything tilted suddenly.

She heard Shiarra drop her bowl, and watched as she turned towards the light with her arms raised and glowing red already with her magic. The move was so fast that Anna had no time to blink and only stood there with a faint smile on her face at the beauty of Shiarra's red magic.

Another loud boom sounded closer this time, and before she knew what was happening, Anna was flat on her back, laying on the wet ground. She turned her aching head and saw Shiarra lying next to her, the apprentice's cloak was on fire.

She reached out towards her friend, her arms and body felt extremely heavy. Everything seemed to slow down as if it was happening in slow motion. Her body felt numb as she slowly climbed to her feet.

She stood there and watched as Doug threw his own cloak over Shiarra to put the fire out. It was then that something slammed hard into her from the back, knocking her face first into Kriston's arms. Instead of releasing her, Kriston threw her cloak over her face plunging her into darkness. She had seen his green eyes burn with anger just before her world went dark.

Where is she?

Somewhere in the Helmand Mountains. I think....

You are not certain?

No, I saw the lake years ago, but I am not sure where they are taking her.

Is she in danger?

Col is not sure. How about Cenzic?

Distance does not do him well. We must find her and ensure her safety. Can you send Su Na?

Perhaps... When she is closer, she can smell her.

If she is lost, so are we.

What should he do?

He knew what he wished to do, but he was worried that if he failed, his head would be detached from his body and his mission would have then failed.

He must use his brain and trust his training. It had taken him many seasons to infiltrate the king's secret guards. Time well spent. But only recently did this position allow him to get closer to his goal.

Revenge.

"Think," he told himself.

When the solution came to him, he almost smiled with its simplicity. But he would have to be careful. Sergeant Bainst was furious now that his first attempt had failed.

After they had reached the lake earlier that morning, Kriston and his men had come up with a plan to trick and then capture the spy they had been sent for. It was a simple plan, one that allowed stealth yet had a high chance of succeeding.

Sash had seen the Sargent's face the moment Kriston had explain the plan, he knew based on his perception of the small man's features that he hated the plan from the moment the young prince has spoken. He had also understood that the Sargent had no intention of following Captain Haddock's instructions to wait hidden in the low hills surrounding the lake until the Captain had secured the woman.

Sash was not surprised when Bainst had instructed him and the other two men, Beal and Ali, to rush their horses through the line of trolls while he, himself captured the women.

Sash had hesitated, but feeling it was not the time to reveal himself a traitor, he followed the other two out into the field but then stopped his horse short before reaching the army of Rock Trolls.

The bombing sound they had all heard next had been one of Ali trying to smash the trolls with his large ax. It appeared, however, that trolls did not cut easily and each time the ax had met with troll skin, the sound had been deafening. However, the damage to the trolls had been non-existent. Sash had seen Ali swing the large ax even harder the second time and watched in amazement as actual sparks flew off the troll's skin along with the ax.

The weapon had heated up, turning a bright red when the man had turned his horse towards the tent.

At first Sash was worried the stupid man was going to try to ram the tent itself, but then he had seen a slightly larger troll heading towards the tent. Sash watched as wizard magic flew towards Ali. The giant man easily ducked the red stream and then overtook the running troll.

This time when he brought his ax down on the trolls head the impact shook the ground as once more, sparks flew in every direction. The troll laid on the ground in a rock heap causing the surrounding trolls to hop everywhere either in fear or rescue of their king.

When he looked up again, Kriston had the spy over his broad shoulder and was shouting instructions to his men who had finally caught up to the Sargent and his men.

Chaos had ensued, Kriston and Timmons had jumped on their horses, the first still flinging orders to his men as they made their quick escape from the trolls. Sargent Bainst had shouted orders too, but no one seemed to pay him any attention as the patrol fled back towards the Deepen forest.

Even now he saw that Captain Haddock's men kept a close eye on the man who had almost cost them their lives.

It had not taken the Sargent long to relay his new plan of deceit. A plan that would surely cost lives this time. Something Sash could not permit, so the time to act was now, but first he had to make sure his plan was solid.

Clearing his throat, he was shocked to hear his own voice. It had been seasons since he had used it, but he must not hesitate now.

Slowing his horse, he hoped the deception would work. When he stopped and then dismounted from the animal, he was pleased to see the young man turn his own horse his way.

"Has your horse thrown a shoe?" Timmons asked Sash.

Sash didn't answer but bent down and raised the animal's back right leg. Giving a huge sigh, Timmons lowered himself off his horse and walked towards the pair, his youthful face half covered with his hood to ward off the cold and rain.

Sash watched as the last of Kriston's men passed, giving them a guarded glance. When Timmons came closer to inspect the horse's raised foot, Sash acted quickly.

"Take heed, young man," he whispered. "They plan another surprise attack ahead." And with this he set the horse's foot back on the ground. "I will travel ahead to ensure the lady's safety. They mean to capture her and kill all." He then mounted his horse once again, turned it quickly, and set off at a run towards the right.

She needed more sleep. Her dreams were so detailed and intense that they were draining her energy as she slept.

She tried to snuggle deeper into the warmth and tune out the conversation going on in her dream, but the shouting wouldn't subside. When she was bumped hard, she realized the voices weren't coming from her dream at all, so she tried to focus on the screams surrounding her.

When she tried to move however, a hard, deep voice next to her told her to keep her head down and stay under the cloak.

"What?" she mumbled, not even sure where she was. Hearing new screaming, she tried once more to sit up. She felt an arm tighten around her middle as the command came again to keep down.

She realized then that she couldn't see anything and started to panic. "What's going on!" she screamed.

"The fool is going to get us all killed, that is what is going on!" the voice said.

"Kr... Kriston?" she asked, "What happened? Did someone attack us? Where is Shiarra?"

"Quiet! I am trying to save our lives!" He grunted as Anna felt the ground give a jerk. Then she realized that they were on the back of a horse. Kriston's arms were tight around her, holding her in the weird sideways sitting position as the horse ran on. Her legs were flung to the right side of the saddle while her body was pressed up against Kriston's chest.

She heard a metal ringing noise as the horse gave a quick jerk. Kriston gave another grunt like he was fighting an attacker off with great effort.

"Cats! The king has them!" he said and Anna swung up with effort and managed to flip the cloth off her face.

The first thing she saw was a huge sword only a few inches in front of her face. It had a curved tip and embellished carvings along the blade, and she knew instantly that the sword and its owner meant to kill. She glanced up into Kriston's face and saw that his green eyes were focused on their escape as he grasped his sword.

Glancing around, she saw that they were surrounded by rocky cliffs. There was no lake to be found. The horse was traveling at a very fast pace down the jagged road.

"What's going on?" she asked again as she tried to get a look around his massive shoulders. She only got a quick glimpse of several men on horses, surrounding them, each bent low on their ride to ensure speed.

Each man had his own sword drawn. Occasionally one would glance behind them as they raced.

Since she couldn't see all the way around Kriston's large form, she had no hope of seeing what was chasing them.

"We waited too long for that rope!" came a voice next to them. Anna glanced over and saw Kriston's brother, Doug, riding alongside them. She noticed an arrow sail past his head and heard a thump as he swerved his horse into Kriston's, bumping them as their horses continue to move along the rocky ground.

"Cats! That was close," Doug said as he glanced over his shoulder.

"Just the three of them? Or has the big one been spotted yet?" came Kriston's response.

"Sash is ahead. He is the one who told me of the attack," Doug yelled. "Look, the forest!"

Anna looked forward and saw huge trees ahead of them as more arrows zipped past.

She blinked a few times as she looked once more at the forest ahead. There were white-leafed trees that were as tall as a four-story building, each with deep black trunks and dark shadows beneath.

It was almost as if all the color had been drained from the forest. She felt a shiver run down her back in fear.

"Wow! Did we just travel back to the 50s?" she mumbled as she searched around for Shiarra. Panic overcame her when she didn't spot the apprentice or their troll friends amongst the horses.

Who was trying to kill them and where the heck was Shiarra?

She tried to turn around once more to see if maybe Shiarra and the trolls were the ones chasing them, but Kriston wrapped one strong arm around her midriff, preventing her from moving.

"Hold still. Do you want to fall?" he shouted.

"No, yes, I want off! Where is Shiarra?" she said, trying to keep the panic from her voice.

"No time to explain," he shouted just as they

reached the first trees. "Timmons, branch formation!" He pulled hard on the reins, turning his horse hard to the left. She felt her body swing hard, and if it wasn't for Kriston's arms wrapped tight around her, she was sure she would've ended up in the mud once more. She cringed at the thought of falling off such a high horse.

"Branch!" Anna heard a shout as she was swung hard to the left with Kriston a second time. She saw two more men flank them, while the other men disappeared somewhere into the forest. About twenty yards into the forest, Kriston and his men pulled up hard on their horses and turned around completely to face the unknown enemy.

"Quiet if you want to live." His facial hair tickled her as he leaned close to whisper in her ear.

His hard tone caused her to shiver. Maybe she and Shiarra had misjudged these men? The voice he'd just used sounded like a killer, not a simple tradesman.

Silence fell and she realized she was being held so close to him, she could hear his steady heartbeat mixed with the sound of his horse's harsh breathing. Everything else was dead quiet.

Chancing a glance around, she saw that they were in a small clearing only about ten feet wide, with the fading sun to their back. Each man surrounding them drew their swords as their horses stood rock still with their ears back and muscles tight, as if excited for the battle to come.

Anna watched in silence as three men came

riding at a slow pace into the clearing. With the black and white trees surrounding them, what color remained seemed sharp and bright to her eyes. The horses with their bright colors appeared unreal, as did the people and their dull-colored clothing. Red and blues stood out, almost making her eyes squint for relief.

She saw that two of the men were larger than Kriston, both with weapons drawn. One held a large jagged, wicked-looking ax, and the other was drawing an arrow into his bow. The third man was tiny and for some reason reminded Anna immediately of the general from Earth. All three wore black uniforms and each had a red star on their chest.

She returned her attention to the small man, who had a look on his face of pure hatred. His little mustache twitched as he sneered.

"Hand over the spy and we will let you live," said the little man.

"Give up this treachery," came Kriston's quiet order, and the little man gave a smile.

"*I* will be the only one handing the spy over to His Majesty. I alone will get the glory of that honor, along with telling the king that his brother died in the pursuit of the spy." He smiled as the man on the right drew the arrow back and aimed it at Kriston's head.

"Beal, Ali, I now give you a chance. Surrender and lay your weapons down." Kriston still had not raised his voice but spoke with a calm sound that caused shivers to run down Anna's entire body. She watched as the other man raised his large ax in a threatening pose, a grin on his face.

"Very well." Kriston said with a nod. "So be it."

Anna didn't see all that happened next, since it happened so fast, but she did see the small man fall from his horse and hit the ground. Kriston's arm covered her as his horse reared into the sky, sending her and Kriston backwards onto the ground.

Legs and arms tangled together as they hit the dirt with a jarring jolt. She heard a loud grunt from Kriston, who had moved to take the brunt of the fall.

She gained her breath back as a shadow fell over them, and glanced up quickly to see the man known as Doug standing over them protectively.

"That's one way to get a lady," he said with a smile as Anna and Kriston struggled to untangle their limbs. He reached down and helped her to her feet and then bent back down to give Kriston a helping hand.

"I usually just use my charm," Kriston said once he gained his feet and slapped Doug on his shoulder with a smile.

"Well, that arrow will need to be taken out," another man said from behind Kriston. Kriston turned with a confused expression on his face.

"That cat hit me!" he exclaimed as Anna noticed an arrow protruding from his broad shoulder.

"Oh no!" She rushed to Kriston's side to assess the damage. She stood on her toes to get a better look at where the arrow jutted out from his leather vest but could only manage to see the shaft sticking out at an odd angle as blood ran down his back.

Seeing her concern, Kriston gave her a confused look as he turned towards her. His hands moved up, no doubt to ensure she wouldn't try to pull the arrow out herself.

"Nothing a quick cleaning and stitch will not cure," the new man said, then bowed slightly as he looked at her. "Timmons at your service, ma'am." Then he gestured to another man to gather their horses.

"I guess camp sets here," another man stated as the sun tipped behind the trees for the day. "If you would be so kind as to follow me, I will provide you with water and food," he said to Anna.

She studied the tall bald man, who had a small mustache and chin hair. She normally would have withheld trust from someone who held a large sword and had knives strapped all over his muscular chest, but she studied his eyes and saw humor and kindness there. Giving a low bow he said, "Brigdon Penn at your service, my lady."

"Anna, at yours," she said with a small bow of her head. "It appears I owe you and these men my life, though I don't know how I got in danger in the first place," she said with an accusing glance at Kriston and Timmons, who had been digging into their horses' saddle bags and pretending not to listen. "I need to know where my sister is and how I came to be in your company," she continued, feeling like the answers were needed before anything else happened.

Turning from the horse, the arrow still jammed into his body, Kriston gave her a quick glance. "After my wound has been tended to. Please, go with Brigdon." He turned and dismissed her.

"A warning...." she said, causing him to glance back at her from over his shoulder. "I expect the full story, and the truth." Her eyes moved to where his "brother" stood by his side. When he nodded slightly, she turned on her heels and marched off in the opposite direction with a swish of her long skirts.

"I like her," she heard Timmons say with a quick laugh.

Next time Kriston saw Anna, she was sitting between Brigdon and Jake on a fallen log in front of a roaring fire. Both men were telling her the story about their quick battle with Pixies in the Kandi forest.

Kriston could see Lazerith through the trees, but only the light of the other moons as he made his way over to the group sitting around the fire.

His shoulder had been sewn up, only three stitches were needed as the arrow head had gotten caught on his leather vest. Luckily, it had hit the seam of his protection garment and only went an inch into his body. Little to no pain was experienced, so he was good as new now.

His temper, however, was more powerful than the pain in his shoulder. It appeared he had waited too long to restrict the sergeant and his men. The fools had attempted to overtake the whole troll army, defying Kriston's direct orders. The man and his fools had almost ruined Kriston's plan at obtaining the woman through stealth. This was a mistake he would not easily forget, or allow to happen again.

As he approached the group, Anna was laughing so hard she didn't even notice him walk up. He was followed closely by Ray and Timmons.

"Then he turns to me and says, 'This one has just proposed marriage,'" Brigdon said in a voice Kriston knew was meant to imitate his own. The large man laughed and quickly slapped his own knees.

"If you have finished telling her of my many exploits, it is time we find out a few things," Kriston said as he leaned against a rather large Austera tree to one side of the fire. He studied the small woman sitting comfortably on the log in a forest surrounded by strangers.

She'd removed her hood so that her pale hair shone in the firelight. Her features were delicate, but it was her pale skin and blue eyes that made him take a second, closer look at her. *Beautiful* was the first word to come to mind. But beauty in a different way, much like the forest they now stood in. Most complained of its lack of color, while Kriston knew that the absence of colors is what made it truly beautiful.

She finished her last bite of yeasty bread, then turned and smiled up at him. Her eyes danced with humor as they scanned him. "It appears you're back to one piece." She leaned back slightly. "I'll be happy to answer any of your questions." She tilted her head slightly. "After you answer mine."

Seeing her determination, he gave a nod of his head. "This is Captain Ray Fielder." He gestured to Ray, who was grabbing his dinner from the pot hanging over the fire. "You have met my other men; Jake and Brigdon, and you remember Timmons, who is the head of my security."

She nodded her head then replied. "I've also met you, Kriston. Or is that not your real name?" She squinted her eyes slightly at him.

Giving her a sly smile, he answered, "Yes," as one dark eyebrow rose in amusement.

"Where is Shiarra?" she demanded, her smile fading as she crossed her arms over her chest in a defensive move. "None of your men would tell me."

He continued to lean against the tree and after taking time to cross his ankles, gave her a quick smile. "We have not harmed your 'sister.' She is quite well, and last I saw, was sleeping off the drugs. She was surrounded and guarded by her troll friends by the side of the lake."

"You drugged us?" she said in shock as she

stood up and marched around the fire to get closer to him. He simply smiled back at her as he watched her movements. "What were the loud explosions? Who attacked us and why have you kidnapped me?" she demanded.

She continued to fire off so many questions that it was hard for him to decide which ones to answer and which ones to ignore. So, he stood back and silently waited until she ran out of steam. After she had finally finished shooting questions to him, he took his time providing her with answers.

"The three men responsible for this attack are now in my control. Your troll friends caused quite a scene at the lake when they saw my men, but no one was harmed." He bowed his head and gave her a searching look. "As to why we drugged you," he took a step closer, giving her a dangerous look which caused her to step back, "that is for later."

When she continued to stand with her small hands on her hips and her face full of frustration, he finally shot off his own question. "Who are you?"

"I'm Anna," she whispered after a slight hesitation.

"No, you are more than that. Tell me or your plight will become far worse than being drugged and chased through a forest," he warned as he loomed over her.

He watched the battle in her eyes as she searched for the right answers. When she whispered the name Reginald, he was so shocked he took a full step back.

"Impossible," came his response as he studied her with new doubts. He quickly glanced at his men and after a moment returned his gaze to Anna. "The princess was exiled," he said, grabbing one of Anna's arms and looked behind her again. "Jake, tell me this is not possible."

"I think we had all better sit and calm down. Lad, release the little lady, I am sure she knows she would not get far if she ran," Jake said, giving Anna a scolding look.

Anna gave a quick nod, and Kriston released her and once again leaned against the tree.

"I answered your questions, now you will answer ours," Kriston said as he crossed his arms while trying to calm his thoughts.

Giving one quick glance at the nearest horse, Anna realized Jake was correct—there was no way she would make it far. Especially since she had no idea where the heck she was in the first place. It also appeared her name was recognized and wondered if she should have kept quiet. Leian never told her that her last name was known, just to keep her appearance hidden.

Panic set in. Had she given too much away already? She should try and stall so she could think more deeply before revealing anything else.

Eyeing Kriston, she settled across the fire from him, sitting near Brigdon again. "Shoot." She motioned for them to take over, but when she only got blank looks from everyone in return, she took a deep breath and replied. "Ask your questions."

"So, you say you are Anna Reginald. Who do you think that is?" Jake asked.

Anna turned to him and thought about his question. This could go bad, but as always, evasion was the best way out of a sticky situation. "Who do you think I am?"

She'd scanned so many psychology books on Earth, she knew more about evading questions than most scholars. She only hoped that Earth methods worked on a bunch of military meatheads from another planet.

"Do not be coy with me," Kriston said as he leaned towards her.

"What the lad means is, we were told the princess of Valorna held the name of Reginald. But rumors of her are conflicting. In some stories, she is dead, in other stories she is sitting high on the throne in Valorna. Others tell of her being exiled to an unknown land," Brigdon spoke up, glancing quickly at Kriston with a warning look.

Anna thought long and hard. Would these men who had already kidnapped her, harm her if they knew who she was? Maybe this royalty business could get her out of this mess. "Do you mean, do I think I am the daughter of King Reginald and Lady Marybeth? Yes. At least that's what I was told."

"Who told you this?" Timmons asked.

"A wizard," Anna said with a lift of both her

shoulders. "And no, I don't have proof, but if you take me to Valorna, I'm sure you will be paid handsomely for my safe return."

"Where did you come from?" interrupted Brigdon, who must have seen doubt in her eyes, as he continued, "We mean no harm to you. Please, where have you come from?" He gave her a reassuring smile.

"That's a really long story," Anna said with a pause. She wished she knew more about the current affairs of Genoa. All she knew is what she'd learned from the books she'd scanned so far.

If she knew what was going on now she might have a better idea why they were asking these questions. "Since it appears I'm going nowhere fast..." When she saw confused expressions, she took another deep breath and proceeded to tell them a short and limited story of how she had lived on Earth, how a wizard had come and retrieved her, and how they had traveled to Byways and now were going to Valorna.

She skipped all the parts about the general from Earth and being attacked by the creature in Byways, along with the oracles' riddle. She felt maybe those details weren't necessary for these men she'd just met.

"Now, I've told my story, tell me why you've kidnapped me. If it's for a reward, then Valorna is where we should head." All the men glanced at Kriston.

Everyone was quiet for a while as they sat

around the crackling fire. The man named Ray took a small pipe out of his jacket and after stuffing something in it, he proceeded to light it up as he leaned back. Smoke billowed out, trailing above their heads in its journey to the stars.

Anna smelled the sweet scent of apples and spices, which brought back a quick memory of her trip to Washington State when she'd been younger.

She remembered that she and Orden had spent a summer traveling the far northern shores along the ocean.

Taking a deep breath, she tried again. "I know you question who I am, where I come from, and my reason for being here. You must understand, a few days ago, I didn't even know of this place. It was only when I passed through the Orick that I found out about Genoa." She stared at Kriston. She didn't know why, but she wanted him to believe her. "Including finding out who I am."

Shaking his head, he stood and walked towards her, only stopping when he was right in front of where she sat. "We have much to discuss. Tonight, my men and I will ponder your words. Until then, you are our prisoner. Do not try to escape." He said this softly, but still his meaning was clear. Then he reached down and gripped her arm, lifting her to her feet.

"I'm a prisoner? Are you crazy?" She glared at him. "Take me back to Shiarra now! She'll pay you the reward if that's what you're looking for. Money!" She spat the last word out. If these men were common thieves, then she hoped Shiarra was awake and well enough to give them a taste of her magic.

Kriston looked down at her with an open hostility. "We are on a mission," he said as he searched her eyes. "I personally have been charged with bringing you back to the King of Matera for answers of treason. It appears you have sights on our land's magic." He gave her a slight shake. "I was told you were a threat to my home. I am merely attempting to stop any damage you would set upon it," he whispered and gripped her even harder.

Anna gave him a stunned expression and stopped fighting him. "Wow," she said and gave a quick look around at the men surrounding her. She noticed the same speculation in each of their eyes.

Giving a little laugh, she shook her head. "Well, I'm not sure what ya'll have been smoking." She glanced towards the pipe and the smoke coming from it as the group just looked back at her. She shook her head. "That's the craziest thing I've heard all year!" She jerked away from Kriston's strong grip and marched towards the horses in the hopes that she could find a road that led north and back to her friend.

She heard him quickly approaching behind her and spun around in a move she'd spent years practicing. His outstretched arm only caught air as she spun and ducked under his reach.

She squared her shoulders quickly and then dipped below his next grab. She put her booted foot on his bent knee, and used her forward motion to swing herself up and around to cling to his back.

She vaguely heard his men laughing as she wrapped her arms around his thick neck.

Kriston's arms reached up and over, gripping the shoulders of her dress, but she held strong, twisting away from his reach. When he fell backwards, she pushed and dropped away from him as he landed with a thud on the ground. Dust and dirt rose around him as he hit the soft ground with a small groan.

More laughter erupted from his men.

"The bigger they are, the harder they fall." She whispered as she smiled down at him, then cocked her hip and turned once more towards the horses and her escape.

This time, her feet were kicked out from under her and she landed in the soft dirt, face first. More dust flew from the ground as the men erupted in gasps.

Her body was pulled and twisted around until Kriston hovered above her on his hands and knees, smiling down at her.

"Yield," he warned quietly.

She jutted her chin up, twisted her hips, and pushed herself downwards using her hands against his shoulders. She moved below his shoulders until she passed easily between his bent knees. Pushing once more against his thighs, she moved behind him. When she once more came up on his back, he used the same fluid moves she'd just used on him and easily sidestepped free.

He swung his massive body around until they were facing each other across the dirt once more. She raised her eyebrows and dipped her head slightly with acknowledgment. "You're a fast learner, grasshopper." She smiled and crouched lower.

He sighed as his men laughed even harder and encouraged him on.

"Enough of this," he growled, causing her to lose her concentration. Before she could dodge the next reach, he had her firmly in his grasp and she was spun around quickly, then flung over his strong shoulders. Both of her hands were tucked tight between their bodies so she was unable to fight back.

She tried to keep the panic in control, but as she kicked her legs, she could tell she was not going to escape his grip without using even more drastic measures.

"I have had enough of your riddles and games, *my lady*," he said with an emphasis on the last word as his men's laughter died down.

Her heart did a fast jump in her chest as she responded. "You want a riddle, here's one. Let go of me now or you'll be singing soprano!" She kicked out harder, but was far too short to hit him where she had aimed. Then she thought of a different tactic.

Bringing her magic forward, she tried to order him to release her. Instead of dropping her, he doubled his hold and gave her a quick shake.

"That will not work with me. I am no commoner," he whispered next to her ear as he continued to walk towards the nearest tent, carting her over his broad shoulder like a small sack of potatoes.

JJ Anders

CHAPTER TWELVE

The Company We Keep

He was finished with fools!

He traveled deep into his home, down stone stairs, beyond the storage rooms and the locked dungeons that held his newest prisoner, opening small metal doors only he had keys to. The farther down he traveled, the colder it got and the stronger the stench was that emanating in the air. Farther down into the black he traveled with only a flicker of the single candle he carried.

He passed beyond the door that held his darkest secret, and even though he was tempted to stop and marvel once more at his possession, he continued because there was work to be done.

When he finally reached the small stone bridge, he stopped to look for what was needed.

Gathering a rather large hairy rat with his magic, he continued as it bobbed behind him, surrounded by a yellow glowing ball.

Over the stench of the sewage below they traveled, beyond the old stone bridge. As he approached the large rocky cavern, he could hardly contain his excitement.

The high stone ceiling dripped with foul water that glowed green with slime and helped keep his footsteps from echoing. The large pool of water ahead reflected his light and cast its glow twenty-fold, making the cavern shine with the water's eerie luminescence.

Finally, he would have control of someone and gain his truest wish.

Power!

He set the rat on the stone altar, which was intricately carved with the ancient words of magic. Dark and evil magic shimmered from the very stone walls encompassing him. He could feel its presence as if it were a living creature that was wrapping its loving arms around him. He shivered with anticipation.

Taking the knife from his belt, he started to work. He kept the rat suspended on the altar, knowing some of his finest work was about to take place.

Reaching down into himself, he felt the rip from his soul and closed his eyes against the temporary pain.

Once he could tolerate the sharp and intense

burning, he continued, bringing his essence and magic forward, running it from the depths, up his torso and down his arms, then finally to his fingertips. He held it there for a moment, hovering inches above the rat.

Finally, adding one more element of himself, he placed his hands on the rat and watched in amazement as it began its transformation.

His mind was beyond the creature's screaming, beyond it flailing its body under his outstretched hands. His only focus was releasing his magic into the animal, building his own creation.

After several minutes, he lowered his arms, which dripped with sweat, as he stood back.

What lay before him would do.

Its size would allow it to access the city in a way it was accustomed to, but would also allow it to bring back the prize he so desired.

When it opened its eyes, he reached out with his mind and gave a small command. When the creature did his bidding by reaching up and scratching its own long nose, the king smiled.

"You are Rodere, and you are mine." The words echoed in the darkness.

What had she been thinking?

Maybe she hadn't, and that was the problem. A sexy pair of forest green eyes came along and her brain completely left her.

She struggled again against the ropes currently tied around her torso and arms in the hope that this time they would loosen.

No luck.

At least she was sitting down, but she hadn't been able to feel much of her lower body after the first two hours of being tied up. She'd tried several times to stretch her legs, but hadn't gotten far.

Maybe she could reach out with her foot and touch the man named Jake. She could pretend she was attempting to relieve herself of the uncomfortable position against the tent pole.

She wiggled her left foot towards the sleeping man and would have jumped if the ropes were not holding her strongly in place when he spoke.

"That will not work," he said in a quiet voice.

Slumping a little with defeat, she stared at him and tried a different plan. "I need the bathroom." When he continued to stare, she elaborated. "You know, go potty, pee, make water...."

"I know what it means," he interrupted. "But seeing as I know you went when we made camp, I think you will make it till morning." He smiled.

"I don't understand why I'm tied up? I thought Kriston agreed there was nowhere for me to go?" She was ashamed at the whiny voice that came out of her as she once again wiggled against the ropes.

When no answer came, she glanced back at Ray, expecting another quiet smile. This time however, he was staring at a point above her head with a vague expression.

"Hello?" she asked in an annoyed voice.

"He cannot hear you," came a voice from behind her, causing her to turn her head around so fast, her neck cracked. "We have hypnotized him so we can deliver a message to you," the newcomer said as he walked further into the small tent, but still staying deep in the shadows so Anna couldn't see him properly.

"Great." She sighed and leaned back against the tent post. "Welcome to the party. And who, may I ask, are you?"

"We are not important; however, our message is." The speaker took a small step forward, then stopped again, still within the shadows. "We are not here to harm." When no further movement was made to show himself, Anna waited, but it appeared the newcomer was not going to make any further move into the tent.

"Okay, you're not here to harm me, just to deliver a message, right?" she asked.

"Yess," came a deeper voice, causing Anna to glance around the tent for the second newcomer. When she didn't see one, her eyes traveled back to the first dark figure.

"What message?" she asked, worried by the change in speech.

"Pleasse, do not sscream," came the voice. When Anna didn't say anything, he continued. "You promisse?"

"Sure, why the hell not. After all, what have I got to lose. It's not like Indiana Jones is going to come rushing into the tent to rescue me." She glanced to the tent opening and sighed. "I wouldn't be so lucky."

She glanced once more at the newcomer, who moved forward a little more. When the light revealed the very large, very scaly man, she had a hard time keeping her promise.

"What are you!" she whispered.

"We are a Scarent, and the message we carry is very important, Anna of Earth. Will you hear it?" he asked as he knelt down before her on the hard dirt, his red eyes blinking at her.

"Scarent? What happened to your voice?" She studied the creature, trying to take in as much detail as possible. Her curiosity took over her fear.

"That is for later," he said and reached a hand towards her face, stopping inches from her cheek. "Will you hear our message?" he asked again.

She studied him. So far it had kept its word. She was unharmed. She glanced back at Ray, who appeared to still be paralyzed.

The creature was close now, as if he seemed to be aware of her magic powers. Maybe he too could communicate by touch. Either way she would have to find out by action. Seeing as she was still tied to the damned tent pole... she had few options.

"What is your message?" she finally asked.

"It is not ours, but it is very important."

Looking deep into his eyes, which had a black vertical slit, she tried to assess his intent, but when no clue was provided, she answered, yes.

As soon as the word left her mouth, he placed his hand on her cheek and waited.

"You know what you must do," he whispered.

He knew! She couldn't believe this creature knew about her power. The only two in this world who knew were Shiarra and Leian and both were lost to her.

What if this was a trick?

She didn't think her powers could harm her or another, so scanning his mind would only result in her gaining his knowledge, but what if there was something hidden she didn't know. This world held so many secrets and magic that she didn't understand yet.

Her internal struggle only lasted seconds before she realized the only way to find any of Genoa's secrets was to gather them the best way she knew how. Magic.

Reaching up with her powers, she felt something shift and found herself standing on the edge of a large lake in the moonlight. She realized then that she was not alone.

"If they get loose one more time, we may have to take drastic measures," Kriston said to Timmons as they walked back to his tent.

"More trouble than they are worth, if you ask me," was the man's reply.

"I do not think my brother will like being

handed his own men in chains," Kriston said as he stepped into his tent with a slight smile on his lips. Then he realized something was wrong and reached for his sword.

Jake was sitting on the floor against the cot with his eyes fixed and unblinking. Anna was slumped over against her bonds with her white hair covering her face. If the ropes had not been holding her against the pole, he was sure she would have been face down in the hard dirt.

Quickly scanning the tent, he found no danger and rushed over to Jake first. He was relieved to feel a slight pulse, but try as he might, he could not get his friend to respond, even when he gave him a good slap.

Moving to Anna, he felt for her pulse and found hers very weak, then he lifted her chin gently to see if she was hurt. He slowly moved her hair away from her face. When he saw that her eyes were open and wet, he sat back quickly. "What happened?" he asked.

"I... I'm tired that's all," she answered as a single tear fell from her pale lashes and ran down her soft cheek.

Knowing there was more to the story, he glanced back to Jake. "What happened to him?"

Shaking her head, she looked over in time to see Timmons throw a bucket of water over Jake.

It was like an explosion! The small hairy man jumped so fast that he banged into Timmons and knocked him backwards into a small table full of supplies.

"What in the king's name did you do that for!" he shouted after giving the top of his head a good rubbing, making his already wild hair stand on end. He glared at Timmons, who was spread across the ground surrounded by pots and maps.

"Had to, you were asleep on the job," Timmons growled as he separated himself from a rather large parchment.

"Do not be silly. I was not asleep," he said and gave Kriston a look. "Was I?"

"No, but you were not responding," Kriston said as he continued to kneel between the two. "Report."

"Report? Nothing to report. I was just sitting here watching the little lady and you two come in and dump cold water on me for no reason," he growled.

"You needed a bath anyway," mumbled Timmons as Kriston stood and helped his friend up from the floor.

"Anna, what happened to Jake?" Kriston asked as he turned back to look down at her.

"Nothing. It's not like he's tied to a tent pole, sitting on the hard ground or anything." She shot a look up at him with resentment.

"I told you why we did this. Until I get further answers, you are our guest and I cannot take any chance of you being harmed."

"Guest! Guest, my butt!" she growled under her breath. Once again, she was reminded how sore her posterior currently was.

First, she'd had to endure a whole night tied like a pig against the tent pole on the hard ground as she'd once more been troubled by weird dreams of dragons and dark rooms. Then the other half of the night she had lain awake, unable to feel her backside. Her mind kept wandering back to the vision she had seen the night before, the one Colab had shown her when she had used her magic on him, or more importantly his snake, Meshi. So many emotions, so much pain and loss, that when Kriston had found her after Colab the Meshi had left, she'd been overcome by sadness and had a hard time hiding this from his sharp green eyes.

In the morning, she'd been given some bread and a quick drink, then had been manhandled up on a horse with Kriston riding behind her. The man had a grip like a vise. Now her sore bottom was bumped against the saddle each time they hit a rock or dip in the weird colorless forest floor.

"Did you say something?" Kriston asked.

"No." She pouted, keeping her head held high, which only managed to reach mid-chest on the man.

"I think you mentioned your... very attractive butt," he prodded with a chuckle.

She decided she wouldn't give him the satisfaction of answering, even as a small smile tugged at her lips. At least she was no longer tied

THE SCHOLAR

up. However, with the gorilla grip he held her with, she may have been better off with the rope.

"Do you have to hold me so tight?" she finally demanded.

He gave her a good yank, bringing her even closer to his chest. "I think so." He chuckled behind her, causing bumps to raise all over her skin.

Wrinkling her nose, she said dryly, "You could have at least showered first."

"Is that an invitation?" he whispered, which brought her full temper to its breaking point.

"No! You... barbarian! If I had a sword I would—"

But before she could finish, his hand clamped over her mouth. "Shhh," he hissed as he pulled his horse to a stop.

Anna could tell by his movements and the way his body had tensed behind hers that something was wrong. Even his horse stood tense, each muscle hard as stone as its ears swiveled this way and that as if seeking an enemy's location.

Captain Ray came up next to him with a wild look on his face.

"How many?" Kriston whispered.

"We cannot tell. Maybe a whole pack, or maybe just a single family."

"That is a chance we cannot take." He drew his sword with his free hand. "How long?"

"Not long," Ray responded.

Anna had started struggling when she spotted Ray's face. His eyes were huge and he had two bright pink spots below them.

She also noticed the other men were gathering closer to Kriston, all wearing the same expressions of fear or dread.

"Formations," Kriston said and moved his horse forward again as each man drew his weapon. They rode in a circle surrounding Kriston and Anna. The horses all held their ears high and their eyes open wide.

"What is it?" she asked. Kriston took so long answering that she wasn't even sure he would respond.

"Cats." The tone of Kriston's voice as he spoke the word sent shivers down her spine. Anna personally loved cats. She'd lived with a few domesticated ones and had once seen a beautiful mountain lion high in the Rockies. However, Kriston's tone spoke of something darker and more dangerous than any cat or lion Anna had ever run into on Earth.

"What kind of cats?" she whispered back, turning her head left and right as if she could spot the beasts. The only things she could see beyond Kriston's large sword were the odd white leaves and the black of the tree bark from the forest. She could hear the men and their horses surrounding them but even this didn't give her comfort.

"The deadly kind," he responded.

"Are we talking lion size or smaller?" she asked but he gave no response. When they had gone over two hundred yards further down the path, he asked, "What is a lion?"

"You know, *The Lion King*, king of the jungle." She shook her head. "Lions, tigers, and bears, oh my..." She sighed just as he yanked his horse to a stop again.

She could feel both the horse and Kriston tense again. Their muscles quivered with hostility as each strained to see beyond the white leaves surrounding them. The horse gave a snort that startled Anna, and she flinched inside her cloak. It appeared to be a sign for Kriston who shouted at his men just as a large animal came sliding into the clearing.

She never could have imagined the beast she saw next. At first it looked like a tall black panther, but then she noticed its jaw and realized it was more like a saber-toothed tiger except with more teeth. Way more. It also had several horns on its enormous head, each pointing directly towards them. When it gave a loud cry, Anna screamed and covered her ears and before she could breathe, they were moving quickly.

Kriston charged his horse directly at the cat. She held on as he stabbed at the animal over her head, then swung past it. He was brought up short when another beast stood directly in their path.

He gave a sharp whistle and the horse reared up and kicked its front hooves at the new beast. She was thrown backwards towards Kriston and he gripped her with his free arm to make sure she didn't fall off.

"What in God's name?" she screamed just as

the horse's front hooves landed a heavy blow to the large cat. They landed back on the ground and circled the wounded animal. The horse and the creature stared at each other. Foam dropped from the cat's lips, which were peeled back, showing its impressive teeth.

"Hold on," Kriston ordered and, letting go of Anna, he grabbed the reins and gave them a hard yank, turning the horse around as he yelled out orders.

It was then that Anna saw his men were each battling their own cats. Some even had two or three of the large beasts trying to dislodge them from their horses.

"Take up formation! Bring up the rear, Brigdon!" Kriston shouted just as they both were thrown forward over his horse's neck. It was Anna's quick thinking that kept them both seated and safe. She grabbed the horse's mane with one hand and put her other arm straight out, stopping Kriston's forward movement with great effort.

Sitting back, Anna turned to Kriston just as another rider came up to their side with his sword dripping with blood.

"Kriston, we need to reach the river to our left. We should head there instead of deeper into the forest."

Anna saw the older man turn his horse and sweep his sword arm out, striking another cat down as he spoke.

"To the river!" Kriston shouted and kicked his

horse into action.

The ride was fast and confusing. Anna only had time to tighten her grip on the horse's mane before they were speeding past the trees with large cats on their heels as they headed towards the water. Although what a little water could do to stop these large animals was beyond her understanding. She knew most cats on Earth didn't like water, but she distinctly remembered learning that some larger cats, like leopards, were good swimmers and enjoyed it.

Minutes went past and still the horses and men sped on, followed closely by the large beasts, who didn't appear to be giving up. In fact, every once in a while, one of the cats got close enough to be jabbed by a man with his sword, then it would fall back behind the horses to lick its wounds.

It appeared the cats could wait until the horses or men were worn down before attempting another attack.

Anna could hear the water before she saw it. The loud rushing was so deafening that at first, she thought something was wrong with her ears. Kriston seemed to hear it too as he bent lower towards her and yelled, "Hang on! We are going to get wet!"

As if she had any other choice?

The next thing she knew, the ground ahead of them disappeared.

"That's a cliff!" she screamed.

"Hang on!" Kriston screamed back at her and wrapped his arms tightly around her waist.

The creature made of iron had used the trans rock to transport itself and the wizard down into the depths of Matera's castle, even as they had continued to battle.

When Leian was finally thrown from the creature's back, he had found himself surrounded by the king's secret guards, all of whom had swords pointed directly at him. The large creature held him down with the eerie green magic that emanated from its hands and eyes.

"Stay down, wizard," it growled.

"What do you mean by attacking me!" Leian shouted from the cold floor. "Release me or feel my powers, demon!" He started to bring his defensive magic forward, feeling it build from his core out towards his fingertips as it begged to be released.

The creature gave a low laugh, then stepped back, giving Leian the pleasure of seeing Matera's king for the first time.

"Please," was all the king said before Leian blacked out.

He awoke chained to a stone wall in a small, dark, windowless room, bound in glowing iron manacles. The irons allowed him to move only feet from the large ring his chains were welded to.

He soon discovered he couldn't release any power to break his bondage or escape.

After several attempts to use his magic, he gave

a quick glance at his prison—no windows and only a small door with a heavy metal knob that held no key hole. He could hear water dripping and smelled death and decay and something else, something that felt familiar, as if he should know its score but it eluded him.

He didn't know how many days he'd been held in Matera's deep dungeons, unable to see light to tell night or day from each other prevented him from being able to count the passing of the sun. But knowing the time wouldn't be helpful anyway. He was getting nowhere in his attempts at escape and was very weak from his efforts.

He knew where he was, he just didn't know how to escape.

After a while he turned his thoughts instead to his arrival at the southern castle and started to worry. His immediate fear stemmed from his knowledge that the king could somehow obtain another's power.

Was he now powerless? Forever?

Had the king acquired his wizard's gift, given to him at birth? What if he had no more magic and escaping this dark place was not in his future? What would become of him if he didn't escape? No power meant he would be unable to help Genoa and her people.

What of Shiarra?

Had his faithful apprentice escaped the city and followed his instructions? Had she guided Anna out safely and were they even now rushing to one of the map's jewels?

After many hours of contemplation, he realized that until he escaped this magical bondage, he would never know if his heart still held magic.

He thought a few times that he could feel it build, coming from his core as usual, but each time he tried to form it, it drifted away from him like a sweet dream floated away right after waking.

He finally accepted that magic would not get him out of his cell. He would have to rely on knowledge and skill instead.

Casting another look around the room, he saw in the chain's faint glow a small drain in the floor. Walking forward until he reached the furthest point of his bondage, he leaned forward with his arms stretched behind him to get a closer look.

What he saw was discouraging. The drain was smaller than his fist and its iron cover was too thick and coated thick with rust. Walking back towards the wall, he looked at the stones themselves. If even one was loose, he may be able to escape. After several hours, he was once again discouraged as none of the stones seemed to be loose.

Maybe he was starting at the end. What he needed to do first was gain his freedom from the chains.

Searching his clothing, he found that all his possessions had been taken. It appeared they had searched his deep pockets and left nothing behind. However, his hope rose when he discovered he was still wearing his own boots.

Of course, the knife he kept on the inside of his left ankle was gone, but the soles of the boots seemed to be intact and unmolested.

Quickly sitting down, he listened for any signs of life beyond his door. It appeared that his captors did not care to provide him with water or food, so reaching down, he gave his right boot heel a hard twist and released the secret compartment underneath.

When his small blade fell out, he quickly replaced the heel and hid the knife. When no movement or sound came from beyond his door, he studied the locks that bound him.

If he could gain freedom from the chains, maybe his magic would work again.

It took him several hours to free his left hand, but his right hand was even harder. His blade kept slipping, causing him to make small cuts in his hand and wrist. The small amount of blood made his wrist slippery and eventually he was able to ease his hand out without releasing the lock.

After ripping a strip of cloth from his shirt, he wrapped his wrist and hand and walked to the door, tense with anticipation.

Before he even reached it, he realized there was more of a barrier than just wood. Magic was here. Though he couldn't see it, he could feel it.

Taking a deep breath, he felt his own magic rise from down deep. Slowing its progress, he tried to stay calm as his joy in still having his magic almost overwhelmed him.

He was weak with hunger and thirst, but he knew that if he focused, he could be free of this room within hours.

Raising his hands towards the door, he was about to send a probe of magic forward when he heard the lock click and was shocked into inaction as it started to open.

"I go to follow the sergeant and his men."

Timmons looked up from his wet supplies and stared at the man named Sash.

After their plunge into the river, most of the men had reached the right bank of the rushing river within seconds. One horse was missing along with Kriston and the pale woman known as Anna.

Timmons had sent scouts, even in their wet state, to find signs of their missing leader, but none of the scouts had returned yet.

It was decided they would take time to allow their supplies to dry and the men to rest from their recent battle before they continued their search for Kriston.

Now, kneeling on the ground as he sorted his own supplies, Timmons quickly looked over the dark man who had assisted them in escaping the trap set by Sergeant Bainst and his two men the day before.

Even dripping with river water, Sash looked formidable as his dark face held anger and determination. His large frame was still covered by many weapons, and even with a few rips in his outer clothing, Timmons could see the man's muscles flexed, anxious to start the hunt.

"They will not get far; we could use you here with us," Timmons stated as he continued to collect his supplies that needed to be hung out to dry.

"My fear…" the large man started in a hoarse whisper, probably the result of not using his voice for a very long time, "is that they will reach the king and betray the captain and his men with lies."

When Timmons glanced back up, he saw the determination in Sash's dark eyes. The man's black brows were drawn together in deep concern.

"Sash. Why did you assist us?" He was surprised when Sash folded his huge frame and sat next to Timmons on an overturned rock.

"My family." He stared off into the distance for a time, the sound of the river and the men setting their supplies right was the only sound. "My family and I lived in a small quiet village across these very mountains. We lived in peace, logging and trading with travelers along the road between Byways and the north trade station. One season, I had been asked to take many logs to a man that lived outside the Pintras Forest. I was only gone three nights." He turned to look into Timmons' eyes. "When I returned, I discovered my village under attack. Most were already dead. I could only save two lives. It took me many seasons to detect who had been behind the attack, and when I discovered the source,

I set out to destroy that man." He glanced down at his hands. "I could not stop the death of my family. My loved ones and village were all dead because of a spoiled and selfish man."

"I am sorry for your loss," Timmons stated and even that sympathy felt inadequate. "Will you need anything for your journey?"

CHAPTER THIRTEEN

Downward and Upward

His head was killing him! It felt like he had drunk more than his share of ale.

A roaring noise filled his head and its echo seemed to bounce around between his ears.

If he could just get the pounding in his head to stop then he could sleep some more. He rolled over to ease the pain in his side and heard a small moan that caused him to open his eyes too fast.

After letting out a few choice words, he realized it was not ale that was the cause of his trouble. No, his biggest problem was lying half underneath him and soaking wet with river water.

He chanced opening his eyes again and realized night was fast approaching. He remembered their harrowing trip down the rapids after their great jump into thin air, all to escape the damned cats.

Each rock he had hit came back to him, as well as the cold water and spray that had hit his face as he tried to keep them afloat in the blasted water, all the while clinging to Rath's back.

Taking stock, he did a quick survey of his own body and realized that most of his skin on his left forearm was missing. He also saw he had two broken fingers. Their angle and color told him the injury wasn't life threatening, but that didn't stop the pain.

Lifting himself above Anna using his good arm, he gave her a quick study. Her face was pale, but it usually was. Her eyes were closed and her breathing seemed even.

He ran a hand down each of her arms to make sure there weren't any broken bones, and she giggled.

He stared at her in amazement.

They had just jumped over a two-hundred-foot cliff, dropped into a raging waterfall, been swept away into a rapidly moving river, and swum for several long minutes in an attempt to reach the shore and now she was giggling?

"Stop!" she gasped and opened her pale eyes. "I'm ticklish!" She gave another giggle and tried to kick out towards him.

His eyes burned into hers and he felt a hint of desire boil up inside him from down deep. Her pale hair was spread out on the dark ground, and her face turned a light shade of pink as she laughed. It appeared her beauty and his fascination with her grew stronger with each moment he spent with her.

When he noticed a look of fear cross her eyes, he cleared his throat.

"You are well?" he asked.

"Yes, well..." She hesitated, then cleared her throat. "You're heavy," she exclaimed just as his horse shoved its nose between the two of them and slobbered all over Anna's already wet face.

"Sorry," he said with a laugh and lifted himself up with his good arm to shove Rath's head back. "He gets excited when he sees a pretty woman," he said and quickly sat up.

When she gave a quick gasp, he spun around, half expecting to see the large cats slinking into the small river bend where they were hidden.

"What!" he shouted, trying to draw his sword even as he couldn't find any threat.

"Your arm?" She scrambled up to her feet, water dripping from the tips of her hair onto her even wetter dress.

Her appearance reminded Kriston of the first time he had seen her. Except this time, she was watching him with her hand on her small hips and a frown on her lips. "What have you done to your arm?" she demanded.

Taking a deep breath, he glanced at his arm. Six large gouges crossed his arm, along with several bruises. Rath kept nudging Kriston's shoulder in an attempt for attention. It seemed the horse had come out of the plunge into the water in better shape than the humans. "Looks like one of those cats got me." He moved to Rath's side and, with his good hand, dug into his saddlebag for his medical satchel.

"It'll need to be cleaned and fixed," she said as she tried to grab her backpack, which had been tied to the black leather saddle. "I'm even more worried about those fingers." She glanced at him as he kept digging into his bag. "Looks like you broke a phalanx on both your second and third fingers. Do you know how to set bones?"

When she only got a grunt from him in return, she tried once more to reach her bag, but his horse was well over ten feet tall, and she couldn't even reach its back. He enjoyed watching her try as she stood up on the tips of her toes. The view wasn't half-bad.

When he gave a small chuckle, she turned around quickly and glared at him. "Can you please hand me my bag? I have a first aid kit that'll help us."

He spared her a quick glance and untied her bag, letting it drop. Luckily, she grabbed it before it hit her in the face and mumbled a quick thanks to him.

She took it over to a rather large fallen tree that ran down into the turbulent waters, sat down, and patted the bark next to her. When he just stared at her, she repeated the motion. "Come on, big baby, it's not like I can hurt you."

He gave her a quick study and walked over to

sit next to her. "What is a first aid kit?" he asked out of curiosity.

She was too busy digging in her bag to answer, but she produced a small white box with a red slash across it.

Now he was more intrigued than worried. As she opened the box, he scooted closer to her and reached into it for a few things that caught his eye. When she gave his good hand a quick slap, he decided he was better off without her help. When he started to stand up, she placed a hand on his arm, holding him still.

"That skin abrasion may need stitches, or... Well, I think I have plenty if I conserve what's left," she mumbled to herself.

"What?" he asked as she pulled a small tin box from her pocket. He was shocked to see a small amount of Winnept sap inside. "Is that what I think it is?" he asked with amazement "How did you get this?" He demanded and tried to grab the tin out of her hand.

"I stole it from a wizard," she answered and rolled his sleeve up then spread a small amount of the purple goo along his left forearm.

She was very gentle and careful not to brush his injured fingers as she used a white gauze to wipe the blood and sap off his arm after the wound was healed.

He noticed she had used less than half the Winnept sap as she carefully placed the tin back into the folds of her wet gown.

When she had finished with his arm, she grabbed a few small smooth sticks and a roll of white cloth. "Well, I guess there is no time like the present to learn," she said as she studied his broken fingers. "I studied medical books every chance I could. Always hoped I would never need the knowledge, if you know what I mean."

He had no clue what she was talking about but felt calm as she continued to hold his hand in her small, soft fingers. His eyes were roaming over her features, watching her carefully.

Her head bent lower over his hand. His middle finger and ring finger were both bent at odd angles, farther left than they should have. Standing one more time, she walked over to the horse and grabbed the water skin that was hung low on the saddle, then marched back across the space towards him.

Kriston sat still and watched the way she moved. He had yet to speak as confused emotions rolled around inside him.

"Here, take these." She handed him two small white stones.

"What are these?" He frowned at the small items.

"They're pills. Aspirin." When he didn't respond, she continued. "They'll help with the pain." She dropped them into his good hand.

"How?" He looked down at the small items with curiosity.

"You swallow them," she said with a sigh. "I

think two will do." Her eyes scanned over him and he couldn't hold back the smile as he let go of the breath he had been holding in. "You're awfully big, but they are maximum strength."

When he gave her a doubtful look, she placed her hands on her hips and called him a chicken.

"What is a chick'n?" he asked, still holding the small stones she'd given him.

"Something that is always scared." She grabbed the pills from his hands and leaned so close to him that he could see the light reflected in her eyes. Then she placed the stones gently between his lips and handed him the water.

When he finished drinking, she placed one hand on his left shoulder and gave his fingers another glance. "Well, here we go."

She frowned when he tensed up. Then he saw a slight smile cross her lips as she sat very close to him. His eyes traveled over her disheveled hair and clothing, and he realized that he was more than just a little attracted to this confusing woman.

Her pale blue eyes widened slightly as she studied him with deep concentration. He watched her irises grow bigger and knew that she felt the same attraction.

His mind became thoroughly distracted, and his eyes tracked to her lips as she moved in closer. He felt her breath on his skin as her lips slightly parted. Her pale eyes dilated even more as she focused on his face.

He took a deep breath as she inched nearer and

felt his heart pound in his head as she closed her eyes and softly touched her lips to his own.

He found his good hand tangled in her hair. This contact caused an explosion of feelings that quickly ran through his brain. None had anything to do with his mission.

He was so focused on the feeling of her soft lips and body next to his that he didn't feel her softly grab his injured fingers, but he did feel the sharp pain when she gave them a swift yank, successfully pulling them back into their proper place.

She landed on her butt in front of Kriston as he jumped up and started cursing.

Pacing back and forth, he held his injured hand and cast evil looks her way. She continued to sit in the soft grass by the log and laughed at him.

"Well, that did the trick," she said after he was finished abusing the air with every known swear word he could remember.

She stood up and wiped the dirt and grass from her skirt. "When you're finished with your tantrum," she said and held out the first aid kit, "I really need to wrap those fingers."

He glared at her and the small box she held out. That was the last time he'd let his guard down around this woman.

She was exhausted.

With the help of the rock troll army, she had spent a full day searching for Anna and her captors.

Shiarra had awoken from the drugs the two men had given her with a slight headache. Clagk had informed her that his trolls had spotted a large group of men approach the lake after she and Anna joined the two men.

It wasn't until after she had taken her first bite of the cursed food that his trolls realized the large group of heavily armed men were heading their way. When the battalion had gotten close enough, Clagk had his trolls set for defense. The troll army had been ready when the first man had attacked them with his broad ax.

Shiarra had attempted to help, but the drug had caused her to send her magic into the troll's shields instead of the men. A large warrior had caused flames to spray about when he kept hitting the rock trolls with his weapon, when he had gotten closer the flames had set her skirts on fire and her world had gone dark thanks to the drugs in the food.

Clagk told her one of the men had stopped and saved her from the fire before they had disappeared with Anna rolled up tight in her own cloaking.

At first Shiarra had roamed the lake's shore and surrounding forests searching for prints or clues as to where the captors were heading.

When she found no tracks, the trolls walked along the small road south of the lake until darkness had fallen and their search was halted.

After setting a makeshift camp in the giant

black and white trees, she had fallen asleep curled at the base of one of the trees with her pride hurt and her skirts burned and tattered. She left it up to the trolls to set watch and keep the fires of the camp lit for the night.

Sometime after midnight, she dreamed a wizard's dream. She knew by the feel of the dream that it was a powerful communication, only used by powerful wizards.

She soon found that the dream was sent from the queen's wizard, Cenzic, whom she had met years ago, on his travel to Tharian to meet with Leian.

She started to tell him of her troubles but was interrupted.

"Apprentice," he said. *"The queen has need of you."*

"Wizard, I am on a quest and searching for Wizard Leian and a friend in the Helmand Mountains," she answered.

"Your friend is being sought as we speak. We have also made arrangements to free your wizard."

Shiarra could not believe her ears. How did Wizard Cenzic know of their troubles? Whatever her doubts, Shiarra had been around wizards enough to know that to doubt his words would be foolish. She had seen wizards rise above problems countless times. *"What would the queen have me do?"* she asked.

"Come," he replied. *"At once."*

And with that, she had awoken.

She jumped up from her sleeping spot and rushed to talk with the rock trolls' king. She told him that their path must now turn towards Valorna once again, that her friend was being rescued and they were being summoned by the queen.

Shiarra was amazed by the trolls that night when the king didn't question her but instead gave her a quick bow and then ordered his trolls to pick up camp.

The entire group was packed and on their way to Valorna within minutes.

During the ride, Shiarra had time to think about her friends. Was someone really attempting to rescue Leian? She assumed he was deep in the bowels of Matera, maybe being tortured. This thought caused her to panic. Yet, she realized, worrying about him from afar could not help him.

Her thoughts moved to Anna, plucked from her grasp just as the two were getting to know each other. She had been Anna's only protector in Genoa and yet she had failed at her task.

She wondered why the queen was summoning her. Did this have to do with Anna's presence in Genoa?

She wished Leian had provided her with more details regarding this quest. Did the queen know of Leian's orders and personal quest?

Thoughts kept swirling around in her head until it started to hurt. Soon her back started to ache too. She tried to keep the hopelessness from overwhelming her, but even that was a battle she was destined to lose.

Their travels towards the trade station were uneventful. They met only a few travelers that following day and the sky stayed dry and clear, allowing a faster travel time.

When they reached the turnoff that led to the dead town of Pinewood, Shiarra hesitated. Pinewood had been abandoned after its destruction when she was a child, but that didn't prevent her from wishing she could take time to travel the short road to where the town used to sit. Maybe she could even visit the shallow grave where her mother's body rested.

Her father had made the headstone himself, using the white marble the area was known for. He had carved only one word in the stone, "Loved." That was before they had fled and headed to Tharian, traveling to a new life and safety.

But some memories were better left in the past. It was growing dark and after a moment, she quickly moved the troll army on and they camped well beyond the turnoff that night.

"So, what is a Keratosis?" Anna asked innocently as she gathered her medical supplies and followed Kriston back over to Rath to set the supplies on his saddle.

He stopped walking so suddenly that she bumped into his back. "Where, may I ask, did a lady hear such a word?" he scolded down at her, still holding his recently wrapped fingers and his own bag full of supplies.

"From your mouth, not five minutes ago," she answered, as she slid past him and tied the water skin back in place.

When he cleared his throat, Anna glanced over her shoulder at him with a small smile. "I gather that it's not a very nice word." She laughed as the tips of his ears turned bright red from embarrassment.

Before Kriston could reply, they heard a shout from the far side of the river bank and turned in time to see Kriston's man Brigdon emerge from the bushes on the other side of the water.

"What in the king's name are you doing on that side of the river lad?" he shouted with a wave.

She saw Kriston look around and they both noticed they were indeed on the wrong side of the river. They had landed on the far side instead of the side that held the road they'd been traveling on before the battle with the cats.

They watched as his other men emerged from the white trees into the day's failing light. Kriston and Anna had a choice. They could either attempt another swim or find calmer waters before crossing.

"How far have we traveled?" Kriston shouted.

It was Jake who answered as he stepped to the water's edge and lifted his voice over the roaring noise. "We are in Draydon territory."

This news caused Kriston to glance skyward.

Anna's heartbeat sped up as she thought about dragons winging above them.

"Any idea where a safe place to cross would be?" When Jake shook his head, Kriston sat down on the log one more time.

Anna watched him and could almost see the wheels in his head spinning as he tried to figure out his next move. After less than a minute, he shouted, "Regroup." She noticed he didn't even look up to see if his men would obey.

She, however, watched the men across the river start scrambling around making camp.

Her stomach gave a good rumble from hunger and she decided food was needed for both her and Kriston. She walked over to her pack and grabbed a small bag that held some food given to her by Shiarra, as well as two granola bars from her fast-dwindling supply.

Sitting next to Kriston, she handed him a chunk of jerky and took a small bite herself. After a few bites, she washed it down with some of their water and handed him a granola bar.

"Thank you," he mumbled and proceeded to peel the wrapping from the bar and then eat it, deep in thought.

"We could swim for it," she suggested.

"No, you and Rath are both exhausted," he said, taking a quick look at his horse, who was still standing nearby.

Anna realized the animal was asleep where it stood and that Rath must have kept them afloat in the raging river.

"I want to thank you," she said, turning back to Kriston. She didn't know many people who would risk their life for her, yet this man had. Even after all he had accused her of, he still valued her life enough to keep her from harm.

"For what?" he asked and continued eating the fruity bar as the sun sank behind the tall trees.

"Saving my life." She took a small nibble from her own bar.

"All part of my quest," he mumbled as color crept into his cheeks and the tips of his ears turned red again. He quickly looked down at his hands.

She was shocked to see such a big man act like a child caught with his hand in the cookie jar. She watched as he squirmed with discomfort.

After finishing the bar, he dropped the wrapper on the ground and she bent to pick it up. She placed it back in her bag without a word.

"I do not understand you," he said.

Anna stopped and saw him studying her with open curiosity. "What do you mean?"

"You travel with a wizard's apprentice, along with an army of rock trolls, have some kind of magical powers, fight like a man, and double talk all the time. What kind of woman are you?" He asked and continued to study her with his deep green eyes.

Thinking about it for a moment, she gave him the only answer that sounded true. "I'm a nomad."

She could see Kriston think about that for a

while.

"Can I ask you a question?" Anna asked.

"What is it you wish to know now?"

"Why do you guys keep using the king's name to curse everything?"

Taking a deep breath, he studied her for a time. "Several seasons ago, the world was almost destroyed by some very evil kings. I guess this curse was a result of the peoples' fear that this type of destruction may happen again." He shrugged his big shoulders.

She could barely make out Kriston's large shape in the dying light. And as he continued to study her he reached into a pocket with his good hand and pulled out a small round object. When he gave it two quick shakes, light poured from his closed hand.

She gave a quick gasp in amazement.

"Easy," he said with a chuckle. "This is a Briar root. The seeds inside make it glow. The light should last long enough for me to get a fire started."

"Why don't you rest that hand and I'll get the fire started." Without waiting for his response, she marched over to a small clump of the fallen tree's branches. She broke them into manageable sizes and set them next to the fallen tree. She gathered some dry leaves and put them amongst the branches, then took some rocks from the river's edge and placed them in a circle next to the pile. She cleared any small dry grass or twigs from the surrounding area.

As she worked, Kriston used his good hand to take Rath's saddle off. He gathered the gear up and laid it in a pile near the fallen tree and hung the blankets on a low branch so they would dry before they were needed again.

By the time he turned around, she'd placed the pile of sticks in a cone shape with the dry leaves underneath. She was leaning over them, holding a lighter and muttering to herself.

He moved closer and watched as the lighter sparked fire into the dry branches.

"What magic is that!" he said and walked over for a closer look.

"What?" she asked and glanced up. "This thing?" She held in a laugh, much like he'd just done about the Briar root. "It's just a lighter. There's no magic in it at all." She smiled as his eyes narrowed.

She continued to light the fire, and after three trips to gather more dry leaves and a few choice words of her own about the forest's lack of pinecones, she finally managed to get the fire going. When she was done, she glanced up with a smile on her face and saw Kriston staring back at her.

"You really were exiled and did not grow up on Genoa," he stated with an amazed look on his face.

Giving him a slight smile, she walked around the fire to sit next to him on the log.

Since her feet were still soaked, she bent down and removed her left boot.

Glancing up at him, she shook her head

329

slightly. "Yes, Kriston Haddock, I'm a new arrival to Genoa." She set her boot close to the fire so it would dry, then sighed as she glanced up at the three moons and all the foreign stars above them. When she reached to tug off her other boot, he stopped her with a question.

"Why are your toes red?"

She glanced down at her unbooted foot and frowned at the wet sock she was still wearing.

She felt him tense next to her and she turned to him, trying to study his eyes.

"How do you know my toenails are red?" she asked, feeling her heart skip.

He glanced down at her small feet and pointed at them. "I can see your toes through your wet stockings."

Following his gaze, she lifted the hem of her wet dress and moved her feet out towards the fire. Sure enough, she could see the bright red toes under the stockings. Giving a chuckle, she relaxed slightly and turned back to Kriston. "A girl has to have some indulgences."

She tugged off the other boot and yanked off the wet socks, then hung them over a large rock so they could dry. Wiggling her red toes, she reached up and started working on releasing the bone buttons on her bodice.

"Wha... what are you doing?" he asked in a voice that cracked slightly.

She stopped and gave him a funny look. "Do you want me to catch my death?" When he shook his head, she continued, "We can't stay in our wet clothing. If you haven't noticed, that water was freezing and since I managed to get a pretty good fire going, I think some of these layers I have on can be cleaned and dried properly." She leaned towards him and gave a little sniff to the air. "Smells like you could use a good wash too. I think Rath smells better than you do," she said, pointing at the still sleeping horse with a smile.

He was getting closer. He could almost smell her now.

After days of pushing onward, night and day, and taking the most direct route, the woman was now only hours away from his grasp. At least he thought so until her trail suddenly disappeared.

It took several minutes to discover what had happened. It appeared the woman was no longer traveling with the wizard's apprentice, who even now her trail continued north. He retraced his steps, and the scent of two men appeared. When he followed their path south, he discovered his quarry was now in the presence of several of the king's men. The apprentice meant nothing to his quest, so he continued south at an even faster pace.

Failure was not an option this time. The king had punished him the last time and sent him back out to track the spy. Its long black robes hid Speculum's metal form from the light of day and shielded its glowing green eyes as it continued its search for signs of the woman.

What he came across instead of his quarry was a scared and running man. Turning its hunting eyes towards the man, he realized he was one of the king's own secret guards. He was large and covered in mud. Most of his weapons were gone, he only carried a large ax in one hand and kept glancing over his big shoulders while he ran through the forest.

Capturing the man was easy. After dodging the huge ax and large fists, the Speculum was on his new prey in no time, pinning the man down in the wet ground.

"What are you?" Ali yelled from under the creature.

"Where is the woman?" it whispered back.

"I know not what you talk about, get off me!" Ali demanded. His large feet tried to kick the beast off his form as fright took over.

"Where is the woman?" it asked again with a growl.

"I lost them," Ali screamed. "I saw them jump off a cliff and float down the falls. They were heading east!" He tried once more to get the creature off his chest.

The Speculum placed a large glowing green hand against Ali's chest. "It appears I am in need of your assistance." It released its fire into the secret guard's chest and watched as the green magic flowed outward. The man started to scream and continued screaming until his voice broke.

When silence settled back around them, the Speculum stood and marveled at his new companion.

There, facing him, stood a creature that looked just like him—metal skin and hair, glowing green eyes, and an evil smile. The only thing missing was the magic he himself had been born with.

"Now, we will find our foe and complete the mission," it whispered.

CHAPTER FOURTEEN

A Good Story

They hung their outer clothing by the fire to dry and she could see that even the men wore more clothes than necessary in this land.

Kriston had on what appeared to be boxers and a long overlay shirt, which hung over his wide shoulders. The garment tied around his narrow waist and had buttons of silver.

After giving his muscular legs a good look, she decided to stay in her corset and long underskirt, both which appeared to be drying quickly.

Throwing her leather apron back on, she felt overdressed but after the sun had disappeared fully, she was glad for the warmth so many clothes had provided.

Kriston had a short conversation with his men

who were making camp on the far side of the river and watched as they posted guards along the path forward and backwards to ensure safety.

Anna took stock of her private supplies in her backpack and was surrounded by her only possessions when Kriston sat down next to her again.

"What do you have in this bag?" he asked, looking at some of the items that she had laid out around her. There were bottles and bags of liquids and even a few small boxes. "Do you have any more of those honey bars?" he asked, reaching towards her bag when he received a stern "No" and a quick slap from her once again so he withdrew his hand.

She confirmed she had the few items she had "borrowed" from Shiarra along with the one picture she carried.

"These are my supplies." She continued sorting items and once she'd done a quick count, started to place items back in her bag. "I only have a few left. We have plenty of food so I think I'll keep these for a rainy day."

Kriston stared at her for a few seconds. "Rainy day?" he finally asked.

Shaking her head, she noticed that her hair had dried completely. "We really must do something about your lack of knowledge of Earth phrases." She continued to place items in her bag. "It means for an emergency."

"Tell me about Earth. Is that where you were

exiled?" He sat back against the log once more, placing his head against a folded-up shirt like a pillow.

When she was finished loading her bag, she placed it to her side and settled down next to him. Her feet were dry and warm, and the rest of her was heading that way too. She felt like it would take weeks to get the sand out of her hair.

"Earth didn't feel like a bad place. I wouldn't say I was exiled, more like misplaced," she said with a shake of her head. She folded a dry shirt and placed it behind her head on the log as well. "There are blue skies like here, a warm yellow sun, and stars in the night sky. I think the two main differences are the moons and Genoa's magic, of course." She thought a minute and added. "Of course, I never saw dragons, but there were old stories of them there."

He was quiet for a few seconds then asked, "Moons?"

She glanced skyward where she could spy three of Genoa's moons. Seeing the smallest, she pointed at it. "See, the small one? That looks a little like Earth's one and only moon." Sitting up, she turned to him. "Do the moons here affect the tides?" she asked as he glanced skyward. The light from the fire cast shadows and patterns across his handsome face.

"Only one moon?" Kriston said as he imagined

what it would be like to have so little light at night. "No, none of our moons affect the ocean's waters, if that is what you mean. At least not that I know about. I have only seen the ocean once, years ago, and from a great distance." He thought of that one fleeting view and wished, secretly, that he could have gotten a better view of the vast body of water.

He glanced sideways at her as she leaned back down next to him. Her hair was dry now, looking much like a soft cloud around her face.

He knew she had royal blood in her based on her magical presence, but she acted like she was comfortable doing chores and living on the trail. Nomad... That felt true, but he wanted to discover more.

"Tell me more of Earth," he asked, liking how her voice rose and fell when she talked. He'd also liked watching her peel the wet garments from her tiny frame. His eyes moved easily over her form now as she talked.

"Earth, well, it sits in the Milky Way galaxy, the third planet from the sun." She glanced skyward again dreamily.

"Tell me about your time there," he prodded. "I want to hear of the people and what happened to you there." He placed his good hand behind his head and glanced at her again.

She gave him an impatient look, but after a moment, she started giving him small details of her childhood.

She was deep into her eighth story before she

stilled and glanced at him. He realized that never had someone held his attention for so long. Especially when the conversation was about herself.

But instead of continuing the story, she interrupted.

"Are you really King Haddock's brother?"

He sat up slightly and threw another log on the fire. He moved over to check on their clothing.

"Yes, Gillard is my brother." He glanced over his shoulder and, seeing her expression of frustration, continued to explain further. "Gillard, or King Haddock, is six seasons older than me. He has been king for eighteen seasons." Taking a deep breath, he turned back to her and handed her the dry dress garments.

"And Matera, what is it like?" She sat still, ignoring the dry clothing he had handed her.

"Matera." He sighed again, knowing stubbornness when he saw it and decided his own limited story may help him discover more about this woman. "She was once the hub of the southwest, nestled between the cliffs of Licht and the Maylin River, whose waters run clear and white. At least it used to." He paused and, walking over to his clothing, grabbed up his garments.

"Used to?" she asked as she finally picked up her dry outer garments and started dressing. She had a small struggle with the clasp along her sleeve, a little battle Kriston enjoyed watching.

"We have tried but failed to find out why the waters are no longer clean. I have heard rumors it has something to do with the disappearance of the surrounding creatures, but my brother insists they are the ones who poisoned it in the first place." He finally turned and finished dressing.

"Creatures? You mean people are disappearing? How?" she asked with concern.

"There have been attempts—no, more like secret missions—to save them, but even my powers have their limit." He finished dressing and sat back down next to her. "My men help, but we are too few."

After she had clasped each sleeve, she asked another question. "Your men." She paused and he watched her face as she attempted to formulate her words with great care. "You trust them and they trust you?" When she only got a nod from him, she continued. "But not all the men who traveled with you have your trust. Those you fought with the other night weren't under your command?" she asked.

Kriston gave a quick bark of laughter and uttered an oath, then stopped and gave her an astonished look. "They were part of the Secret Guard and were taking orders directly from my brother."

She grabbed two of the horse blankets and made a rough bed with them. Then she stood back and gave it a nod of approval.

"Well, it's not the Ritz, but I think it'll keep us warm." She glanced skyward. "As long as it doesn't rain."

Glancing across the river, he noticed his men had made camp in the trees and not along the very small sandy bank on the river's edge. It appeared their own little beach was larger and secluded by a few large boulders and their one fallen tree.

Sitting down on the tree, he thought of his past, all the missions and secrecy that had led him to this very beach, sitting next to this very pale woman. He thought about the secrets she might hold. Taking a leap of faith and a very large breath, he decided it was time for some truth for a change.

"Anna, sit down." When she stopped, and looked at him, worry and concern crossed her face, however she walked over and sat down.

"When I was five, my father took me and my brother to our season cottage up above the cliffs. He left us in his army's care and went away for many days. When he came back and found us at the castle he was..." He hesitated here. Anna placed one small hand on his in a reassuring manner and gave him a quick smile that, he was shocked to admit, gave him courage. "Distraught is too nice a word. He was crazed and kept talking about waste and powers. You could almost see his own power sizzle around him at times." He glanced into her eyes. "He was a powerful king. One of full royal blood and his power was always stronger than most. But when he took us back to the cottage almost a full season later, he was changed. He traveled with only a few of his men and would hole up in a room with his new wizard for hours each day instead of hunting or riding." He paused again. Picking up the water skin, he took a quick sip and continued. "Ten days after our arrival at the cottage we were attacked."

He stood and paced in front of the fire, his good hand cradling the bad one behind his back, his shoulders slumped with his eyes fixed on his toes. "My father was killed first," he said with a deep breath. "Brigdon was a young and eager soldier, one who happened to be at the right place when he was needed the most. He took me from my rooms and out a secret passage that led into the woods and safety. My brother was with our father when he was killed. He was later found buried under the rubble of the cottage, half dead." He stopped pacing and looked at Anna from across the fire. "He was crowned king two nights later, unwilling to wait until he was of age. It was said he threatened the council members with his magic, but no one has ever stepped forward to validate these accusations."

Clearing his throat, he continued. "For too many years, my brother has ruled Matera with his iron fist. He dictates from his throne room and does not think of Matera or her people. I have seen the destruction of many creatures who once called my land home. My brother has no love for nonmagical creatures and has passed laws that condemn them to exile or death." He paused, shocked he was admitting so much to her, yet as he walked back over to the log and took one of her hands in his, he realized some part of him already trusted her. "Matera bleeds from her heart. Her people are sick, the land is sick, and I, along with my men, fear they all are dying. Secretly, we have been attempting to free as many as we can from my brother's reach, all while searching for answers. We had found little until your arrival in Genoa."

Searching her face, he saw doubt deep in her pale eyes, but also something else. "I do not seek my brother's throne; this you must not doubt. Whatever your mission is here—" When she made to interrupt him he continued. "I know you have a mission and you must know I may have to stop you at one point if your mission is to harm my homeland. But for now, my mission is to bring you safely back to my land." Sitting back, he gave her a quick smile. "But until we reach it, there is nothing stopping me from discovering the truth behind your arrival and the fear I saw in my brother's eyes when he sent me after you."

When the tip of a sword appeared behind the door, Leian thought he was finished. He was so weak that his magic, what little there was, would not stop a swamp fly.

He decided his best defense was offense, so he rushed the door. When the sword was dropped to the ground, he saw the man standing behind it. He was dressed all in black, his long brown hair tied back, and his face covered in cobwebs and dirt as he held his hands out in a friendly gesture. A smile touched his lips and eyes as Leian stopped his forward motion. The wizard tried not to fall to his knees as he studied the man not much older than he.

"Who are you?" Leian whispered. His voice was so dry; he was shocked he could speak at all.

"The question, my young wizard, is not who I am, but who I stand for," the newcomer said with a crooked smile. He reached down and grabbed the lantern at his feet. He glanced up at Leian and reached slowly for his sword with his other hand. "Wizard, our time is short, so if you do not mind, we really should hurry. The queen will be upset if I fail at my rescue attempts." With this he picked up his sword, placed it back in its scabbard, and turned around, leaving Leian to stare at the empty doorway with questions flying about his mind.

Taking one last look about his cell, he quickly followed his rescuer. When he caught up to the man, he could only see his outline against a doorway, while he listened for something.

"Wha..." The man turned and placed a hand over Leian's mouth. He released Leian and motioned with his hand. Taking the lantern, he extinguished its light, plunging them into darkness.

A small light appeared a second later, allowing Leian to see that the stranger held a small Briar root in his tightly closed fist. The man allowed a small bit of light to seep through his bent fingers. Leian could see his eyes dart around the empty corridor, and he too could hear something moving about the vast passageway.

Eventually they both headed forward and found the way open to them. The passageways led in multiple directions. The far-left passage headed down narrow and steep steps, dropping deeper into the ground at a sharp angle.

The passage to their right appeared to stay level and disappeared farther than their light could penetrate. Two more on the right led up, headed in opposite directions.

Leian watched his rescuer head straight for the last passageway and followed him up the stairs, holding onto the cold stone walls for support.

When they had traveled over forty steps, the passageway came to level ground once more and the wizard saw two more routes were available.

When the stranger paused at the first corridor, Leian was worried he was lost, but he was only listening for any sounds. Moving on to the next corridor, he listened and after a few seconds went back to the first passageway and they proceeded with their escape.

Leian was dismayed when the cavern kept going. His tired legs and body could not handle such an excursion after being locked away for several days. After several minutes, he had to stop before he found himself flat on his face. When the dizziness almost overtook him, he closed his eyes and tried to remember his last meal.

Shiarra had been there, her face alight with wonder as they talked with Anna in Byways before their trek to see Sayer Otis. Trying to focus on that memory, he thought about how Shiarra had looked. When the dizziness did pass, he opened his eyes to see the stranger kneeling in front of him holding a water skin.

"Forgive me." He passed the skin to Leian. "I forgot you have been imprisoned for six days. Did they not feed you or give you water at all?"

Leian shook his head and slowly drank fresh water from the skin, then his guide helped him stand and they continued at a slower pace.

"It is not much further, my friend, then a hot meal awaits you and plenty of rest." He was helped down the corridor, keeping his arm over the man's shoulder for support.

Even with the promise of food, Leian had a hard time placing one foot in front of the other. It felt like days before they reached an open corridor ending in an iron door.

His rescuer approached the door, knocked three times fast, then followed it with a fourth. The door swung inward and they were met with bright lights and many voices.

"Hurry, lad, we must make the cliffs by nightfall," came a deep voice.

"We may need to carry him; he is in worse shape than I thought," responded his rescuer.

"You three, help the wizard. We have no time to stop now. They will know soon that he is missing," said the deeper voice. Leian felt himself slipping farther into weakness.

"We are lucky the king was otherwise occupied

or they would already be on our heels," someone said.

Leian felt strong hands grip him gently around his arms and legs and lift him and then he finally lost consciousness.

When he woke next, he found himself on a soft grassy bed, a warm soft blanket thrown over him. When he tried to sit up, his vision dimmed and his head felt heavy and he quickly lay back down.

Taking his time, he looked around from his horizontal position. A cave, blankets, cots, and an old wooden table with two chairs stood beyond his feet. The light came from a small lantern on the table. Turning, he saw a cup next to his head and reached over towards it. When he felt the wet water slop over onto his hand he raised it to his lips for a quick taste.

Fresh water!

It was the best water he had ever had. After he drank the whole cupful, he tried sitting again and found the room didn't spin and his vision didn't dim.

Sitting up further he saw an opening behind his head and was just trying to swing his legs over the cot edge when an older man came walking through the door carrying a tray.

"Well, the dead are awake," he said with a chuckle.

"Where am I?" Leian asked and continued to try and sit up.

"Careful now." The man walked over to the

table. After placing the tray down, he helped Leian over to a chair then disappeared though the door again and came back shortly with a bowl filled with liquid.

"My name's Crain," he said.

"Wizard Leian of ..."

"Tharian," Crain finished. He saw the surprised look on Leian's face. "Yes," he said with a nod of his head, "we know who you are. In truth, we were sent to rescue you." He plopped himself down opposite Leian.

"Rescue?" He thought for a moment then sat back with relief. "Shiarra."

"No, no clue who that is. Someone else sent us to rescue you," the old man said.

Leian studied him. This man was shorter than he was and had a big bushy mustache and a little chin hair that was speckled with gray. He had round blue eyes and wore a huge hat that slanted up at the edges.

"Us?" Leian asked. "Who is 'us'?"

Scratching at his chin hair, the man studied Leian. "Well now, you, wizard have just landed smack at the center of the resistance." He slapped Leian on the back. "Eat up and I can tell you a tale."

As Leian ate the bread, fruits, and broth provided, Crain told of how he had been a captain of a training facility high in the Cleveite Mountains many seasons ago. How his teaching had come to an abrupt end with the gnome attacks and how he'd been placed under the king's eye, training his army.

He had later been approached by one of his old students to help discover the king's secrets and start an uprising. The man had liked the sound of that after spending many seasons under the evil king. He jumped at the chance to help lead a group of men, men that stood for the people of Matera, and ensured they were well taken care of, protected.

"We tried to discover if the king had something to do with the poisoning of the Maylin River. Instead, we discovered that several of the training facility captains had gone missing when they questioned the king's orders. Since General Zobo took charge, we have had more disappearances and deaths than any general or king before. Not to mention the killing of innocent beings."

Leian, having finished his meal, could feel his strength slowly seep back into his body. His brain was once again functioning and he could feel some of his magic stir deep down.

A strong panic filled him as he realized where he had been. He thought quickly of the opportunity he had just missed while he was deep in the evil king's lair. If he had been stronger, or had his full magic... After a few moments of punishing himself, he realized some things were meant to be and hoped another opportunity would present itself before the end of the Moonvest.

When his mind cleared, the man named Crain was finishing up his story.

"What does the resistance do to help the people on Genoa?" Leian finally asked.

"Besides freeing the unjustly imprisoned, feeding the starving, and undermining the king's evil orders"—Crain tilted his head— "rescuing wizards, I guess."

Standing, he gave Leian a smile and helped him up. "Come, Wizard, let me show you our hideaway."

"How far?"

"A day. Maybe more," came the reply.

"Can she find her?"

"If she follows the river, there is a chance."

"I leave this choice up to you."

"What of the others?"

"Only she matters." When the other kept silent, she continued. "I have taken steps to ensure they are safe or soon will be."

"What else can I do?'

"When you find her, keep yourselves safe... And come to me."

When this struck deep fear in the receiver of the message, Anna turned in her sleep and mumbled in concern.

Anna's movement caused Kriston's arm to come protectively around her.

He had lain awake most of the night. Even the last three hard and short nights of sleep had not prepared him for sleeping next to Anna.

Her scent surrounded him and teased him, but his thoughts kept returning to her story as the moons circled the sky.

Was she telling the truth? It felt that way to him, but how was he to know? After all, it had taken him many seasons to realize his brother told many lies. Lies that destroyed the lives of the innocent.

Maybe Anna was good at telling lies just like his brother. He didn't think this was the case, as the one or two times he had caught her telling a fib, he had seen signs of distress in her. She tended to look up and over his shoulder when telling a falsehood, and he was relieved that he could pick up on her body language so quickly.

Now, however, wide-awake, he thought about the secrets she kept. *"I will have to do something about this,"* he thought even as he brought her closer to his side in the cold of the night.

Sometime in the night, they were attacked by cats.

It was Clagk's personal guard that woke her. Shiarra had settled in her cloak under a tree some distance from the rock troll's army, hidden away from the road by thick trees and underbrush as the first cries were heard.

The guard came and, after giving Shiarra a quick shake, hopped off towards the sound of battle.

Shiarra had jumped up and was rushing towards the sounds and flashing lights when movement caught her eyes. Turning quickly to her left, her magic already at her fingertips, she saw someone that stopped her heart.

Standing not ten feet away from her was her mother.

Her magic instantly died on her fingertips, seeping back into her as fast as it had come. Her eyes grew huge as they searched out the form, trying to confirm what she was seeing.

She whispered, "Mother?" and was confused when the figure started walking away, not towards her.

"Mother, wait!" Shiarra pursued the figure, which was heading away from the sounds of battle.

When they neared where Shiarra had lain for bed that night, the apprentice did not even stop to pick up her pack, but quickly followed the elusive figure deeper into the trees.

She could see her mother, cloaked in white, walking in the moon's light that reached down between the trees branches. She stayed several feet in front of Shiarra and never stopped. Each time the apprentice ran to catch up, the figure would quicken her pace too. Several times Shiarra called out, but no answer came, so she continued her pursuit in silence over the darkened forest floor.

Only once did the apprentice hesitate.

She had been traveling for quite some time when her mother passed into a tree's shadow. Shiarra thought she saw a twisted shape in the shadows depths, but then her mother was there again, standing in the moonlight, urging her forward.

It wasn't until Shiarra saw the large looming shape of Lehar, the single mountain that resided over the town that had been known as Pinewood, that she realized where she was.

By then the ruins of the town's buildings were all around her. She saw the dark, blackened bones of homes and tattered barns, the old roads now covered with soil and grass.

No longer did the area smell of death and destruction instead the grasses had grown tall, and the undergrowth and vines were taking over, casting an eerie feeling of abandonment across the place.

Shiarra quickly looked around and noticed that her mother had stopped at the end of the road and she stood facing the young apprentice.

"Why have you brought me here?" she yelled.

When her mother stepped forward, the wicked smile on her face made Shiarra step away.

"To die," came the whispered response.

Shiarra shook her head and took another step back. It was then that she noticed the other figures.

"Stoles!" she screamed as she watched the closest phantom leap towards her. Her mother's figure was gone. Now the creatures were in their true form—darkness and smoke, with their large mouths gaping wide open, waiting to get their fill from her emotions.

They attempted to cross the river after the sun peeked above the trees the next morning. Its warm light reminded them how miraculous their escape had been yesterday. Sharp rocks and deep pools filled the ravine with swift-moving cold water. Even this small, narrow valley was beyond Rath's capability to traverse.

"We will keep trying," Kriston stated after they climbed back out of the freezing water, and he informed his men of his plans.

"The river takes us deeper," came Jake's response.

"We will find a spot to cross. It may take a while." Kriston knew both groups would have to travel back into the forest. Both sides of the bank were too steep to walk and, looking down the river's flow, he could see the cliffs getting steeper. "Head down river and we will see you where it opens up again," Kriston said as he turned to help Anna off Rath's back.

She had stayed on the horse's back while he had tried to help walk the animal across the rocky inlet, so she was dryer than Rath and he, who were wet to the bone.

"You can't walk in those clothes; you'll catch a cold," she scolded as he set her on the ground.

"Do not worry, I have a change of clothing in the saddle bag." He proceeded to pull a tan cloth out of one of the bags.

"Why didn't you change into those last night?" Anna asked in astonishment.

Kriston gave her a sly look. "What, and deny you the chance to get me in my underclothes?" he asked with a laugh as he saw frustration cross her face.

After he changed behind the nearest tree, they walked Rath up the bank and into the forest on their side of the river.

"I think walking for a while will help us find a better crossing place," Kriston informed her.

"Sure, no problem."

He watched her kick at the loose black bark from the trees. When she reached out and plucked a leaf from one of the nearest trees, she turned slightly to him.

"What kind of trees are these?" she asked Kriston as she twirled the leaf in her hand.

"Austera. This is the only Austera forest on Genoa. At least the only one I know of." She once again studied the dark trees with their bright foliage.

She stopped momentarily when a bird chirped overhead, her eyes traveling up to the far branches, but he knew she wouldn't be able to spot the creature with her naked eye, and never during the daylight.

"I get the impression you have not traveled much of Genoa's lands." Her words caused him to pause. She stopped beside him and looked up at him. "I would have guessed you were a well-traveled man, but hearing you talk, it sounds like you don't know much about Genoa."

Kriston continued walking and Anna caught up to him again. "Well?" she asked.

"Well what?" Kriston turned and glanced down at her.

"Where have you been? What have you seen?" She folded the leaf and placed it gently in one of her cloak pockets.

"I am not as well traveled as it appears you are," he said as he walked on. "Most of my life has been in military training, within my homeland's borders. However, I have studied many of the known maps of Genoa and know her main geography."

"Real life is always different than what you read in books or see on maps," she said. "I should know."

Stopping, he gave her a hard look. What he saw encouraged him. "I have had training in forests. I spent many years below the goblin villages in the Cleveite Mountains," he informed her with an air of arrogance.

"Military training?" she asked. "I know you said the king has an army. Is Matera at war?"

"Yes and no. We are in a dispute with Malic." He shook his head. "Most of the battles are fought in the Plains of Rith, south of the city itself. However, several smaller scrimmages happen daily within my homeland itself." He paused. "Living under a monarch who carries strong beliefs can divide the people and cause uprising, even revolution." When Anna said nothing, he continued. "Ever since my brother first sat on the throne, he has attempted to segregate the beings of Genoa from the men and women of Matera."

"I know about the kings of old and their attempt to rule all men, but I hadn't heard about Genoa's recent struggles. Are the creatures that live here so bad?"

Giving no answer, Kriston raised his head and studied the forest canopy high above them as he thought of his own heritage. He could see the light dim as rain clouds moved in as the hidden birds sang their songs. He knew his brother detested that Kriston's own mother had been part nymph.

"My brother rules, but he does not hold the heart or mind of his people. It is told that the people of Malic stopped trading, for no known reason, yet I have heard it was Matera who initially closed the roads south. Rumors, that have some truth to them, tell it was my brother who chose to deny commerce because the Malics allowed gnomes and sprites to live amongst the men in their villages." He continued but would not look at Anna, instead kept his gaze upward.

"Why would your brother do that?"

"I told you of my father's death." When she nodded her head, he continued. "It was thought seasons ago that the assassins were from Malic's borders. Maybe even sent by their king himself. My brother says that trading ceased and the borders were guarded to protect against any future attacking force." He fell quiet to consider how he would proceed. "However, working close to my home I have seen that many innocent creatures who cross Matera's border are immediately captured. Most are put to death by the king and his secret guard. Others fair far worse." He paused and considered the sky for another moment. "Rain is coming," he said and went to retrieve a cloak. "You may want to put your hood on."

After placing her hood up, she glanced over as he threw his cloak over himself. "So, these two nations were at a standoff?"

"That is a great way to state it, yes. It lasted several seasons, then over ten seasons ago we had word the king had tried to infiltrate a spy into the north. Word was, he was trying to turn the Queen of Valorna against us." They continued as the sun slid further behind a pale gray cloud above them. "I did not believe this until a messenger came back with a portion of a scroll that left no doubt about their treachery. It seemed that King Malic and the queen were attempting to capture or kill my brother."

Again, he fell silent, and thin rain started falling around them. Its soft drops landed on the forest floor, which was littered with round black rocks.

The trees glistened in the new rain's wetness. He watched with Anna as the large white leaves slowly uncurled until they were completely flat. The tree branches moved slowly upward as if reaching for the life-giving moisture.

Water ran down the leaves towards the trees' black trunks, downwards as it disappeared into the forest floor at the trees' roots. Large black pods started falling softly around them, delayed in their fall by a single leaf-wing attached to its base. The seeds hit the ground and settled with others in the soft mud below.

The rocks on the forest floor were not rocks after all, but seeds dropped from the last rain.

"Amazing!" she gasped as he watched her.

"I did not know these trees did this," Kriston said as Anna moved closer to the nearest tree to watch.

Once finished watching, she continued to walk with Kriston. This time she placed herself on the far side of Rath as she continued to hold onto the pod, which he'd seen her slip in her pocket.

"I think this world has so much to discover," Anna stated. "Even parts of Earth are still being discovered." She glanced over to him. "So, why the attempt on your brother? I get the feeling he's not the best king, but why start a war? Have any negotiations been attempted by them?"

He chuckled sarcastically. "With my brother? The king does not negotiate. Remember, I told you he dictates from his throne," Kriston said as he led Anna and Rath through the forest.

"So why did you capture me? I mean, I know

you said they feared me a spy, but I just came back to Genoa and know nothing of the politics. I don't even remember anything from before Earth."

"The king gave me an order—retrieve the spy and bring you back to him for questioning." His green eyes continued to study the forest, looking for dangers and passage or a ford back to his men.

After a moment, Anna glanced over to Kriston and whispered, "What if I told you that I'm afraid of your brother?"

When he continued to walk without a glance in her direction, she continued. "I have questions about his intentions and worry for my safety. If I'm brought before him..." She pleaded and started to fiddle with her hands. "What's to stop him from killing me?" When she caught Kriston glancing at her hands, she tucked them deeply into her pockets.

"To fail in my orders would cause the king to discharge me from his services." He gave his head a shake. He had a feeling of Deja vu at seeing her twist her thin fingers in worry but could not think of why the movements were familiar to him.

"But you're his brother!" she exclaimed.

"I have no choice. I told you, if your intentions are to harm Matera, or her people, then I must stop you."

"How would I harm a whole kingdom?" she asked.

Kriston did not answer for several seconds. Finally, he stopped and stared at Anna. "The king's wizard stated that you intend to steal Matera's magic."

Anna was not quick enough to hide her reaction. Instead of shock on her face, he saw understanding and something else, something between shock and excitement. "You know something about this!" he shouted.

Shaking her head, she backed away one step but Kriston lifted her in his arms and gave her a quick shake. "You must tell me what you know!" he shouted.

"I—I can't!" she shouted back.

"Tell me!"

"Give me a moment." Kriston saw fear in her eyes and realized he was holding her several feet off the ground. Placing her back on the wet ground, he released her arms and walked back over to Rath. He tied his guide ropes to the nearest tree as the horse licked water from the nearest tree's trunk.

When he turned around, he saw Anna standing in the same spot. She was staring out into nothing, her eyes unfocused with a painful expression on her face. After a few moments, she turned to Kriston with a quick shake of her head.

"I think I understand, but Kriston, what I'm guessing, is only that—a guess." When he only stared at her, she continued. "I don't say any of this to cause you pain. Do you know how your father gained his magic?"

"What? What are you talking about?" he asked, uncertain he wanted to hear her after all.

"The kings of old were defeated, remember.

The three remaining kings, each with their own wizards, went their own ways. I was told that after my birth, my father King Edwin Collin Reginald feared for his life after King Malic had been attacked. He and my mother fled into the country. It is said I was attacked and my wizard, Orden, took me into hiding. To Earth." She grabbed Kriston's arms in turn. "It's said he did this so my magic wouldn't be stolen. That my father and mother were murdered." She paused and looked straight into his green eyes. "Kriston, I was told your father murdered my family."

JJ Anders

CHAPTER FIFTEEN
Moving with Speed

The first thing Leian saw was light.

Then he had the impression he was in a large room. However, after his eyes adjusted to the brightness, he realized he was in a cave that was larger than any room he had ever been in.

The cavern was over a hundred feet tall and appeared to be four times wider than that. Where its ceiling should be, he saw instead trees that were layered so close together that only a little light from the above sky could get through. There were vines hanging from every crevice and homes nestled into the cliff walls. Homes built out of wood, stone, and sometimes even the walls of the caves itself clung to the cave walls.

The floor of the cavern was cleared and used

only for gardens, which were bright green with new growth. He saw all the food staples of Genoa growing inside the large cave. Flan corn, lettuce of every variety, pods, and even fruit trees were layered in rows upon the ground with faint rays of the sun hitting their bright leaves.

Leian thought it the most beautiful site he had seen in days.

"Crain, where are we?" he asked with amazement.

Laughing and slapping the wizard on his shoulders, the short man raised his other arm out in a wide gesture. "Wizard, welcome to the Cave of Abound."

Leian was told the cave was nestled deep in the cliffs of Licht and currently housed over six hundred beings, most were originally from Matera itself. "However, there are many outlanders amongst the population as well."

Leian followed Crain down several wooden ladders and approached a rather large home nestled between two big rocks.

"Where did all the people come from?" Leian asked.

"That, lad, is for our leader to provide."

Leian heard the guards before he saw them. They stepped out of two deep rock crevasses on either side of the home before he and Crain were twenty feet from the house.

"Good day, Captain," one said and Leian noticed both men place their right hand in a vertical salute against their chest.

"Myers," Crain said with a nod. "James. How goes the meeting?"

"They started a while ago," said the man who had greeted Crain.

"Save me some of Bella's pie," said the other as Crain continued towards the home.

When he walked in the door without giving any knock, Leian followed and found himself in a house that could have been anywhere in Genoa. There were walls made of plaster, a ceiling, and highly polished wood furniture. The hallway they entered had a coat tree and Leian saw Crain take his hat off and place it on a free hook. Leian tried not to smile, but Captain Crain was as bald as any newborn baby; not even a hint of hair covered his small head.

"Follow me," Crain said and, turning back to Leian, added, "Make sure to wipe your boots."

They walked down the wide hall and arrived at a set of double doors on the left. Crain grabbed the doors and, before opening them, turned back to Leian. "Mind your manners. All are friends who are in these walls." And with no further explanation, he pushed the sliding doors open to reveal a wide room full of people.

The room itself did not register to Leian until after its inhabitants were fully categorized by him. They were all gathered around a large table. A few sat in chairs around a table, but most were standing and he soon realized why.

He saw tree sprites, wind willows, and gnomes

of all shapes and colors. There were men as well, gathered and mixed in with the creatures of Genoa. He realized the room was not really a room, but the start of a large cave. It appeared the larger creatures had another entrance in the far corner through which they arrived.

Lanterns were placed around the room on high shelves and several more lanterns were set upon the center table. There appeared to be no head of the table. Instead, they all were just mingling around the room and talking to each other. He could hear laughter but also saw several creatures and men in deep conversation.

The click of the double doors closing behind him stopped all conversation, as every eye turned upon the two new arrivals.

Leian's young rescuer stood up from his chair at the table and walked over. "Welcome, Wizard Leian, to the resistance." He gave Leian a slap on the back and motioned him into the large room. "We have a short time for introductions, but then we must jump right into our meeting."

Leian was introduced to Brakko, the leader of the tree sprites. The creature stood well over ten feet tall and had wild twigs and leaves of gold for hair. His torso was made of bark but his face was very much like pale skin. He had black holes for eyes and a small mouth appeared when he welcomed Leian. His mate Lafy was smaller and her twigs of hair flowed down beyond her arm branches and ended with leaves of red. Her small mouth was more apparent as she smiled quite a bit. Leian was told they had traveled down from the forest of Bin. Leian had never heard of this forest and was told it rested east of the Cleveite Mountains, far north of the Abound.

Next, he met the wind willows. There appeared to be several. Before he was introduced to the last one, he had forgotten all their names. Each name had sounded just like the prior one. And all the names sounded like someone blowing their nose.

Leian had seen only one drawing of wind willows, and he took in the detail of their build. They were small, about the size of a child. At first glance, their wings appeared to be made of leaves, but after meeting his third or fourth willow, he realized they must be made of stronger material, as they supported the willows rather well in their flight about the room. Their insect-like antennas stood from the tops of their heads and their large eyes were brightly colored with a large black slit down the middle. Their mouths were seated on the bottom of their heads and even when they talked, you could not see much of it. But Leian liked their little feet the most. When they were not flying, they waddled.

The gnomes gave Leian a start. He had only heard one story about the reclusive creatures. Round in shape, they were larger than him, but had childlike features, except for the horns on their head, which were curved inward where ears would be. Their skin appeared to be made of leather and they did not wear any clothing except the weapons which were strapped about their bodies at odd angles. Bomp, or something that sounded like Bomp, was their leader. He was bigger by a few inches and held more weapons.

"Now, let's start this meeting," voiced Leian's rescuer after all the introductions had been completed.

"But, I have not been introduced to you, sir," Leian stated and looked the young man in the face. The man gave a loud laugh in response.

"I have not introduced myself yet?" He laughed.

"How like my husband," came a sweet voice from the doorway.

When Leian looked over, he saw a beautiful woman with gold curled hair piled on top of her head. She came into the room and carried a large tray of food. Four more women came in behind her with equally large trays.

"You must forgive his manners, Wizard; he forgets everyone does not know Dryna the daring," she said with a smirk on her face.

"Now, it just slipped my mind is all, Hurra," Dryna said and walked over to help her settle the tray and its food on the large table. "What with rescuing him and all."

"Please." She continued, "All are welcome. I think we have thought of food for everyone." She gestured to the table that was being laid with a variety of foods.

Crain stepped forward and after grabbing some

meat cleared his throat. "Are we starting the meeting?" he asked.

Leian was shocked that it was not Dryna who answered but Hurra herself.

"Yes." She turned to the room. "I called this meeting to discuss the queen's request."

Anna wasn't sure how Kriston would react to her statement, but the last thing she expected was for him to draw his sword.

She panicked at first, then she realized he was no longer looking at her. His eyes were directed about three feet beyond her left shoulder. She also noticed that Rath's ears were raised and his nostrils were flared in fear or excitement.

"What is it?" she whispered.

"I do not know. The forest lays still."

Anna turned and could see nothing. She almost squealed when Kriston's big hands lifted her and placed her on Rath's back as the horse knelt to receive her.

Instead of following her up, he grabbed one of the horse's reins and proceeded along the forest floor slowly, keeping his sword raised and his eyes looking in every direction.

"Is it more cats?" she asked and received a small shake of his head.

After what seemed like hours, Kriston relaxed slightly, but then a loud scream echoed from far behind them, causing Rath to tense up and Kriston to spin around at the ready. The scream was followed by loud bangs. After about ten booming noises, they heard something give a final death scream.

"What the hell was that?" Anna asked.

"I think that was the last of the cat pack," Kriston stated and swung up behind Anna on the horse. When he started the horse at a gallop, Anna had a sinking feeling.

"What attacked them?" she shouted above the noise of horse's hooves as they pounded the wet ground.

"I do not know, but whatever it was, I do not want to wait for it to catch us." he said close to her ear.

They ran along the forest floor and caught up to the water's edge only to discover the water was several hundred feet below the forest now.

Waterfalls cascaded downwards, falling hundreds of feet between them and the other side. Kriston spotted a green flag on the far bank and continued along their side of the river.

"Jake and my men were there but continued on," he stated after pointing out the flag.

Their path finally took them beyond the Austera forest and the small path led away from the water's edge.

Deciding to keep close to the river, they continued, Kriston leading on foot and using his sword to clear the underbrush.

Before midday, they finally caught a break. The river slowed its descent and pooled in a rather wide, but shallow pond.

They saw Kriston's men on the far bank finishing a rough wooden craft that Anna assumed was for them to ride in. However, when Timmons stripped and marched into the waters dragging the craft behind him, she realized it was only for their supplies.

After Timmons reached their side of the pond, Anna found herself, for the second time, in Kriston's company, stripped down to the essentials.

They placed all their supplies, even the saddlebags from Rath's back, into the boat and started the cold but quick journey across the pond.

"You sure know how to show a girl a good time," Anna muttered when they had reached the far bank, their bodies dripping with the cold water.

"We do what we must," was his only response as he marched off with Timmons for a quick chat. Anna was left to gather her clothing while attempting to keep the mud off her shoes. Brigdon came over and finally assisted her by giving her a large cloth to dry herself with.

"I trust your night was pleasant," he said with a quick smile.

"Well, it wasn't a picnic," she responded and was in the process of handing Brigdon his cloth back, when her magic gave a quick surge.

It happened so fast. Brigdon reached out to steady her, a simple gesture. But suddenly Anna's powers shot out of her control and launched itself against Brigdon.

She watched in utter amazement as the man's eyes turned white just before her power entered his thoughts without her control.

She was standing in the dark, leaning against a stone wall. She turned her head and heard movement to her right. A light flared a foot away from her and she saw Brigdon's face as he bent down to light his pipe.

"Oh, thank goodness," Anna said. "What happened?" She saw Brigdon glance up, but he wasn't looking at her. Instead, he turned, threw his pipe down, and rushed away from Anna as he drew his sword.

Then she heard it. Someone was screaming and the sound of battle noises grew louder and closer.

She rushed to follow him and saw him disappear into a door. Light spilled out its open frame. She reached the door in time to watch Brigdon run down a hall and enter a door on the left.

More men were running around the large room as she crossed into the building to follow Brigdon. It was a large home, and its high ceiling was alight with a huge chandelier, its candles dripping wax on the carnage below. Men were littered about the huge room, all with swords drawn and fighting each other caught in an eerie death dance.

She couldn't tell what had started the battle, but she knew she needed to keep up with Brigdon.

Racing into the room, she weaved in and out of the battle and reached the door the large man had entered. She rushed in and saw Brigdon leaning over a small bed. He grabbed a small form wrapped in blankets, marched over to the fireplace, and quickly kicked the fire grate hard.

The backside of the fireplace disappeared, and a secret passageway appeared beyond. Brigdon grabbed a small candle from the stone mantel and disappeared into the entrance carrying his precious cargo.

The light faded and the next thing she knew she was standing in a bright field in the middle of the day. Men of every size raced around her. She turned a full circle and realized that Brigdon was standing behind her.

"It is a beautiful thing," he said and turned and gave Anna a quick wink.

"Where are we?" she asked. She had already guessed that her magic was allowing her to see Brigdon's memories. What she didn't understand was why her magic had come forth without her requesting it. She hadn't called it and it appeared that she was not really "driving" at the moment.

"Drills," Brigdon answered. "We are in the heart of Matera. Along the valley floor where our young men learn how to protect our country." He continued and pointed to her right.

There, high above a forest of green, was a huge upland rock. A dark stone castle sat upon the plateau, its many towers twisting upward, piercing *the sky with its sharp points. Few windows set deep in the stone reflected the sun's rays and at the top of the center tower flew a flag of deep red with a black star at its center.*

"Matera," Anna whispered as she looked at Kriston's home. "Why here?" She watched several men mock fighting with sticks instead of swords. A forest surrounded the field they were standing in. She smelled hay and sweat mixed with leather from the men's uniforms.

"I figured this was fitting, given what I showed you in the last...." He gave Anna a quick look of confusion, and she said, "Memory." He smiled and continued. "Ah, I thought at first I was dreaming. Yes, I see now this is a memory." He smiled and pointed to their left. "Watch."

Anna turned in time to see a much younger Brigdon standing a few feet away. His head was no longer bald but had short stubble along his ears. His facial hair was the same and when he turned slightly, she could see he had the same smile on his lips.

His sword was sheathed and a very young Kriston was facing the weapons teacher in what appeared to be anger.

"I will not allow it!" Kriston said.

Anna could see that Kriston had yet to grow into his large hands and feet. She estimated his age about ten or eleven.

"Young prince, you are under my charge. It is my wish, no, my command, that you and Timmons

join Captain Crain's team along the northern borders for further training," Brigdon said.

Anna turned to watch the argument but stopped listening when the Brigdon next to her gave a quick laugh.

"That young lad there was always a handful. Course if I had just told him of the plot I had discovered to end his life, he may have agreed to the trip to Pesha a lot earlier. All with less arguing too."

Anna quickly turned back to watch the young Kriston. "Plot?" she asked with confusion.

"His brother had hired a mercenary to get the young prince out of Matera, but not for any training," Brigdon said with a shake of his head.

"Why would the king wish to kill his own brother?" Anna asked in horror.

Turning away from the heated argument, Brigdon glanced off into the forest. "Why does any man in power seek to end another life?" he asked. "Maybe it was hate, maybe a little fear, but I think the main reason was envy." Anna turned and watched in amazement as a single arrow came flying out of the trees. The arrow arched high above their heads and started a quick descent towards Kriston and the weapons master.

"Watch," he said as his hand rested on her to stop her from calling out.

Anna watched as the younger weapons master caught the movement out of the corner of his eye and, with no time to think, quickly flung his hands out to push the young Prince to the ground just as the arrow embedded itself into Brigdon's back.

Anna gave a loud gasp as she watched the young Kriston scramble up from the ground and rush over to his teacher's side.

Several men came running to surround the young prince to protect him. None hesitated to defend Kriston, each willing to give their lives for the prince.

"You see, even back then, Kriston was loved by the people of Matera, and the men who were in the king's army," Brigdon whispered.

"What happened?" Anna asked.

"I spent two months in bed, recovering from the arrow, and Kriston went to Pesha for training the following season," he said with a chuckle. "He never doubted my guidance after that."

Anna could feel her magic falter, so she quickly closed it off, sending them back to their spot along the pond.

When her eyes cleared of the images, she saw that she was not standing along the shoreline with Brigdon anymore, but was in fact lying face up on the ground. This was a new experience for her.

She blinked a few times to allow her eyes to focus, and then noticed that a large sword was pointed directly at her face. When she tried to move, the sword moved closer.

"Do not move, my lady, not until we have figured out what you have done with Teacher Penn!" came a deep voice. It was one of Kriston's men and it appeared there were two more behind him with their weapons drawn.

"What happened?" Anna asked. If she had used her magic, that meant she had been touching Brigdon, but it appeared he wasn't even near her now.

She remembered they had touched when she had gotten dizzy, but knew she had not brought her own magic forward. Maybe here in Genoa her magic was stronger? She had never entered another mind without knowing what she was doing or having complete control of the memories she selected. Worries circled in her mind, as her head throbbed. She needed answers but feared only Leian could help her with finding them.

"Stand back!" Kriston ordered. Anna watched as the men guarding her moved aside. She started to sit up and was shocked as Kriston lifted his foot and planted his boot in the middle of her chest with force, successfully pinning her back down to the wet ground.

"What have you done!" he demanded. "If you have harmed Brigdon, I swear on my father's grave, you will pay!"

"I don't know what happened," Anna pleaded, raising her hands in surrender as she tried to see beyond Kriston's large form. Was Brigdon unconscious? Where was he? He couldn't be far from her; he had just been next to her a second ago. After all, her powers only took seconds to reveal memories. "Where is Brigdon?" she asked weakly.

Kriston turned after hearing a shout from behind him.

Lifting his boot off Anna, he rushed over to a group of his men. Anna quickly scrambled up and watched as Kriston helped Brigdon to his feet.

After having a quick whispered conversation with him, Kriston turned back towards Anna with anger in his eyes.

"Tie her up," he ordered.

Far to the south, in a small village named Pavia, the people went back to their hard work of farming and carpentry after their midday meal. Husbands kissed their women and children as they left to toil in labor to provide for their families.

Pavia had some of the finest forests surrounding the small village and held many generations of wood carvers, it was known far and wide for its wood materials.

Belent was one of the town's best carvers. He enjoyed making furniture the most, however, his weapons were traded the most. Today as he approached the towns' work barn, he had a slight lift in his step. His Mala was carrying again.

Most men would worry that this meant another mouth to feed, but not Belent. He was still amazed that the prettiest girl in the village had chosen him to settle down and raise a family with.

They had been married now four seasons and

here they were, already on their second young. She still greeted him each evening with a smile and a kiss.

Her cooking could not be beat, either. Even the village elderly relied on her baking during the holidays. Last season it was Mala who had cooked most of the Mid-day's feast. She had had help, but the way Belent saw it, his pretty dark-haired wife could do no wrong.

Belent walked into the barn and smiled at Croan, the manager of the carving barn, then settled his tall frame at his end of the worktable.

Belent and Croan had been friends since they were no taller than the table itself. Croan, being single still, held the town record for most ladies dated. Right now, though, Croan and Tapel, a fine-looking lady who happened to be the daughter of the town's doctor, were seeing a lot of each other. Maybe that was why Croan was in such a great mood this morning and had agreed to let all the carvers go home early for their meal.

"Finishing up that bow today, or will it take another day?" Croan asked as he peered at the intricate carving that ran along the handle of the bow that Belent was working on.

They had received a special commission from a lord, two villages over only a few days ago, and now Belent had the rather large bow carved. Its belly curved wide and the tips ended in intricate carvings of trees. The nock on each end would eventually fit the finest bowstring made from the best rawhide around.

The grip of the weapon is what held Belent's attention now. He had smoothed the grip itself, but the detailed carving that the owner had requested included two large bucks rearing in a deadly battle with each other, their horns raised in their struggle. He had taped and tied cloth around the area to ensure no damage to the already finished arrow rest and bow's arms. But his knife never slipped; that was why Belent was the best.

"No rush. I think tomorrow will yield a finished product for our eager buyer," Belent said with a smile.

Belent saw Croan looked out the nearest window as if he had heard something, but when no other sound could be heard, he continued down the large table to talk to the next carver.

He had just passed old man Nepan, when Belent saw him cock his head again and walk back to the window.

"Kids should be back inside. What is that young fellow doing?" he asked just as one of the men near the door gave a shout from behind Belent.

Spinning around, Belent saw a black-clad man run a sword through old man Nepan. Too shocked to do anything, the room watched as the sword was slowly pulled from Nepan's chest. Both the sword and Nepan were now covered in the darkest blood he had ever seen.

None of his friends had moved a muscle during the death of their friend. However once Nepan's body hit the floor Belent moved.

When he realized his friend was dead he pushed up on the table, upending its goods all over the floor and successfully getting every man in the room on their feet.

Grabbing the nearest wood staff, Belent moved to the door just as another cloaked figure came from the outside.

He could hear shouting now from outside, and also from inside the barn.

"Who are you?" he shouted just as the man raised his large sharp sword towards Belent's head.

Two clicks away, General Zobo's first-line man, Nathaniel, ran up to him with his report.

"The village is finished. We have what we came for," Nathaniel provided.

"All have been eliminated?" the general asked as he reached up to rub at his short mustache, turning his head to the right to see his man and confirm his answer. All his men knew never to approach from the general's left, as he had lost his eye to a cat several years ago. He was still angry about the loss. A small black patch covered most of the damage, but the scar was still a deep purple mar running from the back of the general's bald head all the way down to behind his left ear. If the general caught a rookie staring, that man usually found himself dealing with the most unpleasant chores,

383

then he was usually transferred to another regiment.

"The town is a wasteland. Not even minimal resistance was received. We have gained exactly what we came for," Nathaniel answered.

The general studied his first man. Nathaniel wasn't a large man, but he blindly followed every order the general gave him.

"Very well," General Zobo said as he watched a runner behind Nathaniel dismount his horse and come running up to his second in command.

After a few quiet words, Nathaniel cleared his throat. "General, word from the king." He handed Zobo the parchment from the runner.

Taking the paper, he turned from the runner and Nathaniel, dismissing them without even a second thought.

Walking some feet away, he studied the seal on the rolled paper. He noted it did hold the king's seal, and he broke the black wax and magic seal and unrolled it to discover his next mission.

"Get the men ready," the general shouted as he turned back with a smile on his lips. Then he whispered, "It appears we leave at once to meet a lady."

Here she was, tied up once again.

This time she was sitting on top of Kriston's horse Rath, but she was still tied up.

They had used big thick gloves to handle her,

tying her hands in front and binding her arms to her body, leaving no room to even scratch her nose. Which, now that she thought about it, had started to itch like crazy.

Why had her magic acted up?

She had never lost control like this before. Maybe something was affecting her here?

Could the place itself hold some answers? Maybe Genoa and its magic were twisting her own, causing it to build or mutate. Maybe she had just watched too many movies and she should just realize this was an accident?

She bet Leian and Shiarra would have ideas into her magic's outburst, but she still had no idea where they were or if they were safe.

What had she been thinking when she had touched Brigdon? She had been struggling all day with her hope that she would get to know Kriston better, understand more about the man who had captured her. The man was an enigma to her.

Anna now had time to ponder Kriston's words about his brother, along with the details from Brigdon's visions. Her impression was that King Gillard Haddock did not take well to creatures other than humans. It appeared he also had no qualms about hiring a hit man to kill his own brother.

And what, she thought, did this all have to do with Colab the Meshi's vision from the other night? The Scarent had told her that his snakes visions were important, hinting that she would have need of the knowledge found within the short, but powerful memories. If the king was indeed unfavorable towards Genoa's creatures, how would the Scarent tribe, who lived so close to Matera, fare? His vision gave her great insight into life on Genoa, but no details about Kriston himself, only more assurances that King Gillard was an evil man.

Man, her nosed itched!

"Great!" she exclaimed.

"You brought this upon yourself," Kriston said from in front, as he led Rath along the narrow path that wound next to the river.

Kriston and his men had taken a short time to determine which direction they would head, and all had agreed to go down the river and then out of the Deepen Forest. Since the path was narrow, they were leading their horses in single file along the path.

"My nose itches," she stated, sitting a little taller in Rath's saddle.

How humiliating. First her powers had exploded out of control and now she had been thrown on the back of a horse, left to rely on someone else to scratch her own nose. She was currently crossed eyed, wiggling said nose, and trying to ease the excessive itch.

"I guess you must suffer," came his response. Even though Brigdon was well and leading his own horse in front of them, Kriston still seemed uneasy towards Anna.

"I told you, I've never done that before. I'm not even sure that was me. Does Brigdon have any magic in his family?" she asked.

Instead of answering her question, he asked one of his own. "What happened?"

"I'm not sure. It felt like...." She stopped and thought, then felt she should not continue. Maybe she was a danger to others now. If her powers were increasing now that she was back in Genoa, would she no longer have control over them?

"What, Anna? It felt like what?"

"Like someone else was in charge of my magic," she exclaimed. When Kriston stopped Rath and turned to look at her, she knew she sounded crazy.

CHAPTER SIXTEEN

Keeping Evil in Your Sight

He gave her another glance, then continued down the trail. Was she telling the truth?

At this point, all he could worry about was his men. Seeing Brigdon flat on his back, white as parchment, was something he hoped not to see again.

Sure, when his friend had awakened, he was his own spry self. He had even cracked a joke. But since Anna had recovered faster than the weapons teacher, he had taken the only action he was trained for.

Capture and question.

He knew from experience that if you allowed danger to continue, some innocent person always got hurt.

His brother had been sure to teach him this hard lesson at a young age. Not a day had gone by that he hadn't felt his older sibling's scorn, which could have been rooted in Kriston's heritage. His mother had been one-fifth land nymph. Her mixed blood had not stopped his father from falling for the beautiful, soft-spoken woman. If not for a shared father, Kriston worried he would have joined many of the half-elemental beings in either exile or prison, maybe even death.

Had he not spent several seasons cleaning up after his brother?

Even now, while he was away from Matera, his men continued Kriston's chore—keeping the innocent creatures and magical peoples out of the king's reach.

He had talked to Anna about his brother segregating the people who lived around his home, but it was not the king who did this. No, it was Kriston and his men who ensured separation. Kriston was not proud of this, but he knew there was great need for this action.

However, he could not keep all safe, a fact that ate away at him every day and night. He and his men had learned this lesson the hard way when a tribe of wood willows had been captured by the king's men several seasons ago. How was he to know that Gillard had ordered his men to kill them all?

It had been even more devastating when Kriston had learned that not all had died. Even before the willows had been found, he had heard rumors of what his brother did deep in the dungeons of their home.

Magical beings, it appeared, were enslaved by Gillard for reasons that were unknown by Kriston. His men had attempted to find out if the stories had any truth to them.

What had his men gained in their search of the dungeons?

Nothing.

The men who had volunteered to attempt infiltration into his brother's dungeon guards had all disappeared and never returned. After the third volunteer failed, Kriston put a stop to the investigation and attempted to go himself.

Instead of finding out the king's secrets, he had ended up with new orders from the king before he could even start. These orders had taken him to the far western reaches of the kingdom and kept him gone for two seasons.

Now he feared Gillard's secrets, feared they were harmful to Matera's people and all of Genoa's creatures.

With Anna, he was also seeking some answers and now feared he would not like what he would find.

However, it seemed that Anna did not have any answers about her and Brigdon's adventure, and neither did Brigdon. All he remembered were dreams.

The path led up and away from the flowing

river. Ahead the trees thinned as they moved out of the forest and back toward the road leading to Matera. As each man and horse reached the opening, they mounted up to speed up their travel.

Kriston was just about to climb up behind Anna when one of his men gave a loud shout.

Spinning around, he drew his sword and watched as a nightmare of a creature came running at them from the dark trees.

Anna saw the first of their attackers streak out of the forest near them. She was so shocked that it took precious seconds for her brain to realize what she was seeing.

"It can't be!" she shouted as the beast came barreling into the midst of Kriston's men, knocking over two of them, along with their horses, before the rest of the group even knew they were being attacked.

Within seconds, Kriston's men were overpowered. Each man drew his sword and started up their formation, but they were easily cut down.

She feared the men would fare just like Leian in the struggle with this creature from Byways. How could normal men fight this magical creature when even Leian's wizard magic couldn't stop the metal man.

She watched as the brute continued to plow through the men with ease. This time it swung a huge ax about its head in its attempt to cut the enemy down.

She watched in horror as Kriston stepped in front of Rath, his large sword already drawn, his feet planted wide in anticipation of the attack.

Even though he was ready, he was not prepared when a second beast emerged and started an onslaught from their right.

Anna knew she had to do something to save them all. Thinking quickly, she moved Rath just as the creature lunged towards them, causing the creature's metal body to ram into the horse's head instead of Kriston's vulnerable body.

When Rath reared up in his own defense, Kriston had time to turn and meet the new attack head on.

Anna watched Kriston's sword flash and a green light emit from the creature where it had been struck. She heard Kriston give a grunt and the being gave a low growl from the contact.

Past them, Kriston's men fought the second creature and appeared to have it surrounded. Jake and Ray were using long spears to jab and cut at it. She couldn't see Timmons or Brigdon but knew they would also be in the crowd around the other beast.

Seeing the battle rage on, she realized, with a sinking in her chest, that this fight was a losing battle.

Hadn't she seen Shiarra and Leian try their hardest to protect her with their magic. If a wizard and his apprentice couldn't stop one creature, how can a handful of military men hold back two of them?

She had to stop this fight and quickly!

But how?

She knew the creatures were after her. Hadn't the one in Byways said, *"Give me the girl and I will let you live."*

That was it!

As Rath settled his front feet back to the ground, she reached for his reins with her tied hands and gave them one hard tug as she scanned and found the best escape.

"Creature!" she screamed and set her eyes on the closest one, who was actively throwing Kriston's sword away. "I'm here!" she screamed and without waiting for its response, kicked Rath into action. The horse ran off to the right, heading down a narrow opening and into the dense forest.

She prayed she was correct, that one or both metallic beasts would follow her, leaving Kriston and his men safe or at least buying them time to reform their defenses.

She spared one quick glance over her shoulder, and instantly knew she was right. The closest creature was chasing her.

Perfect. Great. Hell! she thought as it gained ground.

The path was narrow. After ducking to miss several branches, she knew she wouldn't get too far. She needed a good plan or time to come up with one.

Making a quick decision, she turned the horse back towards the clearing she'd just left, making sure to execute a wide left turn.

She would just play cat and mouse for a while and hoped this would allow Kriston and his men to regroup.

She could hear the creature gaining on Rath, and after giving another quick glance behind, realized the metal being and horse were matched in running speed. She just didn't know how long Rath could keep up the pace.

She broke into the clearing where the battle continued with the remaining creature and noticed that it seemed to be going rather well. Two large spears and a single sword were lodged into its chest and back.

She had bought Kriston and his men the time they needed to subdue the second beast, but another quick dip into the forest was still needed.

"So, they can be killed," she thought as she passed the group of fighters currently hacking at the first creature and took comfort in this fact as she raced back into the forest closely followed by the second monster.

Kriston was in full military mode, except the part of him that was in full panic.

Seeing Anna racing away on Rath, and the huge

shiny creature tearing up the ground to pursue her, caused his heart rate to double.

What was the fool woman thinking of?

She had her body low over Rath's back and her tied hands wrapped around the horse's reins. She had no chance.

Kriston saw that his men had the first attacker injured; green ooze seeped from its wounds and poured into the ground beneath where it stood.

But his main thoughts were of Anna. Could he reach her?

Where was she running to and how soon before the powerful being gained on Rath and captured or killed her?

"Grab the long staffs!" he shouted to Jake and Ray as the rest of the men continued to battle the remaining creature. "Go after her!" he ordered and was racing over to a free horse when he heard a commotion and realized that Anna and Rath were racing back into the clearing.

"Surround her!" he shouted and hoped there were enough men to battle the beast that followed Anna.

His brief battle with it had proven to him how strong and powerful it was. He knew that the creature also held magic, which had given Kriston a great burn on his forearm.

Before he or his men could near Anna though, she had swung Rath about and he watched in horror as she lowered her thin frame over his powerful horse and once again headed into the forest.

Once again, she bent low over Rath's neck, clinging tight so she wouldn't be swept away by a low branch. After several yards, she made another sharp turn and headed back to the clearing.

Before she had reached it, she realized her mistake. She'd forgotten to make sure the creature was following her.

Suddenly, she was thrown from Rath's back and landed with her feet up in the air, her head settled against a tree trunk at an odd angle. Her limbs twisted about her thin frame as her short hair covered her eyes. The ropes that bound her wrists were ripped and hung from her bleeding hands. She tried to stare at the creature from her upside-down position, but her long skirt kept flipping into her face.

"Witch!" the creature hissed. "Speculum has finally caught you," it said in a deep metallic voice as it slowly approached her.

She scrambled to right herself and saw a quick flash of green. Bracing for impact of magic or pain, she was shocked when she heard Kriston's scream from far away and felt a body land on top of her.

Panicked now, she struggled even harder to right herself and see who was covering her body, protecting her from the creature's magic.

She could smell blood and hear metal on metal, but still couldn't see anything.

Finally, she freed herself from under the heavy body and realized with quick pain and sorrow that Brigdon Penn had thrown himself in front of her, taking the creature's killing magic full force and saving Anna from the blast.

His large frame was twisted and burned as a broken spear fell from his lifeless fingers. His empty eyes stared at her in shock. No hint of humor was left in them. Anna screamed in pain and cried his name over and over again.

She heard the Speculum laugh as she tried beating on Brigdon's chest.

Then she was yanked around as Kriston came and ripped her from Brigdon's body.

"Run Anna!" he shouted. "Run!" he shouted again as he turned back to face the Speculum.

"He's..." she cried.

"I know!" he said and turned back quickly towards her. "Run," he whispered and raised his sword towards the creature, a short sword held firmly in his other hand as his armor shone dully in the afternoon light.

Blinded by sorrow, she ran.

She hoped she could get the creature to leave her new friends alone by following her once again. She didn't even care if it caught her this time, as long as no one else was hurt.

She stumbled along for several minutes, each second expecting a green flash and then nothing more. But each second only brought pain and sorrow deep in her heart.

She ran so hard and so fast that she lost track of where she was. The tears running from her eyes blinded her and the sobs from her chest were the only sound she could hear over the pounding of her heartbeat.

When she burst out into a clearing, she was so confused that she thought she was back where she had started. She expected Kriston's men to be scattered around in the clearing, but instead found a lone dragon the color of gold.

Stopping in the center of the small clearing, she stared at it without realizing what it was. With her bleeding hands, she used her cloak sleeve to clear her eyes.

When it moved, she took a quick step backwards in fear and confusion. It only took moments before she realized the dragon was the same one from her dreams.

"My lady, I come to retrieve you. Climb on," it said in a voice that sounded deep, like a bass drum.

She gave her head a quick shake. "Must have hit my head," she mumbled.

"My lady, you must come now!" it said.

Yup! She was officially crazy.

The huge dragon was golden with stripes of dark blue on its chest. It had a bright red jaw and matching eyes. It was sitting at the edge of the clearing, talking to her like it was a most perfectly normal thing to do. Well, she hadn't seen its mouth move, but she had heard its voice loud and clear in her mind. It was easily the size of a semi-truck and was perched on a low crop of rocks, calm and still.

Taking a step towards it, she was momentarily distracted by a clashing sound and turned in time to see Kriston and the Speculum fighting through the trees.

Kriston had an odd-shaped shield and short sword in his hands and was beating the Speculum with the sword every chance he could. He would then use the shield as protection from the creature's magic when it would shoot the green killing light at Kriston.

They moved closer to her location while their death struggle continued. She could see Kriston's face contorted with effort as he kept up the hand-to-hand battle with the powerful creature.

"My lady!" the dragon urged as Anna took a step towards the battle.

"I have to help him!" she screamed back. Turning once more towards the battle, she thought about a lesson she'd learned long ago from a very old book.

"He who fights and runs away, may live to fight another day; but he who is battle slain can never rise to fight again."

Her mind screamed those words as she thought about Brigdon's body laying at the base of the tree.

Turning back to the dragon, she studied its clawed feet. It took only a second for her to make up her mind, and she ran towards the dragon.

She climbed up into the saddle, which was set before the large leathery wings, and was so distracted by the battle she didn't stop to think about why it felt so comfortable or familiar.

"I need you to fly over and grab him!" she screamed to the dragon as she saw Kriston get blasted by a green flash and fly clear across the forest clearing. He landed in a heap on the edge near some thick underbrush.

The dragon lifted immediately, its huge powerful wings blowing the air about its body as it rose off the ground. Her hair lifted from her face and the breath was almost knocked from her lungs by the sheer force.

It took only seconds before the dragon's dark blue claws reached out towards Kriston's unconscious form.

They lifted fast after his body was nestled between the dragon's large claws. Then, before she could blink, they were above the treetops, as the metallic creature below gave a loud scream in anguish.

"My lady, I am Su Na. I am here to take you to Faro where my Draydon tribe lives," the dragon explained.

"Who sent you? How did you know where I was?" Anna asked while holding on to Su Na's reins, which were made of red leather and matched the dragon's saddle.

Anna tried to lean over the side of the dragon to get an eye on Kriston, but Su Na's chest was too wide for her to get a good look at him. She thought for a moment about leaning further down, but then guessed that falling off a dragon was way worse than falling off a horse and tightened her grip on the reins.

"That is for my mistress to tell you," Su Na responded.

"Su Na, can you tell if the man you carry is alive?" she asked.

Su Na shifted his head down and looked at Kriston. "He sleeps, my lady. I fear the creature poisoned him with its magic."

"Poison?" Anna asked quickly. Her concern for Kriston increased. She may have been kidnapped by Kriston and his men several days ago, but that had all been a misunderstanding. Since then he had saved her life several times. She felt responsible for his injuries. After all, the Speculum had been after her.

First Leian had been lost to the creature in the streets of Byways, and now it had tracked her deep into the Deepen Forest and had attacked her new friends.

Maybe it, just like Kriston, had been sent to capture her, not harm her? But if that were true, then Brigdon wouldn't be dead.

She couldn't fool herself into thinking it was not her fault that Brigdon was dead. He'd died saving her life, something she would never forget.

She had to make sure Kriston didn't pay the same price for her safety.

"Will he be okay?" she asked.

"We must hurry if our wizard is to help him,"

the dragon responded.

"How far is it to... Where did you say we're going?" Anna asked as her eyes searched the cliff faces and river far below them.

"The Cliffs of Faro are at the end of this river. It is not far. We will be there before Grenata sets in the east."

Anna knew Grenata was one of the moons, but didn't have any clue how to tell how much time that would be. She needed to trust that they'd make it in time.

Anna continued to watch the river below and wish the miles away. She was worried about Kriston hanging below Su Na. She listened to see if she could hear him, but could only hear the wind whistling past as the dragon flew on.

She couldn't believe it! A dragon!

She guessed from what she could see of Su Na that most drawings of dragons on Earth were very close.

Su Na's head was horse-like in shape, but instead of ears, the dragon had small leathery webbed flaps, and instead of hair, the dragon had two large blue nubs that reminded her of the top of a giraffe's head. It was covered in large golden scales and its wings were bat-like. The body past its wide chest was very long and ended in a tail with its own wings, except they didn't flap. She assumed these end wings were there to help steer the creature, like a rudder.

She guessed that this was the same dragon

she'd dreamed of and her curiosity increased. How had she dreamed of Su Na? Who was its mistress?

They flew on as the miles stretched below them, forest and river passing by, as time slowly ticked on.

Finally, the dragon dipped its wings and headed closer to the ground, causing Anna to squeeze her knees tighter to the saddle.

It was odd, but the saddle seemed to fit her perfectly, a fact that she now considered. The stirrups were the exact length she needed for her feet, even with her skirt and cloak whipping around her. It all felt familiar.

As Su Na flew even lower, Anna could hear waterfalls before she saw them. The dragon leveled off several feet above the river, and she held her breath as the river fell away below her in a splendor of beautiful waterfalls.

The rushing water fell over large rock outcrops, green trees and vines clinging to any moist spot as it created over twenty huge waterfalls hundreds of feet down.

The view of the river dropping left her breathless as small beads of moisture hit her face. She pulled her cloak closer with one hand and felt the straps of her backpack against her shoulders. At least Kriston had allowed her to keep her lifeline to Earth with her when he'd tied her up.

Su Na used the fall's uplifting wind to rise higher, which allowed Anna to see the full extent of the falls, which were in a crescent shape formed from the mountains surrounding them. It was the most beautiful sight she'd ever seen, either here or on Earth. The sound of the massive falls was deafening; she even felt its rumble deep in her chest.

Below the waterfalls, hundreds of feet down, she saw a grassy area that leveled off and moved into the vast ocean beyond. She turned to either side and watched the cliffs rise.

She knew, even before she saw them, that the cliffs held hundreds of homes and nests. She could see smoke rising from fires, their smells mingled with the scent of the salty waters far below.

Su Na headed towards the left of the falls, angling near an opening at the top of the cliffs where the forest intruded on the rocks. As the dragon landed its massive body, Anna saw small cones or teepees and was reminded of the American Indian villages she'd seen in one of America's old history books.

In the middle of the clearing, surrounded by the teepees, were several people, all dressed in bright-colored clothing. Each face looked up at her as Su Na laid Kriston's body gently on the ground before setting its massive claws on the grass next to him.

Anna scrambled off the dragon and rushed to where Kriston lay. She checked for his pulse and, finding it very weak, then she stood and addressed the people gathering around her.

"He needs help! Where is your wizard?" she asked.

When no one moved, she screamed. "This man needs medical assistance, please! Where is your wizard?"

Even before she finished her questions, the people moved aside as two figures emerged from the crowd, walking towards her.

One was a tall man with a black Mohawk and a rather colorful dragon tattoo that ran from the top of his right eye and then disappeared around his head, and reappeared along his neck. He wore no shirt, but had leather pants and many odd belts strapped about his thick chest, each holding many weapons.

He moved aside and Anna saw something that almost made her pass out. She sucked in a huge breath and was so shocked by the appearance of the woman before her, that she almost forgot to let the breath back out.

She stumbled back a step until she came up against Su Na's chest.

There, before her, stood... herself.

There were slight differences. The other woman had a Mohawk much like the man's. However, instead of her head being shaved on the sides, it was pulled back so that her white hair was braided and piled atop her head in a thick twist making the Mohawk.

She wore a leather tunic with a gold tank top under it and tight pants of bright red. The woman's muscular arms were exposed and she had the same belts and straps about her as the man wore.

When she approached Anna, she smiled and

raised both hands to her forehead, touching it with her fingertips.

"Welcome, Anna. We are glad you are safe." She even spoke in Anna's voice.

"Who are you?" Anna whispered, then swallowed the lump that was in her throat.

"I am called Té. I am you."

Deep in the bowels of Matera, King Gillard glided down the foul-smelling steps. Each level brought him closer to that which he held most dear.

He was pleased to see the increase in guards. After losing his newest prize, he had killed five of his old dungeon guards in anger. But they were easily replaced and he hadn't given any thought to them, other than the order to dispose of their bodies.

Now, however, his hands twitched as he thought of what lay even further down, deep in the dark, hidden for many seasons while he savored the power he yielded from it.

Restraint was not his strong suit. Tonight, he would travel the full length of these steps. Just one more level and his hunger would be cured.

Inspecting the new guards that lined each level, he was pleased with their girth. The bigger, more muscled men intimidated the prisoners. Not that the poor souls saw much. Only the occasional food trays that would keep them alive until he was finished feeding off their talents.

After reaching the last door on this level, he withdrew the small key and slid it into the well-oiled lock.

Either the click of the lock or the light from the torch startled the man crouched inside. The king did not care which, only that the sign of defeat and fear crossed the scarred face that looked up at him with haunted eyes.

Without a word, Gillard boldly walked up and, without even touching the filthy man, started to suck the magic from his body.

The rush of pure power flooded into him, which caused his back to straighten, his head to lift high, and his eyes to close in pleasure.

Yes, here was true royal power. Power that mixed and added to his own, twisting and coiling into his body. Power that combined with the diminished power he had collected only two days before.

When he was finished, when the shell of the man huddled on the floor gave a small whimper, Gillard turned without a backwards glance and locked the cage once more.

Even after collecting what little power the man held, he still felt empty.

The quick thought passed through his mind that he should visit the dark cell several doors down, but then he dismissed it. It was not time for that; he would keep those visits for another night. A night when his enemy and savior was closer, a night when he would have need of the raw power his dearest secret held.

No, he was not much on restraint, but plotting was one of his biggest assets.

That and keeping secrets long lost.

With a quiet chuckle, he turned to leave the foul smell of the dungeons behind.

He had much more plotting to do.

BOOKS BY J.J. ANDERS

The Scholar
The Warrior
The Queen

FOLLOW J.J. ANDERS

www.jjanders.com
fb.com/jjandersauthor
twitter.com/jjandersauthor

ABOUT THE AUTHORS

JJ Anders is the pseudonym used by the powerhouse writing duo of NY Times & USA Today bestselling author, Jill Sanders and her identical twin sister, Jody. Hailing from the Pacific Northwest, these two talented ladies have merged their creative forces to craft an amazing new fantasy series that will leave you begging for more.

With over forty bestselling romance books and counting, Jill alone is a force to be reckoned with, boasting thousands of glowing reviews with a cumulative 4.7 star rating. Jody's powerful imagination and newfound love of writing has spawned the thrilling new world and enchanting characters of Genoa. As a furious reader and devoted mother, Jody's passion for storytelling reaches full bloom by teaming up with her talented twin to bring her magical stories to life for the enjoyment of readers everywhere.

Made in the USA
Middletown, DE
04 October 2020